PENNANT MAN

Also by Daniel Wyatt

Two Wings and a Prayer
Maximum Effort
The Last Flight of the Arrow
The Mary Jane Mission
The Cotton Run
Pennant Man
Route 66

"The Falcon File" series:
The Fuehrermaster
The Filberg Consortium
Foo Fighters

PENNANT MAN

Daniel Wyatt

Published by
Bladud Books

First published in USA in 2004 by Waltsan Publishing, LLC

This Paperback edition published in 2018 by
Bladud Books, an imprint of Mushroom Publishing,
Bath, BA1 4EB, United Kingdom

www.bladudbooks.com

ISBN 978-1-84319-489-7

Foreword

America is obsessed with the grand game of baseball, and with good reason. The sport is played by boys, girls, men, and women. All ages. All races. It is played at various levels; amateur and professional. 'Talent can take a player anywhere, if he chooses to work hard developing his athletic craft. The sky is the limit.

In the land of the free, home of the brave, where all people are assumed equal under the constitution, it is hard to believe that well into the twentieth century black men were barred from entering the major leagues because of the color of their skin. The honorable and unofficial Gentlemen's' Agreement was the code that the white owners lived by. The majors would stay lily white. Because of this, the colored were forced to languish in their own leagues, where they had their own game, their own stars, and their own name. The Negro Leagues. Some called it Blackball, or Raceball. Jim Crow ball. Whatever the name, it existed for a purpose, an essential outlet for those players to flash their talents, although under less than ideal conditions, including poorer pay than the majors.

The year 1945 saw a shot in the arm to the grand old game. The following is that untold story.

One

Due to war-time travel restrictions forced on major league baseball, the Brooklyn Dodgers held their third consecutive spring training camp in the north, instead of in Florida. This year's camp was unique. Two ball players arrived unannounced, demanding tryouts.

Terris McDuffie was a pin-point pitcher who won five and lost six in 1944. Dave "Showboat" Thomas was an agile, hard-hitting first baseman. Thomas and McDuffie had thirty-seven years combined experience in the pro ball circuit. They were also dark skinned, seasoned veterans of the Negro Leagues.

On this cool, bright day, Dodger president Branch Rickey came out to the diamond to scrutinize the tryout. It was the first time since Charlie Grant performed for the New York Giants in 1901 that a black baseball player had vaunted his abilities before the watchful eyes of a white major league team.

From the stands alongside first base, Rickey called an end to the two-player tryout after forty minutes. No one in the game knew how to attach a dollar sign to talent the way flamboyant Branch Wesley Rickey did. Feared by a handful, revered by many, Rickey was a giant in baseball boardrooms, the most successful executive in the major leagues. In his early sixties, associated with the game for forty years, he was a combination preacher, politician, reformer, orator, lawyer, loan shark, and charlatan. His fiercest opponents called him a con man. His players referred to him as a cheapo, for the way he bargained so fiercely at contract time. He never drank potent liquids and the strongest language he ever used was "Judas Priest." A shrewd judge of talent, he was a saint to hayseed high-school kids, farmers, and ploughboys who were offered more money in one month playing baseball for him in the minors than they could make in a year back home on the farm slinging bales with a pitchfork, spreading manure across a garden, or driving a beat-up old tractor over some dusty summer fallow field.

Rickey had learned the major league way of doing things from the ground up. Inept as a catcher as well as a manager, he was offered a job in the St. Louis Cardinal front office. There, behind a desk, sporting white shirt and black tie, he blossomed. Tradition didn't mean a hill of beans to him. The game had to change to survive. In St. Louis, he devised the major league farm system, the overall scheme that brought six pennants to his Cardinals between 1926 and 1942. By the start of the Second World War, he had at his disposal eight hundred players assigned to thirty-two minor league teams. Before he departed St. Louis, with the war escalating around the world, he signed a load of young boys to Cardinal contracts.

Taking on the position of Dodger president in early 1943 at $100,000 yearly plus a piece of the team's stock, Rickey continued signing players, this time before they went into the service, mindful that quality in quantity hadn't failed him in St Louis. "Some of them might be killed, but most of them will be back. And they'll be Dodgers," he told his critics. He was already proving himself right. Most potential Dodgers had survived the war so far. Determined to see the Dodgers become a future powerhouse, Rickey was thinking years ahead of his competition. However, his greatest innovation was yet to come.

Thick cigar in mouth, Rickey turned his attention to his colored friend, Art Powell, a former Negro Leaguer of some note, whose leg injury had halted his playing career many years before.

"Art, what's your opinion of the Negro Leagues?" There was a boom to Rickey's voice, like a smoothbore cannon firing off. "Is there talent out there?" he asked, his bushy eyebrows fluttering over his glasses.

"The talent's always been there, Mr. Rickey." Powell spoke slowly and carefully, punctuated with breathy pauses. "At best, the leagues is Double A or. . . Triple A. But in any year there's a number of players who could step right into the majors. . . with little or no minor league

3

training. I'm certain of that. There's not much depth in the lineups. Each team"—he shrugged—"has only one. . . or two. . . good pitchers. The others don't cut it. Even the strongest teams I've seen is weak at one or two positions. . . Maybe three."

"What else? What about the game itself?"

Powell looked at the bow-tied executive in his suit, long coat, and fedora. "Bunting and base-running is outstanding. Every runner thinks extra bases. Run. . . run. . . run. . . There's more daring in Blackball. Two bases on a bunt or a long fly ball. Cool Papa Bell has done it. I seen him. Runs like a rabbit. The infielders are fast and limber. The pitchers throw slow curves on full counts. There's some mighty fine catchers around too. Outfielders is another story."

"In what sense?"

"Blackball is lacking in outfielders. A lot of 'em have the range. . . but they don't have the arms. And as far as long ball hitters, there's only a few real good ones. Josh Gibson. . . Buck Leonard. . . and Brown."

"Brown?"

"Yes, sir. Willard Brown. Only he's in the service."

"What do you think of these two. . . Thomas, McDuffie?"

Powell shrugged. "To begin with. . . sir. . . they're too old fer the Brown Dodgers. McDuffie is in his thirties. Thomas. . . he's forty. They're long, long past their prime."

Rickey nodded. He respected his friend's opinion. They sat and watched the activity on the field in silence.

Powell was ash-haired and chunky, in his fifties, slow-moving, slow-talking, a perpetual sad grin of a face. Although uneducated, he was a man full of wisdom and down-home smarts. For the last fifteen years, the South Carolina-born Powell had managed winter teams in the Caribbean, Mexico, and South America. For thirty years he had seen quality black players come and go. Called up on the telephone to Bear Mountain by Rickey, Powell was told he'd be scouting for the United States League, a new and much-heralded Negro League started by Gus Greenlee, the numbers racket king and the owner of the once-powerful Pittsburgh Crawfords.

Established in January, the new league was set to open this season. Everything about the United States League sounded too good to be true. Nevertheless, franchises had been granted to Greenlee's Pittsburgh

Crawfords, the Toledo Rays, the Philadelphia Hilldale Club, the Detroit Motor City Giants, the Chicago Brown Dodgers, and the Brooklyn Brown Dodgers, financed by Rickey's Brooklyn Dodgers, who would play at Ebbets Field when the Dodgers were out of town. Unlike the past colored leagues, the United States League would be run—so the stories went—in a more business-like manner, with uniform schedules, valid contracts, and better accommodations for the players.

Yeah, Powell had heard that before. He was not impressed.

Rickey flicked his cigar. "That's not all," he said. "Thomas swings at too many bad pitches. Hitting is combination of stride, hitch, and keeping your bat level. Meanwhile, the secret of pitching is throwing the ball as far from the bat and as close to the plate as you can. You know the biggest difference between a major league hitter and a minor league hitter? More than anything else?" He cut in before Powell could answer. "His judgment of the strike zone. That's what."

Powell nodded. He agreed. Good observation. "Right, sir. I agree."

"Simple isn't it. Too simple, really. Now, take that pitcher, McDuffie. He has control and can mix up his speeds with an array of pitches including a high, hard one, but he doesn't know how to get off the rubber in time. He has no footwork. I'm surprised he hasn't been killed by a batted ball before this."

"What footwork. . . sir?"

Rickey stood to demonstrate. He was quick for a man of sixty-plus years. The art of pitching was his favorite baseball subject. A scattered few men in the stands looked over. Although he measured only five-foot-nine, Rickey, with his wide shoulders, seemed taller to Powell. He reeled into a wind-up, then stopped cold, stomping his foot down on the wooden floorboards.

"Some pitchers move wrong after they finish throwing to the plate," Rickey said. "He has to bring himself to a proper fielding position in order to grab a line drive through the box. The pivot foot"—Rickey slapped the back of his leg—"the one on the rubber, must be brought even with his lead foot. Then the pitcher is evenly balanced. Like so." He placed his feet together. "Far too many pitchers, even in pro ball, leave their pivot foot dangling in mid-air. They're asking for trouble. Some pitchers don't think out there. Their arm is ahead of their brain. There's more to pitching than just throwing a baseball."

Powell was moved by Rickey's knowledge of the inside part of the game. Rickey could talk people to death. The trouble was, he was usually right. "I get yuh, Mr. Rickey. I ain't never paid it much attention before. But I will now."

Rickey sat down. "Art?"

"Yes, sir."

"There's a revolution across this country. The war will be over soon. Times are changing for the better. Baseball and the Brooklyn Dodgers have a glorious future. We have some good young players coming up through the farm system and some coming back from the war." He paused. "I don't want to get ahead of myself. Let me tell you a story:

"In 1904," Rickey began, "I coached the baseball team at Ohio Wesleyan University. Charles Thomas was our catcher, our best player, one of the better players in the league. He was a black man. No relation to Showboat, here, that I know of. He was the only black man on my team and one of a mere few in the league. We took a trip down to South Bend, Indiana, to play Notre Dame. When we booked in at the hotel, the hotel clerk refused Thomas a room. So I told that clerk I'd move the entire team out on the spot, if Thomas couldn't stay."

"What happened, sir?"

"I decided to call for the manager," Rickey continued, glancing at the diamond, eyeing McDuffie and Thomas standing idle near the dugout. "We finally settled for a compromise. He agreed that a cot would be put in the room for Thomas. So, I told Thomas to go up to the room and I'd be up after I settled the accommodations for the rest of the team. When I got to the room, there was Thomas crying. His whole body shook. Then he began to scratch his skin. I was shocked. I asked what he was doing and he told me, 'I'm scratching my skin until it turns white. If only I was white.' And I said to him that the day will come when a good ballplayer won't have to be white." Glassy-eyed, Rickey turned to the black scout beside him. "That day is now, Art, my good man, I didn't call you to Bear Mountain to look at these two players. Not at all. It was a mere coincidence they showed the day you arrived. I didn't call you to scout for the Brooklyn Brown Dodgers either."

"Yuh didn't, sir?"

"Absolutely not. I called you to scout for the Brooklyn Dodgers of the National League." There was now a fire in Rickey's voice. "There is an

6

untapped source of talent in America. Fifteen percent of the population. I can see a string of pennants flapping over the Ebbets Field facades in the years to come. We are going to sign colored players. And we are going to fill the park with millions of people. Soon. We are going to start signing colored this year."

"Yuh are?" Powell stared off into space. He prayed his heart wouldn't stop pumping blood to his brain. He never dreamed of seeing integration in his lifetime.

"Art, I need a black scout who can get closer to the players than a white scout can. Someone who can get to know people. Establish a network. Make connections. The United States League is only a front for what we're really up to. Use it to our advantage. If anybody asks questions, make the players and press think you're scouting for the Brown Dodgers."

As Powell smiled, his lips quivered. "I'm at yer service, Mr. Rickey. It. . . will be a pleasure. When do I start?"

"Are you kidding? Immediately. Art, I'm looking for that one player to lead the way for the others. I have the secret backing of the Dodger directors on this. Our man has to be the right one on and off the field. He has to receive favorable reaction from the press and public, and the backing of the Negro community leaders and from the race in general. And," Rickey sighed, "he has to be accepted by his teammates. That could be the toughest of all."

"You are right about that."

"He has to be many things. He has to have character. He has to be a leader. A competitor. A model citizen. He must have a clean background. An example to others of his race. He has to be willing to pay the price with sweat and hard work. He has to be saturated with the desire to excel. He has to strive to be more than mediocre. I need someone with three things on the field. Arm, legs, and power. I want to see speed on our team. Base-running is another key. And I don't want a pitcher to be the first, although I value pitching. Our player has to be someone who will be visible, in people's faces every day."

Powell nodded, and said, "Yes, sir."

"Scouting, Art, is sixty percent of the success of any ball team. Finding the right players. If it was the outside—a player's talent—than it would be a whole lot easier. But a scout has to look into a player's heart.

Seek and evaluate, that's your job. Project what he could do outside his current league. Next year. The year after. Can he move up? Does he have the heart?" Rickey pounded his chest. "For a year now several scouts have been out there for me looking over the colored players. Tom Greenwade, George Sisler, Wid Matthews, Clyde Sukeforth, and Oscar Charleston, whom I'm sure you know."

"Yes sir, I surely do. Played with him. . . in Mexico. Best center fielder I've ever seen. Some say he was better than Joe D."

"Oscar is going to manage the Brown Dodgers for me. So, his scouting will be rather limited, due to his own workload. You'll be one of my main scouts. I'm counting on you."

Powell smiled. "I won't let you or the Dodgers down, sir. Are there any players who yuh already have in mind?"

"A few, yes," explained Rickey. "The trouble is the best ones so far are too old, like Thomas and McDuffie, here. Two of the best are still in the service. Larry Doby and Monte Irvin."

"I've seen me a messa great ones."

"No doubt, Art. No doubt." Rickey puffed on his cigar, crunching the end with his teeth. "Cool Papa Bell, Josh Gibson, Satchel Paige, Buck Leonard. All four are too up there in age to be pioneers. Then there's the younger ones. Sam Jethroe, Roy Campanella. But there's got to be more."

Powell jerked up. "Campanella is a great one. Best catcher in the Negro Leagues. He's only twenty-four or twenty-five. Better than Gibson, I'd say. Seen 'em both in South America and Cuba."

"In your estimation then, is Campanella a good prospect?"

"Of course," Powell's voice rose. "Catchers that good are hard tuh come by. He's played on integrated teams before in his hometown of Philly."

"Good. Put him on our list. This spring and summer will be the end to our hunt. Whoever rises to the surface will be our man." Rickey stamped out his cigar butt under his shoe. "Now, I'm off to New York to a press conference to announce my support to the United States League. It will be official. I know I'll get a backlashing about it, from whites and blacks, exploiting the poor black ballplayers and all that. But what about Clark Griffith in Washington. I know he'll be the biggest screamer. Meanwhile, he rents his ballpark out to the Homestead Grays for $100,000 a year." Rickey chuckled. "For years he's sat there and watched Gibson and Leonard smash homer after homer and he can't touch them, all because of the Gentlemen's Agreement. Too bad for him."

"Yeah, too bad," Powell agreed. "Gibson and Leonard should be finishing up their major league careers. Instead... if they were only white." Over the years, Powell had confided with a dozen black owners of the Negro League teams, many black media people, black players, and black managers. There were too many crooked owners and booking agents. Contracts were generally verbal. Games were canceled without notice. Umpires and official scorers often arrived at the games drunk or didn't show at all. The leagues had always lacked proper organization, unlike the structured majors, where games were canceled only due to rain.

"Judas Priest, Art! It's high time this Negro League baseball comes to a screeching halt. It's a paradise for bookies and schemers. It's a mafia, that's what it is. A mafia. A racket."

"I'll say," Powell added, dumbfounded that Rickey was almost reading his own thoughts.

Rickey stood, his hand on Powell's shoulder. "Rest assured, that's going to change. And you're going to see it. This year will be the last year of Blackball as we know it. It might be the last year of America as we know it, too. The colored are fighting and dying in this war. If they can take a bullet and bleed alongside whites, they can at least play with the whites on the same ball field."

Powell looked up, his eyes full of tears. The former player-manager began to picture a conglomeration of black faces belonging to the players he'd managed or seen over the years, spirits of the past, who were good enough for the majors, but were forced to waste away their baseball careers receiving a quarter of what they would make in the white leagues. No more. Hopefully. Providing Branch Rickey was true to his word. Somehow, though, Powell didn't doubt the man. If Rickey said he was going to integrate the Big Leagues, then he was going to do it. But still, the pressure on the first colored player going up to the Dodgers would be unbearable. Powell had wanted to see black men in the majors all his life. Now, faced with the real possibility of it, he was suddenly scared silly for his race.

"It sounds like a real fight tuh me, Mr. Rickey."

"It will be, yes. The wrong man could set this back a decade or more. We have to pick the right man. Our pennant man."

"Yes, sir." Powell wiped his tears with the back of his hand. From this day forward, he knew baseball would never be the same.

"Everything, I mean everything, must be done in secret."

Powell cleared his throat. "Yes. . . sir."

"Good luck, Art."

"Thank you, sir."

Two

Denver, Colorado—May

The black cab driver wheeled over to the curb. "There she is, there, lady." He got out, took the money, handed the passengers their luggage and roared off.

Ramona and Chester found themselves in the colored section of Denver. From what they could tell at first glance, the ratio of blacks to whites in this modern western city was far less than they were used to in the small towns in Louisiana. A lot less. The Denver black neighborhood—known as Nigger Alley to the whites—was tidier by comparison to anything they had seen in the Deep South. Most of the houses here had a fresh coat of paint. Boulevards were reasonably well kept. Trees were pruned, the grass and the bushes trimmed. The people seemed happier, including the black cab driver who had dropped them off in such a hurry. All he talked about along the way was the latest news of the day. Germany's surrender to the Allies. The war in Europe finally over after nearly six bloody years. The driver didn't need to tell Ramona and Chester that because they saw it for themselves. Downtown Denver was coming unglued. Screaming, drunken people blocking the downtown streets. Everybody whooping it up, it seemed, except for Ramona and Chester, two small-town Southerners out of place in the North country. A couple of square pegs in two round holes.

"Let me do the talking," said Ramona, suitcase in hand, pondering the beige, three-story house with the blue shutters. "I have me a good story."

"I was hoping you might, mama." Chester rubbed his hands together.

He was cold and the sight of snow patches on the distant mountains made him shiver all the more. Denver felt like another planet to him. How would they ever fit in? What were they doing here?

"This is one harsh part of the country, boy."

"It sure is, mama."

"Come on, son."

Chester grabbed his suitcase and hurried after her, up the porch, to the wide, shiny, wood-grained door. Chester ranged nearly a foot over his mother at an inch past six feet on a frame that tipped the scales at an even 195 pounds. He had his father's solid build, his mother's mouth and nose on a friendly, trusting face. Light-skinned like Ramona, he appeared to be a well-tanned white man if not for the kinky hair under his fedora.

Ramona knocked and waited, peering over her shoulder, a habitual quirk she had picked up after leaving Louisiana so suddenly.

A black woman's face appeared, transfixed through the window. "Ramona!" she burst out, swinging the door open. "Oh, God. Ramona! The war's over and my sister visits me on the same day. I don't believe it!"

The two women hugged for a long time.

"And Chester! I do declare. It is Chester, ain't it?" the woman said, as she broke away from her sister.

"It's me, Aunt Anna."

"Lordy, Lordy. Such a handsome young man. Yer all grown up." The woman hugged Chester.

"Well, sis, aren't you going to invite us in?" Ramona asked.

"Of course. Come quick and set yerself down. I still don't believe it!"

They placed their suitcases on the area rug inside. A black man in his twenties walked by, smiled, and proceeded to a room around the corner on the main floor.

Anna was the older sister of the two, shorter and overweight. She'd been widowed for a year. She removed her tomato-stained apron and held it in her hand. Her flowery dress had tomato stains on it, too. "What in blazes are yuh doing here in Denver? Why didn't you tell me yuh were coming for a visit?"

"I couldn't."

"Why? What's wrong? I always could tell when there was something wrong, girl. I can read it in yer eyes."

Ramona cleared her throat. "It's Clyde." She held her breath. "We're. . . fugitives."

"Fugitives? What you mean, girl?"

"We're on the run."

"Pretty far to run. What did he do this time?"

"Let's just say things haven't gotten any better."

"Uh huh, honey. Can't lay off the liquor. Gosh, sis. Fool man."

Ramona hoped her sister would believe the story. "He threatened to kill me and Chester with a shotgun. We left Grambling and Louisiana too, for good. Sold what we could. We've had it with the South."

Anna sighed, looking to the ceiling, clapping her hands once. "Thank God, you finally came to yer senses and got outta there. Didn't I always tell you that you were too good fer that place?" She shook her head. "But, wasn't this Chester's last year in senior high?"

"It was." Ramona stole a glance at Chester, relieved that Anna had fallen for the story. "I was forced to remove him early."

Anna pouted. "What a shame. So, you two need a place to stay, do yuh? I just happen to have a room for each of yuh, until yuh get on yer feet. Or if yuh want to stay a spell, that's just fine too."

"We're thinking of being around for some time."

"That's OK, honey. Men on the first floor. Women on the second floor. Those are the the rules."

"Fair enough."

The door opened behind Chester, bumping him in the elbow.

"Oh, I'm sorry." It was a woman's voice.

Chester turned around to see a young lady in a bright, white dress and brown hat. She had plain features, yet pretty in her own way. She was slim, with dancer's legs, medium height, and rich, dark eyes with a whisper of pink make-up.

"That's quite all right, ma'am. I was in the way," he said to her, shyly.

"Agnes, what yuh doing back so soon?" Anna asked. "Come home to celebrate?"

The girl smiled at Anna, shaking her head, her long hair swinging back and forth. "No, ma'am. They closed the pharmacy down early."

"Did they now?"

"What with the war news and, of course, the ball team coming home tomorrow."

"Ball team?" Chester asked. "What ball team, ma'am?"

"Don't you know?" the girl told him. "The Black Sox."

"They ain't from around here, Agnes," Anna said. "This is my sister, Ramona. Moved up from Louisiana way."

"How do you do? I'm Agnes Hudson."

"Pleased to meet you. I'm Ramona. . . Parker."

"And this is her boy, Chester," Anna said, glancing at her sister then to Chester. "He's played a hot game of baseball down in Louisiana."

"That so? How do you do, Chester?" Agnes held out her hand. Her smile showed off perfect white teeth.

Chester pumped her hand gently. "Fine, ma'am."

"I know a couple of the players. I hear they need a player or two. What position you play?"

"Outfield, ma'am."

"What do you know? I think they're looking for another outfielder for this summer, come to think of it. They're professional. Barnstormers. They pay good, too, I hear."

"They do?"

"Now, Chester. Remember your schooling."

Chester grinned. "Mama, you know there won't be any schooling for me until the fall."

"That's right, honey," said Anna.

"You stay out of this, sis," Ramona said to Anna.

"I don't want to start a family squabble," the girl smiled, moving gracefully up the flight of stairs. "Pleased to meet you both."

"The pleasure is ours, ma'am," Chester replied, watching her until she was out of sight.

"Supper's on in thirty minutes," Anna shouted up the stairs.

"That's swell, Anna," Agnes called down. "Thank you."

"Come on," Anna said, an eagerness about her. "Let's go to the kitchen. Coffee's on."

"Anything to warm us up," Ramona said. "It's going to take me a spell to get used to this weather. It's freezing."

Anna laughed. "You'll get used to it. Most Mays are like this. It'll warm up soon enough." She lowered her voice. "Ramona Parker, huh. How did yuh come up with that one, girl?"

"We're on the run, remember."

Anna winked. "Oh, yeah. I'll play along."

"Aunt Anna?" Chester asked.

"Yeah, boy?"

"Tell me more about this baseball team?"

Anna talked nonstop as she poured strong coffee in the kitchen. The Denver Black Sox were run by a well-to-do black man real estate operator, the owner of the boarding house that Anna had been running for him since she had moved from Joplin, Missouri almost a year ago. Dead in winter, the colored section of Denver came alive during baseball season, especially when the Sox came to town off a road trip. The players and their families and girlfriends always needed a place to board. The team traveled most of the time, but returned once a month for a few days. The merchants, of course, looked forward to it because the players always had money to spend.

"You'll like Denver in no time. You'll see," Anna went on. "It's a nice place for blacks. No KKK around neither. No lynchings, that I know of. It's not perfect, but not bad either. The air is dry and sometimes hard to breath seeing that we're up so high. Like everything else, it takes some getting used to. The snow in the winter, well, let's take that step when we come to it. It can snow here in September or October, and stick around till April."

"Snow!" Ramona winced, her forehead creasing.

"Yeah, snow! What you expect in the Rockies, honey, palm trees?"

Chester couldn't sleep. He just lay there, staring at the ceiling. After what Anna told him earlier about the ball team, Chester decided that Denver wasn't going to be such a bad place after all. Like she said, it'll warm up. It always did every spring, she said. And what luck. A professional team, all the way out here. Chester grinned to himself in the darkness. Every spring, the urge called out to him. The smell of green grass meant the smell of baseball, no matter where he was.

He was hooked. And he knew it.

That one day did it. April 9, 1936. The Pittsburgh Crawfords were touring the South, and expected to play an exhibition game at Shreveport against a local colored semi-pro team. Ten-year-old Chester, older brother Billy, and their father made the trip across the state to catch the game. In his Denver bed now, Chester closed his eyes and could still see it all. . . nine years later. The more than 13,000 fans did not leave disappointed. That mild afternoon, the great Satchel Paige hurled an 8-0 shutout, striking out fourteen men. Chester was stirred by Paige's performance, but he was absolutely awed by the catcher, Josh Gibson, an all-muscle six-foot, 200-pounder. Chester loved how Gibson kicked up his lead foot like a bronco before he swung at the ball with a vicious, yet controlled, compact swing. He had a fluid way of moving his huge arms and meaty thighs into the ball. In his first two times at the plate, the right-handed Gibson hit two line-drive homers to left-center. Then he walked twice. But in the ninth inning, he ended the day by hitting one loud, tremendous blast over the grandstand roof in left field.

Never in his life before or since had Chester heard such an explosive sound, and never had he seen a ball get so small so fast. Once he saw Gibson in person, Chester Henry made up his mind then and there he would one day be a professional ballplayer.

Three

It was easy for Chester and his mother to take the five blocks to the ball field the afternoon that the Denver Black Sox were in town for their first long practice in weeks. What luck Kramer Park was a mere fifteen-minute walk from the boarding house.

The two were clad in their Sunday best on a Tuesday, Ramona in a clean, blue dress and Chester in a black suit, white shirt, and black tie. Chester was carrying his canvas bag with him, containing his glove, two bats, socks, cleats, and Beckford High uniform. Anna was right about it warming up. It was a fine morning, marred only by Ramona's nagging along the way. The majestic snow-capped Rocky Mountains glistened against the bright, sun-filled western sky. The temperature was near seventy degrees. Chester took his mother's remarks one at a time, then stopped her suddenly.

"Now hold on, mama," he explained, slowly. "I have to do this. I just have to. And I wanted you to come along. You haven't seen me play since my junior year."

She looked behind her.

"Mama, nobody's following us. OK?"

"I can't help it. Habit."

"Louisiana is a long way off. We're safe here," he tried to assure her.

"Don't be so sure, boy." She unbuttoned the thick coat she had borrowed from her sister.

"Come on."

They walked on.

"There it is, mama. The park."

She saw the lights and the grandstand roof. "Baseball is a waste of time, Chester."

"Why do you say that?"

"It won't take you anywhere. Education and a good job will do it. That Miss Hudson knows that. She finished her high school and took a university course to be a pharmacist. She graduated near the top of her class. And she has a good job that pays her one hundred and fifty dollars a month. Smart girl for twenty-two. She'll marry some college boy and do just fine. She won't marry no wood-chopper or cotton-picker. No, sir. It's a decent suit-and-tie man for her."

Chester took his mother by the hand. "Mama, I was ready to finish high school, too."

Ramona lowered her head. "I know. I don't need to be reminded."

"I never told you this. But I better now." He swallowed. "That day. . . you know. . . I came home to tell you something."

Her eyes bulged. "I thought we weren't going to discuss that day. Billy took care of everything. Isn't that what he said? That subject is closed. Forever. It never happened!"

"Sorry, mama. But listen to me. After my last game, a professional scout found me and offered me two-hundred and seventy-five dollars a month to play for the Birmingham Black Barons."

"Goodness me, boy." She was obviously surprised at the amount of money. "What did you tell him?"

"I said my mama wanted me to finish my school year first."

"Good boy."

"And he told me to call him as soon as I graduated. Don't you see, mama. I have to try out for this team. They're professional. I have to know if I can make it. I have dreams, too, mama. Just like you had yours."

"A long time ago, boy. Dreams fade when reality sets in."

"I'll tell you what I'm going to do."

"Now you sound like your daddy."

"Listen, mama. Let me play for the summer, and I'll go back to senior high in the fall and finish my final year."

"And go to college the next year?" she asked.

"Well. . . I can't promise that."

"Why can't you promise me?" She shook her finger. "Chester Henry, don't try and sweet-talk me the way your daddy used to. Anyway, you don't know if you're going to make this ball team. Your Aunt Anna said they are good and they're all older than you. Besides, ball players have no morals. They play on the Lord's Day. They gamble. They run around. And they carry on. And they don't have any schooling."

"Oh, mama, stop it!" He raised his voice at her, cutting her short. "I'm trying out, whether you like it or not."

She folded her arms and stood firm. "Is that so?"

"Yes."

"Well, then, far be it from me to argue."

"That's right." He took a breath. "Are you still coming? I really wish you would."

Ramona had to think about it. She was a proud woman of practical principles with a strong Southern Baptist background who believed in going to Church on Sunday and keeping the Lord's word the rest of the week. In her early forties, she, with her smooth, youthful skin, could pass for a woman ten or fifteen years younger. She was slim, firm-figured, with delicate features and a light complexion from a hint of French ancestry two generations previous. Upon graduating from high school, the only one in her family of four girls, she dared to marry a man of mixed race, a mulatto, thinking it would get her ahead. It didn't. He was too incompetent and too hard drinking. And here she was now. On the run, a fugitive, hundreds of miles away in Denver, heading to her son's first pro baseball tryout.

"I'd better keep you out of trouble," she eventually said, after a lengthy silence.

"Thanks, mama."

"Besides," she grinned, "I might get lost trying to find my way back home."

A few players had already arrived at the park. Chester wasted no time. He quickly dressed under the stands, passed the duffle bag stuffed with his suit to his mother, then leaped over the wire fence near the third-base dugout.

He stepped a few feet onto the field, looking in every direction, absorbing the beauty of Kramer Park situated half-way between the middle-class white and the black section of northern Denver. It was the cleanest ball field he'd ever stepped onto. The infield and outfield were held together by a soft, thick, liquid green sheet of grass under his feet. Unlike the Louisiana high school fields, there were no pot holes anywhere to dodge. Off to the side, he saw the inside of the two newly-painted dugouts. The outfield fences were a see-through steel mesh. No chicken wire and cracked fence posts like back home. The raked infield, with white bases in place, was a deep, reddish-brown loam. A set of tall oak trees in bud hung over a large flower bed on the other side of right field, seventy feet or so from the 350-foot sign down the line. Beyond that wound a narrow creek. Chester looked around at the stands where a dozen people were sitting. The place would seat 10,000 fans, at least. Maybe more.

He let out a whistle.

"What yuh doing here, boy?"

Chester turned to the third-base dugout, where three uniformed players were eyeing him. The oldest one, about forty-five or fifty, with a double chin and paunch, his cheek bulging, plodded up the steps and marched towards Chester. At close range, his leathered, unshaven face gave evidence of a widely-traveled man who may have seen the inside of many a smoky liquor bar, as well as the bright glow of an occasional sunrise.

"Hey, boy, I'm talking to yuh. State yer business." The man's legs appeared unsteady, his voice gruff and hostile.

Chester straightened his shoulders. "Good morning, sir. I'm looking for a Mr. Garrett."

"You found him," the man barked, spitting brown juice on the ground. "They call me Cap. What yuh want?"

"Are you the manager?"

"That's right, boy. I said, what yuh want?"

"I came to try out for your team, sir."

The man was taken aback. "Did yuh really?"

"Yes, sir." Chester nodded, pointing to the stands. "That's my mama over there."

The manager looked over his shoulder at the woman and caught her glancing down at them. "Your mama, huh? Is she trying out too, boy?"

"No, sir. I brought her along. I told her I can make this club. And I'm going to prove it to her."

20

The manager smiled for the first time. His teeth were brown from chewing tobacco. "Oh yuh will, will yuh?"

"I heard you need an outfielder because one of your boys went lame and you had to send him home to Georgia. I was a left fielder in senior high."

The manager studied Chester's cleats, socks, cap, and scuffed uniform. "High School, eh? What's that big ol' B stand fer?"

"Beckford Senior High, Grambling, Louisiana."

"How old yuh, boy?"

"I'll be nineteen in August, Mr. Garrett."

"That's young fer this club."

"I know, that's what my mama told me too."

"You got one smart mama. What's yer name, son?"

"Chester Henry Parker. I can hit, run, and throw," he stated boldly, then hesitated. "And I think I can make this club."

Garrett slanted his head at the youngster. "You let me be the judge of that, boy."

"All I want is the chance."

"Hmm. Yuh sure yer black? Yuh look kinda white too me. Talk white too."

Chester removed his ball cap to show the manager his black kinky hair. "See."

"All right, Chester Henry Parker, I believe yuh. You're one of us, I guess. Let's see what yuh got. Better warm up first."

"Much obliged, sir." Chester saw more players piling out of the dugout.

"Yeah, yeah." Garrett spun towards the dugout and beckoned a player. "Chick?"

"Yo."

"Get yer boney ass over here, and warm this boy up," Garrett grunted with a gesture of finality, spitting a full mouthful of juice on the ground.

The player grabbed his glove and slowly banged up the stairs. "Sure thing, Cap."

Garrett felt his head. "Hell, where's that Joe Schmo trainer of ours? I need a ice pack!"

"He got fired, yesterday, remember," replied the player, trotting past. "Mr. Jeffries made you the trainer."

"Oh, yeah. Shit. I forgot. Another job fer me. Man, as if I don't have enough now."

Chester didn't get into the full mood of the tryout until all the players were on the field. The stands were filling up with two-hundred or more fans. They even had a mobile batting cage. This was a first-class operation compared to his native Louisiana.

Cap called to Chester. "Grab yer bat, boy."

In the cage, Chester rolled his sleeves up and cocked his bat, peering over his shoulder at the player throwing batting practice with the same menacing stare that struck fear into the pitchers back home who faced him. The Sox player reached into a pail behind him, grabbed some balls in his fists, and bore down from the mound at the left-handed hitter. Chester took a few cuts, as naturally as he always did back home. He quickly realized—after four solid smacks—that Denver was a hitter's delight. The ball was taking off on him. Then he put more strength into his swings. Now he was knocking line drives to the fence and beyond. Two balls sailed to the opposite field. Over and out. This thin Colorado air was really something.

Several of the players stopped to watch. Standing behind the third-base dugout was a thick, dog-faced black man in his forties, his disposition suggesting a cool, calculated intelligence set under thinning hair and dark sunglasses. He had a cigarette in his mouth and was backed up by a muscular man in his mid-thirties.

Garrett came up, an ice pack on his forehead. "Yo there, Mr. Jeffries."

"What's yer problem?" The man in sunglasses asked. "Yuh look like hell."

"Feel like hell, too. Got me a humdinger of a headache."

"Too much of that celebrating, huh? So, who's the kid with the crazy peek-a-boo stance?"

"Says his name is Chester Parker. From down Louisiana." A loud crack of the bat made Garrett look to the outfield fence. "Shit, man, there goes another one. And we got Rabbit in there, our best pitcher."

"Straightaway center. The kid can sure hit the long ball."

"No kidding. Says he's an outfielder."

"Looks young. How old is he?"

"Coming up nineteen in a few months. August." Garrett took the ice pack off his head and held it in his hand.

"Get him out to the field. Hit him a few. Let's see his arm."

"OK, boss."

Four

Horace Jeffries sat down with his bodyguard in the first row behind
the dugout, where he lit another cigarette, and eyed this new boy. He
squirmed to find a comfortable position as his bulk filled the seat tightly.
It took him only a few minutes to see the talent in Parker. The kid had
the speed, the range, and the throwing arm, although he was a bit
erratic. They could use him in the outfield.

Horace Jeffries was the mastermind behind Denver's colored section,
owning several pieces of property. He printed his own black community newspaper, *The Denver Examiner*, operated his own nightclub, and
controlled the city's numbers racket. He was friends with the white
politicians and businessmen of the area. He also knew all the city coun-
cilmen by their first names.

Jeffries was raised in a high-crime section of coastal Texas, where
dropout and suicide for colored were common occurrences in their
miserable lifestyles. Jeffries belonged to various ghetto gangs from the
time he was eight. He only got as far as the third grade before he quit
school completely. His marks were horrible, anyway. His parents didn't
seem to care. They were never around. His father was a card shark and
pool hustler; his mother a prostitute, who deserted the family for greener
pastures northeast. The young Horace was left to look after himself.
He did, receiving a solid schooling in the rackets as a street fighter, an
errand boy, a whiskey runner, and a protection collector.

During the Depression, Jeffries swung north. At Pittsburgh, he found

23

a job as a numbers runner for Gus Greenlee, a nightclub owner in town and the biggest colored name in the east. Jeffries worked his way up to be Greenlee's right-hand man, taking care of odd chores that needed some arm-breaking. He also became the secretary for Greenlee's baseball team, the Pittsburgh Crawfords of the Negro National League. When the stars—Satchel Paige, Josh Gibson, Judy Johnson, Oscar Charleston, Cool Papa Bell, Leroy Matlock, Jimmy Crutchfield, and Sam Bankhead—up and left for the Dominican Republic in the summer of 1937, the team disintegrated, never to rise again to such stature. Jeffries departed too, packing up and going west to fertile territory, with his own ideas patterned after what he had learned inside the Greenlee operation.

Some locals called him the "Saint of Colored Town" for his charity during the Great Depression, when he set up soup kitchens for the poor, white and black. For ten years, he had been wintering in Mexico where he ran an integrated winter baseball league. The barnstorming Denver Black Sox was his latest brainchild. His first year—1944—was the experiment. And a successful one at that. He made money, especially when he sold two players to the Homestead Grays of the Negro National League. Now there was this new United States League starting up by his old mentor, Gus Greenlee. They'd be looking for players too. At a price. Jeffries' price. And this summer the Mexican League that was in the news lately would also need players.

A man of infinite ambition, Jeffries dreamed of being the "King of Baseball West of the Mississippi River" and thus steal the headlines from the Kansas City Monarchs. His future plan was to eventually find his way into the Negro National or American League with a team of his own from Denver. For the time being, the Black Sox was a perfect screen for the tax man. The profits were invested elsewhere, in his real estate. Jeffries was not one to sit on his cash. He was caught up in a cycle. He spent. He owed. He spent. He invested. He profited. It was the only way he saw to make money in a white business world where one had to make it on his own merits and damn awful good luck.

Jeffries snapped his fingers at the bodyguard. "Duke."

"Yeah, boss?" the bodyguard twitched. Duke Johnson was a former prize fighter, a confidant of Jeffries for six years.

"Get Cap up here."

"Right, boss."

The bodyguard jumped the rail and went into the dugout.

Garrett soon leaned over the first-row seats. "Well? Yuh wanna see how he looks in a game? We're gonna split in two soon."

Jeffries shook his head at the manager. "Nah. Sign him now. We need an outfielder, anyway, don't we?"

"Yeah, we sure do. OK, Mr. Jeffries."

Garrett shouted to Chester and waved him in. They waited. Chester legged it to the stands, glove under his arm. "Chester Parker, meet Horace Jeffries, the owner of the Black Sox," Garrett said.

"Pleased to make your acquaintance, Mr. Jeffries," Chester answered, slightly out of breath from the fast jog, shaking the fat man's hand.

"Chester. We'll come tuh the point. We wanna sign yuh to a full season. At some good starting money."

Chester studied Garrett for a moment. "Will I be playing on Sundays?"

"Of course," replied Jeffries.

"My mama won't like that."

"Oh, she won't, huh?" Jeffries said.

"Nope."

"Mama's boy, are yuh?"

"No, sir. It's just that she's all I have left since my daddy. . . left us."

"What if I talk tuh her?" Jeffries said.

"Go ahead. There she is." Chester pointed to her in the stands.

Jeffries nodded at Garrett. "I'll take care of 'er. Come on over with us and rest up a spell," he said to Chester. "Yuh look tuckered out."

"Thanks."

"Don't mention it. Let's go."

"Yes, sir."

Jeffries, his bodyguard, and Chester all gathered around Ramona in the stands. Jeffries stood directly in front of her, blocking her view of the playing field. He undid the buttons on his gray flannel suit and cracked his suspenders. His round stomach strained to burst through his monogrammed shirt. In his hands was a piece of paper. "Mrs. Parker?"

"Do you mind, mister? You're in my way."

"How do yuh do? I'm Horace Jeffries, owner of the Denver Black Sox." He stuck out his sweaty hand.

She looked down at his outstretched hand. He quickly took it away when she didn't respond.

"We wanna sign yer son to a contract. Right now."

She glanced up with no special interest at the scar-faced, dapper-dressed black man. "Do you play on Sundays?"

"Yes, ma'am, we do."

She turned her head to the side. "Then he won't sign."

"Let's get down to brass tacks. What if I tell yuh he can make three-hundred and fifty a month?"

She cocked her head sharply at Jeffries. "You mean three-hundred and fifty dollars!"

"That's right, ma'am. Every month. Yuh have to admit, that's no chicken feed, Mrs. Parker."

Chester was ready to buckle at the knees at the sound of the figure, much better than the Birmingham offer. "Say yes, mama."

Ramona pursed her lips. Her voice shook when she said, "May I please see the contract?"

"What!" Jeffries snorted. "Why?"

"I want to read it."

"Do yuh know who yer talking to?"

"I don't care if you're George Washington Carver back from the grave. I want to read it first."

"Read it! What's this? What's tuh read?" Jeffries' words had the potency of a gun shot. "Just sign. He gets three-hundred and fifty smackers and two dollars a day meal money. What do yuh want?"

She held out her palm, taking in his flaring nostrils with a glance. "Let's see the contract," she demanded.

"Oh. . . all right then. Here." The owner slapped down the standard Black Sox one-page contract in her hand. "What are yuh, his lawyer?"

"I wish I were." She devoured the contract in seconds. Searching, her eyes were suddenly glued to one clause near the bottom. "I don't like this," she remarked, pointing.

"What?"

"Says here he has to stay until September 30th, unless you choose to sell him to another team. You really can't do that."

"I can sell him to another team if I want."

"No, no. I mean make him play until the end of September. He's going to high school at the beginning of September and finish his last year. He has to enroll and be in class weeks before that."

The owner sighed, his tough stance softening. "I know some mighty fine people in town, Mrs. Parker. I'll arrange one of them there correspondence courses for the first month. And I know a real good school for him too. Best colored school in the state."

She looked up, squinting in the sunshine, using her hand as a visor. "You'd do that for my boy?"

"I sure would, ma'am."

She cleared her throat. "What about the money? I don't want him to squander it like his daddy does."

"I don't want him tuh. . . ah, throw it round, neither. What do yuh say tuh him sending home two-thirds of every pay check? The manager will make sure he does."

Ramona thought it out. "Three-quarters," she suggested.

"Mama!"

"Three-quarters it is, ma'am."

"I don't want him to gamble at cards or chase women."

Jeffries was smiling now, two gold teeth flashing. He stole a glance at Chester. "Yuh won't gamble at cards or chase women, will yuh, boy?"

Gawking, Chester shook his head, mouth open. "No, sir. I came to play ball. That's all I want to do."

Then Ramona said sharply, "We never miss church on Sunday either."

Jeffries put a hand up, his smile wider. "Neither do a few of the players on the team. Sunday church is important tuh them. If we find a colored church, someone will see that he goes."

"Preferably Baptist."

"We'll try. How about Methodist, in a pinch?"

"They'll do, yes."

"I wish there were more like yer son, Mrs. Parker."

"Oh, really?"

"Yes, ma'am. Yuh have a bright boy there. Probably picks it up from his mama. So, do we have a deal?"

Finally warming to the idea, Ramona found a smile, and handed the contract to her son. "All right by me. Put your ink to it, Chester," she said. "Before Mr. Jeffries here changes his mind."

Jeffries stuffed the signed contract inside his jacket. He had the Parker boy signed now. He'd be worth something to another team someday.

"Quite the woman," Jeffries said to Johnson, as they watched more of the practice from the stands behind home plate.

"She drives a hard bargain. For a while there I thought yuh were going tuh lambaste her a good one."

Jeffries flicked the suspenders under his jacket. "Me? Nah." He glanced across the seats to where Ramona was seated, watching her son return to the batting cage. "She is one of them there intelligent ladies. And I do mean lady."

A crack from the batting cage turned them to the playing field.

"There goes another one, boss. That kid can sure as hell hit."

"Yeah. Lookit go!"

"That one's over the trees. . .and into the crick."

"So it is. By the way, who's this George Washington Carver?"

"Hell, boss, yuh asking me? I dunno."

"I got your message. You wanted to see me, sir?"

Chester, in his shirt sleeves now, saw the white man at the end of the parking lot where the road led out to the street. He was blonde, in his thirties, dressed in clean coveralls.

"You the one hitting those balls over the fence?"

"Yes, sir. I was the one."

With calloused hands, the man dug into a canvas bag by his feet. "Here." He thrust a bat at Chester, barrel out. It was no ordinary bat—it was varnished in a glossy, dark red tone and had a small white oval painted on for a trade mark. Chester held it in his hands and twirled it. He liked the feel of the handle which was a tiny bit thicker than regular bats. It seemed lighter than anything he'd ever tried.

"Go ahead. Swing it."

Chester stepped back, and took a few cuts. "Pretty good."

"Pretty good. I honed it myself. It's indestructible."

Chester grunted. "Mister, no bat is indestructible."

"This is. It's a secret wood, from a tree grown right here in Colorado. They don't make bats like this back east."

"Are you in the business of making bats?"

The man in coveralls grinned. "No. It's just a hobby. But that is one special bat, buddy. Once I saw you hitting them out here, I thought it should belong to you."

28

"Chester!" Chester turned at the sound of his mother calling him. She trotted up. "What are you trying to do? Go without me?'

"Oh, no. I was just—" He looked back to the man, but he'd already walked away to his truck. "Well, what do you know? Why did he take off so darn fast?"

"Who?"

"That white man in the coveralls."

"What about him?"

"He gave me this bat."

"A white man gave you a bat! Why would he do that?"

"I dunno, mama." They watched the man drive off.

"Let's go," Chester said, shrugging.

He admired himself in the mirror, holding up the uniform over his chest and feeling the two words BLACK SOX in raised letters across the thick wool cloth. There was a certain magic to the cloth. It was his size, his uniform. He was now a professional baseball player. "Nice."

Chester caught Agnes Hudson peeking through the open door.

"Oh. . . Miss Hudson. . . Hello." He stumbled with the words, as he took in a whiff of her pleasant perfume drifting into the room. "I didn't. . . hear you come in." Embarrassed, he tossed the uniform on the bed beside his two-tone, black-and-white Denver team jacket and the new baseball gear he had purchased with an advance. He now had three thirty-four-ounce bats, a glove, and long- and short-sleeved sweatshirts.

"Hey, what you go and do that for? You're looking good." She stepped into the room, barely making a sound. She appeared more attractive than she did that first day, her gray skirt and white blouse accenting her slim figure. "You made the team. Congratulations. And you got a single and a double in the practice game. Tell you something, though. You better give way to your center fielder next time on a fly ball. You call off a center fielder—any center fielder—and you're dead, boy. Especially Quincy. He can get ornery."

Chester laughed cautiously, avoiding her piercing dark eyes. He looked past her to the wall. "You sound as if you were there?"

"I was. I got off for my lunch and went to watch. They're still talking about you uptown."

"They are?"

29

"Yes, sir. I ain't never seen a stance like that at the plate. They're calling you Peek-a-boo Parker."

"My manager told me my stance stunk, but he won't change it."

"Cap, you mean?"

"Uh-huh."

"You better listen to him. He's been around some."

"Yeah, he looks it. How do you know so much about baseball?"

"I've been around too. Kansas City's my hometown."

"Kansas City? No kidding?"

She nodded. "No kidding. I used to watch the Monarchs. My older brother used to play for them." She smiled, eyes flashing. "Ever see Satchel?"

"Once."

"Did you now?"

"Uh-huh, in Shreveport. Ten years back. Boy, what I'd give to face him some day and get a hit off him."

"Who knows. Maybe you will meet up with him." Agnes turned for the door. Then she saw it. . . the glossy dark-red bat on the floor. "What is that?"

"A baseball bat," he grinned.

"I know that, silly," she smirked. "But what a strange color. Like mahogany. Where did you get it?"

He shrugged. "Somebody outside the ballpark gave it to me. A white man. Said he made it himself."

"A white man?" she frowned.

"Honest. Then he went and took off before I could pay him or anything. Couldn't even thank him properly. He said it's special."

Her eyebrows fluttered. "I had better go. Anna doesn't like the women on the men's floor."

"You're right, she don't."

"See you at supper. Smells good," she said, excusing herself. Then she was gone.

Chester swallowed hard. She was the one who smelled good. She was one nice, good-looking woman. There was something out of the ordinary about her. He grinned, slowly. The word to best describe Agnes was 'class'.

In a sassy sort of way.

Five

The pitcher pointed at the black runner standing on second base. "Don't you try and steal third on me now, boy, or I'll fix you good."

"We'll see," rookie shortstop Jackie Robinson hissed under his breath. Opposing white pitchers who called him boy didn't scare him. They were the enemy. So piss on them. Robinson glared at the tall, boney white pitcher with the Southern accent, then took three long pigeon-toed steps off second base and looked around. He had just finished stealing second on a close play and had received the green light from the bench to steal third. He liked stealing third. Closer to the catcher, it was tougher, more of a challenge than second.

Robinson dared a few more steps off the bag, taking everything in. The pitcher kept looking back. In a runner's crouch, Robinson took another stride towards third, glancing over at the second baseman, then at the shortstop. Neither had made a move for second. Robinson relished this type of combat of the minds. Only a month with the team, he had already established himself as the fastest, most daring runner on the squad. When he got on, the base paths were his.

Out of the corner of his eye, Robinson caught the second baseman moving slowly for the bag. Robinson made two quick fakes just to bother the pitcher, who turned and rifled the ball to second. But Robinson anticipated the move and dove head-first for the safety of the base. The tag came too late. Robinson popped up and brushed the dirt from his uniform. Hands on his hips, he stood, defiant.

31

The pitcher chuckled, staring at the man with the shock of rich, coal-like black skin, his eyes white and large. "I told you, coon. Don't try it."

"What did you call me?" Robinson's voice was high-pitched and nasally, ironic for such a husky man.

The pitcher laughed. "Are yuh deaf? I called you a coon!"

The umpire strode in front of the plate. "Let's play some ball out there!"

Seething inside, Robinson didn't say a word. No pitcher alive was going to tell him not to steal. Or get away calling him a coon either. Robinson would find his own form of vindication. He would embarrass the pitcher. He deserved it. Wearing his anger on his face, Robinson merely went through the routine again. Maybe, he'd tolerate a white man's "hate stare" on the streets, where he could do nothing about it. But not here at the ball park. He took three long steps towards third and glanced around, then took another step for good measure. His mind had absorbed the pitcher's moves from the beginning of the game, picking up little leads that would help his base-running and break up the pitcher's concentration.

Robinson wondered if the catcher would try a pitch-out.

The pitcher looked back. Once. Twice. Then jerked into his windup.

Robinson was very open about his purpose now. Third base was only ninety feet away. He clicked his taut body into high gear and broke into a run.

"There he goes!" the shortstop yelled, pointing. "Get him!"

Robinson dug in after five feet, and retreated. The pitcher spun and planted his cleats in the mound for a throw to third.

"Balk!" roared the umpire. Then he pointed to Robinson to take the next base.

Robinson grinned.

The pitcher flung his arms skyward and cursed loud enough for everyone in the park to hear. Robinson calmly strutted to third base, head up high. He knew he had the pitcher upset now, right where he wanted him. He enjoyed that.

Now, stealing home would be the icing on the cake.

Robinson glanced over at Satchel Paige casually stepping into his shiny red Cadillac by the curb outside the park. Robinson loathed Paige for not having the time of day for rookies like Robinson. Who the hell did he think he was? Where was he going, while everyone else was taking the bus? Probably out on the prowl. He didn't travel with the rest of the team on the bus either. Too preoccupied with himself, he drove his own car to the games. Robinson knew from his teammates that Paige's companions were either other pitchers or women, sometimes white women, which was definitely not good for many other's views on race relations.

Robinson clambered aboard the team bus in his suit and tie and headed for the rear, ignoring the empty seats available at the front.

"Hey, college boy," cried a veteran player. "Where yuh going? Take a load off. Sit up here."

Robinson stopped, turned, and shook his head. "Not until I earn it."

"OK... suit yerself."

Robinson angled himself into the right-rear corner over one of the big tires. The bus was his safety room, his protection from Jim Crow and the outside white world, where he was a third-class citizen. For now he sought comfort with his peers. He could draw the shades and lock ol' Jim Crow in until the next game, in Cincinnati. Then it would start all over again.

Shortly after the bus pulled out of Springfield, he closed his eyes, listened to the hum of the power train and the tires, then fell sleep. Only six months earlier, November 1944, Second Lieutenant Jack Roosevelt Robinson was in another uniform. Uncle Sam's U.S. Army. Stationed at Camp Breckinridge, Kentucky, waiting for his discharge papers.

One day he played catch with Ted Alexander, a member of the Kansas City Monarchs colored baseball team before the war. Alexander said there was good money in Blackball and that the Monarchs were looking for players. He went on to say they played in front of big crowds, and that half of the fans were white, with money. Blacks had money too. Money they made in defense plants. Quite a few of the best players were not drafted into the service, unlike the white leagues where the best were in military uniforms. The most exciting and entertaining baseball in America was found in the Negro Leagues. Upon his discharge, Robinson reported to the Kansas City Monarchs spring training camp in Houston and made the team. The contract was a verbal one for $400 a month, a better than average wage for the majority of working black men.

Show up, play, get paid was the deal.

In 1945, twenty-six-year-old Jackie Robinson was considered one of the best athletes in the nation. He was a household name in California, fresh off a publicized tryout that spring with the Boston Red Sox, arranged by influential black media men. He and two others of his race performed for manager Joe Cronin. Although the Red Sox staff saw talent in the three, very few expected anything to come of it.

UCLA graduate, the husky, handsome, six-foot Robinson became the school's first four-letter man, excelling at track, football, baseball, and basketball. Baseball was actually the least favorite of his sports. And here he was, ironically, a professional baseball player with black America's team, the Kansas City Monarchs of the Negro National League.

The Monarchs were the New York Yankees of black baseball, the most profitable of all Blackball teams. For the last fifteen years they had played as many as 150 games a season against pro, semi-pro, and amateur competition every spring, summer, and early fall, thanks to their own portable lighting system. With the lights, they survived the Great Depression, while many other colored teams collapsed. Owned by J. Leslie Wilkinson, a white man, the Monarchs had dominated Blackball for two decades and were the pride of the Mid-West farm belt. Everywhere they barnstormed, they were heroes in black neighborhoods, their red caps and red-and-blue-trim uniforms familiar sights. On the road, they flopped out in the best hotels and ate in the best restaurants. The best black hotels and black restaurants, that is. Robinson hated that side of Blackball. The accommodations.

Robinson was a loner, avoided by the others on the team. He was a different breed. He didn't fit in. He was a college man. He was also branded a big-head, a trouble-maker. Too head-strong. He was not popular with his peers after management moved out Jesse Williams, an all-star at short, and shuttled him over to second base to make room for Robinson. Although grateful for the job with the Monarchs and the money, Robinson was not pleased with what he had seen to date in Blackball.

It was below his dignity.

Alexander had said he'd enjoy the life of a black ballplayer. For Robinson, what was to enjoy? The road meant long bus trips in the middle of the night, with sandwiches, pickles, and warm bottles of soda pop for breakfast before an afternoon double-header. Then back in the bus. Hot meals were as common as polar bears in Florida. On top of that, spring training each year in Houston was a joke. As soon as a player threw his uniform on, he was in a game. There was little time for the manager to instruct players on the fundamentals of hitting or pitching or the double play or the pick-off move. They were a colored team on the road. They had to keep moving. They needed the money. They had to learn as they played, and play themselves into condition.

Robinson despised the clowning side of Blackball, where pitchers like Paige called the outfield to the bench then would more often than not strikeout the next batter. And where the players performed such tricks as play with an imaginary ball or wear their uniform backwards or catch the ball in a hat. Robinson had no time for such carnivals. He was out to win.

His ideology was clear and uncomplicated—kick the shit out of the opposition before they could kick the shit out of you.

Six

When the Dodgers president arrived at Ebbets Field, he was handed
a sealed Western Union telegram. Without breaking stride, he closed
the door to his office and ripped the envelope open.

ROOKIE SHORTSTOP JACKIE ROBINSON KC MONARCHS HITS WITH A
VENGEANCE STOP RUNS LIKE A CHEETAH STOP PLAYS LIKE GANG-
BUSTERS STOP TOP PROSPECT STOP GEORGE

Branch Rickey nodded. It was from scout George Sisler. Rickey knew
Jackie Robinson was an excellent football and basketball player, but this
spring his baseball ability was the issue. Rickey didn't doubt Sisler's
assessment. A former major league first baseman, George Sisler was
an excellent judge of talent, especially anything to do with infielders.
His opinion reflected still another scout's analysis, that of Clyde Sukeforth. The report in Rickey's hands was also similar to the one he had
received from Tom Greenwade. The Dodger executive smacked his
lips. He'd send colored scout Art Powell to see what he thought of this
Robinson fellah.

Rickey gawked out his office window. Rain clouds threatened over
the heart of Brooklyn. Rickey knew that if Robinson was to be the
man, then Brooklyn would be the perfect place to kick-start integration to the major leagues. The people would accept a black man, if he
was the right one. If he could play. If he could win. If he could bring
the people to the park.

Rickey's Brooklyn was a unique American city of five boroughs with over two million honest, dedicated, hard-working people, next to the Big City of New York. Brooklynites were proud of their city. They would stick up for it. And they would defend their Dodgers, as they did in the days when they were the worst team in baseball. That lasted for decades. A team synonymous with losing and famous for bonehead plays, they were tagged Dem Bums, having the distinction of never winning a World Series. Casey Stengel managed the Dodgers for a time in those deep, dark days and once said, "Brooklyn is a borough of great churches and bad ball clubs."

Then the Dodgers won a pennant in 1941, the first since 1920. They nearly won again in 1942, losing out in the last week to the Cardinals. The Dodgers, now on their way up, had united the city with a special bond. New York City held claim to the Chrysler Building, the Empire State Building, Grand Central Station, and Yankee Stadium. Brooklyn had their steel and concrete band box, Ebbets Field.

And they had the Dodgers to play in it.

Rickey saw his personal blueprint for Brooklyn. Nothing would be left to chance. Brooklyn would soon be the anchor of the baseball world, a new brand of post-war baseball. The Dodgers would win their first World Series, then another, and a few more. And they would fill Ebbets Field to capacity doing it.

Rickey would see to it, before somebody else around the league cashed in on integration.

Grambling, Louisiana

Tommy was forced to push a gaunt, stray dog away to get a better look at what was lying in the vegetable garden near the high weeds.

"Hey, Marv, come over here," he said. "Shit!"

Marv wiped his brow on this hot day at the rear of the vacant country house. "What you got?" Then he saw it and walked over. "Oh, God."

The two policemen stared down at the shallow-graved body of a bare-chested man in police trousers, his skin the color of ash.

"Looka here what the dog dug up."

"Get outta here, pooch," said Marv, throwing a stick at the animal. "Beat it."

The dog growled and vanished into the high weeds.

"Best to leave the body where it is until our crew comes in. Whew, it smells."

"Right," Tommy said, appalled to see the sick gray skin and the decomposition on the neck. He fought his churning stomach to keep his lunch down. While he and his partner kicked at the dirt, he flicked out a hat and a shirt with his boot toe and slid them to the side. "Is it him?" he asked.

"Yeah, it's Herbie."

"Your hunch was right. You knew where to come."

"But I didn't expect to find him here. Hell, in the yard. Whoever it was who buried him didn't dig too darn deep." He looked at the house and the weeds in the long field. "And so close to the house. Maybe he had to work fast."

They walked a few feet away.

"What do you think happened?"

"Hell if I know."

"We still don't have the car."

"Yeah. But it's probably close by, too." Marv scanned the open field. "At least we know where to concentrate."

"How did you know where to look? This-here place, I mean," Tommy wanted to know. He had come from out of town to help the police in Grambling find the missing policeman, Sergeant Herbie Collins.

"I did some checking."

"So, who lives here?"

"The Lee family. At least they did. The mother, Ramona, and her son, Chester. Niggers. She used to clean our station. She was one of them uppity colored. Educated family. From New Orleans, I think. Thought she was better than the others. The father left some time ago. Clyde. One of them half-white mongrels. We had trouble with that one. Did some damage to more than one bar around here, he did. As soon as I heard that Ramona and Chester up and left more than a week past, I got to thinking. Why would they move before Chester got his senior high diploma? He had only two months to go. It just don't figure."

"No, it don't."

"His principal said he was an honor student. And they didn't try to sell their house. Just left it, even though they had the deed to it. The place has to be worth something. Paint will do wonders. It's in better

38

shape then most nigger homes I've seen around here." Marv pounded the wall below the window frame.

"Do you think one of them did it?"

"Neither seems like the type to stir up that kinda ruckus. But when you look at the evidence, what else could you think?"

Marv loped up to a window and stared in. "Come on. Let's go in for a gander."

Under the veranda, they stopped to glance down at the old porch boards. Together, they noticed long stains deep in the cracks. The back door pushed open easily. The two policemen didn't know what to expect. In the kitchen, Tommy bent over the white tiles of the kitchen floor. In the cracks were the same dark stains.

"Do you think it's dried blood?" asked Marv.

"Could be. Our lab boys will check it out."

On the second story, two dog-eared magazines were in one corner of a bedroom painted in a pale green. The closet still had some clothes in it.

"Must've been Chester's room," Marv said, picking up one of the magazines. "Baseball. That figures. He was quite the ballplayer."

They returned outside to find the dog creeping back to the yard.

"Get outta here!" Marv yelled. He threw a tree branch. The dog raced into the nearby woods.

"Where did they go?"

"That was the clincher that brought me this way. They left no forwarding address. My guess is they are trying to get as far from here as possible."

"Outside the state?"

"You got it, partner. You know what this means?"

"What?"

"The sheriff's office will take over. Those whipper-snappers from Ruston. It's under their jurisdiction. Those bastards can have it." Marv fanned his face with his hat. "Sure is hot."

"You're not kidding."

"I better call the station and tell them what we found." Marv shuffled off to the car.

Tommy sighed. "Yeah. Looks like some damn cop killers on the loose."

Seven

The Monarch second baseman tossed the ball to Robinson. "Go two, Jack!"

Jackie Robinson stomped on second, kicking up a whiff of dust. He saw a clear view of the black Cincinnati Clown runner bearing down, attempting to break up the double play. Robinson quickly took the relay from his teammate, pivoted, and instead of throwing on a line to first, he deliberately rifled the ball right at the runner's head, knocking his cap off. It still wasn't enough to stop the runner from ramming Robinson. Spikes first.

The runner had been out to get Robinson all day, sliding too hard the last time into second. Robinson wasn't about to take it again. The runner got up and swung. Robinson ducked and swung back, connecting. The runner crashed to the ground.

Then both dugouts cleared.

"Eat shit, college boy!" The runner dragged himself up, swung, and missed again.

Robinson punched the runner to the dirt for the second time. "Come on. Get up!"

"Give me a chance, college boy."

Robinson stepped back, giving him space. "Come on," he taunted the runner, as a tidal wave of players rushed up.

Vince Basser watched the police car being winched out of Willie's Creek in the mid-afternoon heat.

Basser's office was the chief administrator for Lincoln County. They took charge of prisoners, oversaw juries, and did their best to prevent breaches of the peace. This breach of the peace was serious. Murder of a policeman. In his five years as a Lincoln County deputy sheriff, he had not seen anything quite like this situation. A sedan pulled up close by. Basser glanced over at the Grambling Chief of Police behind the wheel.

"There she be," the chief said, emerging from the car, approaching Basser. "Number eighteen. Herbie Collins's squad car. Gives you a chill, don't it?"

"Sure does. Got the file for me?"

"Yep. Anything to help the sheriff's office out. It's in your mitts now. Here you go."

The overweight chief handed the tall, skinny Basser a manila folder filled with paperwork and photographs. There was no love lost between these two factions of the police, going back years. The Grambling city police force resented the confident, better-paid, better-dressed civilian-style deputy sheriffs from the county capital in Ruston. Today was no exception. Basser had a certain air about him—a young, composed professional, ready to solve any problem.

"Thanks." Basser removed his suit jacket, threw it over his shoulder, and rolled up his sleeves.

"Don't mention it."

Basser spread out the file on the car hood and rummaged through it, extracting information a piece at a time. "This Chester and Ramona Lee moved away did they?"

"Yep. The house is down the road, yonder. Vacant."

"No forwarding address?" Basser asked

"Nope."

"Any kin folk round here."

"Yep, a husband. Clyde. A half-white drifter. Drinker, gambler. You name it. Lives in Monroe most of the time."

"Got an address for him?"

"I do, but his mind is so bad he don't make sense no more. Too much booze."

Basser faced the chief. "I'd still like to see him, though. What's the address?"

"Call the station. They have it there somewhere," the chief said stiffly.

"Thanks. I will. Any other kin?"

"Older son. Billy. Big trouble, that one, like his daddy. Nobody's seen him in ages. Left town about five years ago."

"Where to?"

"Georgia, I think."

"Where did you get the snapshots?"

"The nigger high school gave us the one of Chester. The one of the mother was found in Herbie's desk. It was taken at the station."

"In Herbie's desk, huh?"

The chief grunted. "Yep, that's what I said. I hope you're going to get them niggers."

"We will." Basser studied the picture of the mother one more time. "By the way, I hear that Collins liked his. . . let's say. . . sugar brown."

"Meaning?" They were eye to eye, toe to toe now.

"Do I have to spell it out?"

"Lookit here, Mr. Fancy Deputy Sheriff, we've gone out of our way to help with your investigation and set everything up for you."

"The way I see it, you didn't have much choice."

The chief's face was flushed. "Ain't so."

"Is so. We can confiscate anything we damn well please. The governor's office has priority over all police work in this state. I can get his permission. And I'll tell his office why. I asked you a question. Putting it in other words, did he make advances towards her?"

"All right. I don't know about any advances, but he seemed to be hanging around her a lot. He said once that she was right pretty for a nigger woman."

"She cleaned the station, did she?"

"Yes, sir. Quite regularly. Had her own small cleaning company. What else can a nigger woman do around here? She really thought she was something."

Basser's eyes fell to the file, as he removed some high school records. "The son has quite the academic record. Excellent student and a damn good baseball player. My nephew played against him. To up and move like that before the school year was over sure is mighty strange."

"Yep, it sure as hell is, mister. What now?"

Basser tucked the file under his arm. "We plan to catch up to them and find out exactly what happened."

"Isn't it obvious what happened?"

Basser frowned. "Maybe. Then again, maybe not."

CINCINNATI, OHIO

Robinson loped down the bus aisle, weary-eyed, uniform torn.

"That's the way, college boy," manager Frank Duncan said, slapping the shortstop on the shoulder as he passed. "How's the knuckles?"

Robinson smiled, and flicked his hand. Punching someone in the teeth hurt all the way back to his shoulder. "It might need a little mending."

Duncan liked having the controversial Jackie Robinson on his team. "At least the other guy looked worse."

Robinson grinned. He did look worse, he recalled, a large swelling above the eye. "You don't think I hit him too hard, did yuh?"

Duncan shrugged. "Nah. I think yuh hit him kinda. . . just right."

Robinson laughed. He got along well with Duncan. Robinson proceeded to the back of the bus. There, he curled into a corner where he started writing a letter to his fiancée in California. After Dear Rachael. . . then he suddenly didn't know what to say to her.

He had given her a ring some months back to become officially engaged. But they were drifting apart. And it wasn't the miles between them. She was pursuing a nursing career. She had a sense of the future. Her future. Meanwhile, his future seemed mired in doubt. All he was doing was getting into fist fights. He should have been a boxer, like Joe Louis.

GRAMBLING, LOUISIANA

Basser drove to Monroe. Clyde Lee, recovering from one of his daily hangovers, was of some help. He remembered that Ramona had a sister living in Joplin, Missouri. Basser followed it through with a few phone calls. She had moved. No forwarding address.

The next day, Basser sought out the employees at the Grambling bus depot, and spoke with them one at a time.

"Did you see these two in here in the last couple weeks?" he said to the fifth person, a clerk, a white man about forty.

The clerk examined the photographs, then his eyes turned to the tall, dark-haired man in the expensive suit. "You a cop?"

"Deputy Sheriff Lincoln County." Basser reached for the pocket of the jacket slung over his shoulder and showed his wallet identification.

The clerk nodded. You know, come to think of it. I do remember."

"You do?"

"Yeah." The clerk's forehead wrinkled as he looked to the black and white photographs. "A muscular boy, twenty, maybe. Looked like an athlete."

"Sounds like him."

"And the woman. Good-looker, for a black woman. Both were light-skinned. I sold them their tickets."

"Can you recall where they went?"

The clerk pursed his lips and scratched his ear. "I think it was. . . St. Louis. Yeah, St. Louis. That's where it was."

"Thanks."

Eight

She arrived home, dog-tired after a full cleaning day at the police station, and plunked herself down on the couch.

A car door slammed. She went to the living room window and pushed back the curtain to see Sergeant Herbie Collins emerging from the bushes across the gravel road. Fat-bellied, bow-legged Collins, the one who was eyeing her in a strange way only an hour before at the station. What did he want? Where was the police car? In the bushes?

He banged up the porch steps and tapped on the door. Ramona opened up, slowly.

"Mrs. Lee," he said, looking up and down the roadway through his dark sunglasses.

"Yes."

"May I come in?"

"What's this concerning?"

He removed the glasses. His badge glinted in the sun. "Your husband, ma'am."

She laughed. "Clyde? That no-account white trash hasn't been around here in months." She began to close the door.

But Collins stuck his foot out to block the move. "Just a minute, woman. You sure?"

"Yes, I'm sure. You police boys already came around here looking for him, after that trouble in Monroe. I told you I haven't seen him. Why didn't you question me at the station?"

"I want to see for myself. Move aside." He pushed his way in and stared at her.

She took a step back. "If you came to look for my husband, then look."

He kicked the door closed and moved towards her. "That's not why I'm here."

"Then what?"

"You know."

"I'm sure I don't. What you want?"

"You're right pretty for a nigger woman. I guess it's because you ain't a full nigger. That French blood and all that I've been hearing about."

She glared at him. "You can leave now, sergeant."

"Like hell I will. Feisty nigger woman, ain't yuh?" He gripped her arm.

She struggled. "I'll scream!"

He whipped her around and slapped his hand over her mouth. "I'll tell you when I'm ready to leave," he barked. "Come here!"

"Stop it!" she shrieked in terror, pushing his hand off with all her strength, catching her breath.

"Come on, woman. I know yuh fancy me."

"Leave me alone!"

Then. . . she woke up. Suddenly, jerkily.

Through bleary eyes, Ramona glanced around the room, confused. It took her a moment or two to register. She sighed, brushing her hand through her hair. She was in Denver, thank God. The dream was all too close, too real. She wiped the perspiration off her face and dragged herself out of bed. The sheets were soaked. She looked to the window. The first rays of the morning sun filtered through the curtain. It was dawn, and the only sounds outside were the birds.

Then she realized that today Chester was leaving her.

Two days had passed since the tryout. Chester had his duffel bag and black suitcase packed and by his feet.

"You take care of yourself, Chester Henry."

"I will. You look tired, mama. Didn't you sleep well?"

"No, I didn't. I'll go right back to bed, I will."

Tears filled Ramona's eyes on the front steps of the boarding house. Her boy was growing up. He'd be on his own for a whole month. He

46

had never done anything like this before. There was a chill in the dawn air, fifty degrees, if that. The neighborhood was still asleep. She saw the polished-silver Ford touring bus hugging the curb across the street, loaded with equipment and players, geared up for another barnstorming trip through the west. The red letters on the side were large enough to read from the porch.

THE DENVER BLACK SOX. THE CROWN PRINCES OF BASEBALL WEST OF THE MISSISSIPPI.

"Come on, Peek, let's go," a voice rang out. It was the bus driver, bald-headed Bennie, poking his head through the driver window. "Gotta get this heap going." His schedule was tight. Afternoon game in the hot-spot of McCook, Nebraska, to kick off the heavily-booked schedule. Night game in North Platte.

"Yeah, Peek. Hustle your butt."

"Who's Peek? That you?" Ramona asked, buttoning up her sweater.

"Yeah. They already have a nickname for me. Peek-a-boo Parker."

"My word." She wiped her tears with the back of her hand. "I still don't like the idea of you playing on Sundays. But what can I do? I forget, you're a man now."

"Mama, ballplayers always play on Sunday. They're the biggest crowds."

"You remember your prayers, Chester Henry, and get to church."

"I will." He looked back. He was anxious to board. The driver motioned for Chester to get on with it.

"And always wear clean socks and underwear."

"I know, just in case I get into an accident."

"And no gambling or card playing. That's what ruined your daddy."

"Don't I know it. Gotta go. Bye, mama."

She reached out and put her arms around him. One of the ballplayers blew a wolf-whistle. Ramona laughed, and let go. "Sorry, I suppose I shouldn't embarrass you in front of the players."

"They're a good bunch, mama. Really they are."

"Yes, I suppose they are."

"Good manager, too. Although he can sure cuss. Doesn't even have to get mad to do it neither," Chester said. "I can't complain about the money."

"No, you can't there."

"I can't do anything for now. Until September classes, anyway."

"You get going now, boy." She pushed on his chest. "And sock some of those home runs for Aunt Anna and me."

"You bet, mama. Say goodbye to Auntie."

"I will. Oh, dear, look! The bus is pulling away. You better run, boy."

The bus was moving slowly down the street, the players laughing, calling out to Chester.

"They're going to wake up the whole block," Ramona giggled.

"Hey, you guys, wait for me!" Chester clutched his baseball bag and suitcase and tore across the front yard, jumping clean over a set of low bushes.

Two players taunted the rookie. One of them extended a hand out a side window. Chester ran up and tried to reach for it. It was no use. The faster Chester ran, the faster the bus went, until he lagged behind the machine several feet.

"Whoa! Stop!" Chester screamed.

Suddenly, the driver slammed on the brakes with a loud screech, and Chester banged hard into the back bumper.

Inside the bus, Garrett laughed and said to a veteran, "Shit. We get them rookies every time with that one."

"Yeah, don't we. It almost ain't fair. But I kinda like it."

"Yeah, me, too."

Agnes woke up and watched the antics with amusement from her bedroom window facing the street. She smiled, then winced when Chester ran into the bumper. He appeared shaken, but quickly boarded the bus. Poor Peek-a-boo. Boys will be boys. Just having fun.

Despite the little they had seen of each other over the three days, Agnes had taken an instant liking to Chester. He was polite, almost to the point of being clumsy and awkward. He was a decent young man, well raised, with manners, rare for the majority of ballplayers she had known. He didn't even talk like them. She could tell he wasn't some hot-shot or a high-tone. Flash Barber was the worst. The fastest hands in the west, on the field and off. Then again, maybe, bashful Chester hadn't been around women enough to be as obnoxious as some of the other young men.

She closed the curtain and found her way to the bathroom. She knew it was too early to freshen up before her day, but she couldn't sleep anyway. So why not take her bath now? She ran the taps, undressed, braced the sides of the tub and slid into the hot, steamy water. She thought of the day's work. She'd be putting in some late hours today at the job.

At first, Agnes chose the pharmaceutical field for family reasons. In college, she was the only woman and one of two black people in her integrated class. That was frightening enough. Many of her race were suffering for years, due to lack of proper drugs. Her brother died from receiving the wrong medicine, the fault or even the intent of a white counter man. The family never knew the truth, whatever it was. But that was 1935, in the midst of the Depression, when proper drugs and money to pay for them were scarce. Now, 1945 was the dawn of a great new era and she was a part of it. Antibiotics were the new thing, especially the recent miracle drugs like penicillin and this new streptomycin. Although a decade had come and gone since her brother's death, Agnes wanted—in her own way—to correct the wrong to her kin and her race. She was a pharmacist, in a field she had so far found challenging and rewarding. And it paid not too bad, too.

KANSAS CITY, MISSOURI

This was Art Powell's first trip to Kansas City to see the Monarchs since he played against them way back in September 1924 as a member of the Chicago American Giants. In 1945, the Monarchs were still a powerhouse, now managed by Frank Duncan.

Bullet Joe Rogan had struck out sixteen Giants that cloudy afternoon in 1924, Powell a three-time victim. Rogan's speed would forever stick in Powell's craw. He remembered second baseman Newt Allen, another star, and Frank Duncan, at catcher. All three were of major league caliber. It was too bad they were born too soon.

Powell was at the ballpark early for the doubleheader between Kansas City and the Cleveland Buckeyes to familiarize himself with some of the players on both teams. Especially Jackie Robinson. Between games, he talked with Cleveland general manager, and Duncan, two old friends from the Caribbean days. Powell wrote little quirks, and habits of the better players, as he saw them in the warm up. Soon, his scorecard—front and back—was heavy with scribbled notes.

In the first game, five-foot-nine Gene Bremmer had shut out the opposition 4-0 on a three-hitter. Bremmer looked good, Powell noted. But too old at thirty. He was a pitcher anyway. Mr. Rickey said the first player had to be a fielder, be visible every day. With a pencil point, Powell now eyed down the list of Buckeye players. Catcher-manager Quincy Trouppe was a perennial all-star, but in his thirties. Sam Jethroe had possibilities. Only twenty-three, he could hit and had speed on the bases, as well as in the outfield. He stole two bases in the first game. Powell put a checkmark beside Jethroe.

The Monarchs had two top pitchers on their roster—Satchel Paige, nearing forty, but still effective, and Booker "Cannonball" McDaniels, a six-foot-two righty from Arkansas in his thirties. Jesse Williams at second base was a rock. Nineteen-year-old Hank Thompson was a comer. Jackie Robinson at shortstop definitely had some stuff. He and Thompson were the only possibilities under thirty. The others were scratched due to age.

In the second game Satchel Paige squared off with Cleveland's George Jefferson, a tall twenty-one-year off-speed pitcher from Oklahoma who mowed down the Monarchs until the fifth. Kansas City put a runner on second and up came their muscle-bound shortstop, Jackie Robinson, with one out. Powell watched Robinson in the first game and beside his name etched, agile shortstop, throwing arm suspect, outstanding speed, pigeon-toed, college man, twenty-six, first year of Negro ball. Powell remembered that Robinson, Jethroe and another player tried out for the Boston Red Sox only a few days after he had met with Branch Rickey in Bear Mountain, New York. According to Duncan, Robinson was one of those all-round athletes. With great interest, Powell leaned forward in his seat between first and home and peered over his round-framed reading glasses resting on the bridge of his nose. With his pocket-size binoculars, he studied Robinson's footwork and hands at the plate, then reached for his stopwatch.

On the field, Robinson took the sign from his third base coach. Cap to arm. The bunt was on. Given the situation, it was meant to be a safe-hit bunt, and not a sacrifice bunt. Robinson considered the field alleys. Either he'd put it to one side of the pitcher or down one of the lines. The third baseman was behind the bag. Down the line to left was the most obvious.

Jefferson jerked into his windup. Robinson gave no indication he was going to bunt until Jefferson threw. Then, he quickly turned his body to the pitcher, and slid his top hand up to the bat's trademark for better balance and control. He started the bat at the top of the strike zone, tilting it at a forty-five-degree angle to prevent a pop-up. As the ball approached, Robinson bent his knees slightly, and dropped the ball perfectly along the third-base line, half-way between the catcher and the fielder. Robinson raced for first at reckless speed. The runner on second slid into third base, kicking up a cloud of dust. The third baseman picked up the ball with his bare hand. . . too late to make a throw or a tag.

Robinson had caught the defense by total surprise with one beauty of a bunt.

Powell slouched in his seat and rubbed his chest. The butterflies were there in force once more. His doctor had said it could be a heart murmur. One thing was for certain, the murmurs were increasing. Road life was probably not the best thing for such a condition. But he just couldn't back out now. Mr. Rickey was counting on him. This was the greatest thing for the black race since Lincoln emancipated the slaves in the Civil War. Powell was going to see it through, and face the consequences later, if there were any. All he had to do was take it easy. And not get too excited.

The fans filed out of the park.

Kansas City won the second game 3-2 in the ninth on a double by Jesse Williams. Robinson impressed Powell the most, except for the long throws he made. One from the hole in the seventh inning stood out. The ball skidded into the dirt before the first baseman snagged it for the out. To Powell, the majority of Robinson's throws didn't have enough mustard on them. And he didn't seem to pivot properly. He just didn't have a quality enough arm at short. Quick release, though. Maybe a change of positions would be the answer. But where? He needed an arm no matter where he played.

A major league arm.

Powell smiled. Robinson's bunt, then a quick steal of second grabbed the thunder. Then he took the extra base on a single and bulldozed Quincy Trouppe, the big six-foot-three catcher, knocking the wind out of him and the ball from his grasp. Robinson then said something to Trouppe and the umpire stepped in. Before putting his glasses away, Powell stroked a check mark and another note beside Robinson's name. Not afraid to mix it up. He liked the way the rookie shortstop tucked his hands on his hips between breaks, as if to say that he was one son-of-a-bitch. . . which he was. Robinson and Jethroe had the stuff, and were within the age group.

Powell had clocked them. The times were better than average. Batting right, Robinson made it to first in three-point-five seconds; Jethroe, a switch-hitter, recorded his best time at three-point-two, batting left-handed against right-handers Jefferson and Bremmer. Robinson and Jethroe were the fastest to date. But Powell still had one doubt about Robinson.

That damn arm. Maybe second base could work.

Nine

It didn't take Chester too long to discover that Ted Garrett's bark was worse than his bite. The youngster was gradually getting used to Garrett's varying moods and his favorite four-letter word starting with the letter S. Beyond his bronze exterior, Garrett was a man oozing with baseball, a walking, talking wealth of information.

"Did you say Josh Gibson was your teammate?" Chester asked, fascinated, while sitting with Garrett on the bus.

"Shit, yeah, boy. Down Puerto Rico."

Garrett cleaned a set of wire-rimmed glasses with a handkerchief, then put them on.

"What's he like?"

"A nice feller." Garrett chomped on some tobacco, handing Chester the pack. "Chew?"

"No, thank you."

"Yuh, sure? It's good fer the rheumatism."

"I shouldn't have to worry about rheumatism at my age."

"Yeah, guess not."

"You were talking about Josh Gibson."

"Oh, yeah, yeah, Josh. I can remember I never saw him get mad at anything or anybody. Quite the beer drinker, too. Shit, man, could he hit. Best hitter I ever saw. And that's the pearly truth. Haven't seen him in, oh. . . seven years or so. I hear he's not the same anymore. His knees are shot. Yuh know, I once saw him drink six beers before he

53

finally got up and went to piss. Hear he's worse now, now that he got down to more serious drinking."

Chester was crushed. His idol a drunk, like his daddy?

He turned in his window seat to catch sight of a small herd of cows and the dry, rolling Colorado prairie through the glass. There was a poker game behind him, the players laughing. The driver was racing flat out along a long stretch of endless highway, the tires thumping to the beat of the cracks in the road. To Chester, this alien countryside could easily be half-way around the world, instead of only a three-day bus drive from Louisiana. It was hard to fathom this was the same United States.

"Isn't he driving kind of fast?" Chester asked.

"Shit. Don't worry about it. Bennie's like that all the time. He got his license from the Indianapolis Motor Speedway."

"Did he really?"

"It's a joke, son. A joke."

"OK." Chester smiled gingerly, fidgeting in his seat. "I knew that."

"Yeah, I bet yuh did." Garrett belched. "Getting right anxious tuh play?"

"Sure am, Mr. Garrett."

"Lookit. Stop the Mr. Garrett stuff! Not so formal. Call me Cap. OK? Cap. Don't make me look bad now, yuh here?" Garrett stretched his arms and cracked his knuckles.

"OK, Cap. I hear."

"Anyway, yuh won't be playing the afternoon game."

"I won't."

Garrett shook his head. "Nah. Just watch and get tuh know the routine. I've decided tuh put yuh in at right field for the second game. You'll be batting fifth, behind Night-train."

"Much obliged."

"Don't mention it."

"With that there rocket arm of yours, right will be yer position. Another thing, I've been going over something in my mind."

"What's that?"

"Crowding the plate. If you could learn tuh pull the ball more, yuh can take advantage of them short fences down the line."

"I don't know the first thing about pulling the ball. What do you do?"

Garrett laughed. "Swing early. And hit those inside pitches. Don't let 'em go by, boy. Try 'er out in the night game."

"You play night games?"

Garrett reached under his seat for a paper cup, and spit a mouthful of juice in it. Chewing and spitting tobacco was enough to almost make Chester throw up.

"Whoa, man, didn't anybody tell yuh? Shit, yeah, we play night games. Got our own portable lights and our own technicians who look after 'em to boot. They left a day before we did. They're already up in North Platte with the midway and dance band," Garrett explained. "Quite the operation Jeffries has. Trouble is, the midway and band are only licensed for Nebraska. So far."

"A midway and dance band? What is this, a circus?"

"Pretty damn close. Yuh see, kid, Jeffries is a business man. Like all businessmen, he likes tuh make money, naturally. And he pays it out pretty damn good too. This is his second year with this. Listen up. It works like this. He moves his midway and band into one of the bigger centers. A place where they can draw well. They stay there two, three, or four days, depending on the size of the town, while the baseball team—us—tour round the town, drawing off the smaller centers, playing two or three games a day. Then we finish up at the same place that has the dance band and midway for a wing-ding bash. We start off the last day with an early afternoon game. We charge fer that. I put up four-hundred dollars tuh any local team that can beat the Sox. If they win, they get the money. We hardly lost a game last year, or so far this year. Three, this year, I think it is."

"That's a good record."

Garrett spit into the cup. "Hell, can't lose. We got our own umps." He winked at Chester.

"Isn't that kind of dishonest?"

"Dishonest?" Garrett grinned. "Hell no. Just gooood solid business. Jeffries sells entertainment in an area that is starving fer it. After the game is over, they open up the midway, and charge fer that. There's rides, vendor machines, shitty food, the whole bit. Then they shut the midway down about nine. And we have another game. A rematch or we take on another team or we break into two squads and have ourselves a game. We make adjustments, too. We might not arrive in town until just in time for the night game. So the midway will open earlier tuh make up for the loss of the afternoon game. The four-hundred bucks thing still goes. Anyway, this goes on until eleven o'clock or so, then the dance band comes out and goes until one, and charges fer that too. Slickest thing you ever did see."

"Sounds like it."

"And we're all colored. Thanks tuh Jeffries, a black ballplayer can keep his head up. It's not this good any place else in the States fer us. Sure, the prestige is playing in the colored leagues back east, but they treat you like shit, man. Piss-poor food. Dirty hotels, when you can find 'em. Travel all night on those lousy buses or beat-up cars. A lotta times we don't find accommodations neither and have tuh sleep on the bus, but at least the prairies don't have that damn humidity. The nights are cool and it's easy tuh sleep. Can't bitch about the pay." Garrett's voice dropped to a whisper. "But he owns yuh."

"You mean Jeffries."

"Yeah. Don't cross him. See that man up at the front?"

"Where?"

"There." Garrett pointed, his hand close to his chest.

Chester leaned forward in the seat, head peeking over the top, and saw the back of the man. He noticed earlier that he couldn't be a ball-player because he was too fat.

"Yeah, I see him."

"Name is Clem Rowe. He's a gorilla."

"Huh?"

"A gorilla. An arm breaker." Garrett let fly with another batch of juice into the cup. "He works fer Jeffries."

"An arm breaker!"

"Hush! Keep yer voice down," Garrett whispered. "He travels with the team and keeps an eye on things fer Jeffries. Dumb as a post, though. Just tough, that's all. Once you sign up with Jeffries he owns yuh fer the duration of the season, unless, of course, he chooses tuh sell yuh tuh some colored team back east before the season is out."

Chester shrugged. "Why does he have to go through all this trouble? Who is this Mr. Jeffries, anyway? He seems to act pretty high and mighty to me."

"Well, let's just say he's a. . . mobster."

56

"What!"

"He runs the Denver underworld in the colored section. Owns everything. The numbers racket. A gambling hall. Couple cat houses."

"Cat houses?"

Garrett rolled his eyes. "You know, brothels."

"Oh, for harlots."

"That might be the biblical name fer them," said Garrett. "Boy, you ain't been around much, have yuh." He stopped chewing. "And he owns that there boarding house where you and yer mama stay at. He knows people in high places. White people. They look after him. He accommodates them, if yuh know what I mean. Some people he's rubbed the wrong way. But that's his problem."

"Now I know why he needs a bodyguard."

"He doesn't have tuh worry about no gas rationing fer this here vehicle, either. He gets everything he wants. Don't look so scared. What's bothering yuh?"

"Who says I'm scared?"

"Yer mouth was wide open. You're a good ballplayer. Just keep yuh nose clean, boy, play ball, and take the money. Don't rock the boat. In the winter yuh can play some more ball if yuh like to, down in the Caribbean. Cuba. Mexico. Or Puerto Rico. Yuh can play ball year round."

"My mama wants me to go to school."

"Shit, yeah, that's right." Garrett said. "Can't agree with yuh more. Get an education if yuh can, boy. It's important. Don't be like me. Yuh know, yer mama there wants yuh tuh do a lot. Things like go to church on the road. The truth is there's very few colored churches in these here parts."

"Really?"

"Fact is, none that I know of. Closest thing to church for us is we Praise the Lord and pass the hat at game time!"

"Mr. Jeffries lied then?"

"Well. . . yeah, he tends tuh exaggerate sometimes."

Chester asked more questions, and soon the conversation got around to Garrett himself. The team player-manager was born and brought up in Pensacola, Florida. He began to smoke and drink at twelve. He ran away from home at fourteen to work on a shrimp boat in the Gulf of Mexico. He played ball from the time he was six and started playing semi-pro ball at fifteen. He was in and out of jail before twenty, caught stealing once, vagrancy the other time. Married at twenty-one, he was divorced at twenty-three. He married a second time at thirty, to a woman who hated Denver enough to stay away from the Wild West and keep house in St. Petersburg, Florida, instead, with their three daughters, two dachshunds, and Cap's aquarium stocked with dozens of tropical fish.

Garrett had played his baseball in the deep south with various teams, and throughout the Caribbean and some summers on the dry Canadian prairies, all year long until he was thirty-five. In the last ten years, he slowed down to be a manager and occasional first baseman. With Denver, he was doing what he did every spring and winter for the last ten years, sifting through the player talent available to him and trying to mold them into a formidable team. He didn't believe in luck. Instead, he knew that hard work would always produce good results. He realized long ago that baseball was a young man's job. To stay in baseball, he needed something else going for him. And that something else was managing. Cap ventured north again in 1944, his first year with Jeffries' Denver Black Sox. Now, he was also Jeffries' road manager, trainer, and treasurer. Jack of all trades, master of none, as Garrett referred to it. He paid out the salaries, the meal money, and kept the advances to a minimum.

"My first year of managing was a disaster," Cap said, a twinkle in his eye. "A winter league in Cuba. We finished dead last. All we needed was one thing."

"What?"

"Ball players," Garrett laughed. "So, yuh ever play white, Chester?"

"Twice in senior high."

"It's not so bad, right?"

"Right. It's not so bad."

"That was Louisiana. Here's what we do out here. These boys are farmers. Cowboy-hat country. The range. Pointy boots. Buckskin and leather. We have tuh get the feel of the crowd and try a few things. If we clown and showboat and get a few laughs, then we clown and showboat for 'em. If they are serious and really want that money bad, then we play straight up and whip their asses. But don't taunt 'em."

"We don't?"

"No. Unless yuh want 'em tuh lynch us. I don't care what they say

58

to yuh or call yuh or try and do tuh yuh on the ball field. Don't step outta line. Yuh hear me?"

"Yes, sir."

"Remember, Chester, it's Cap."

"Right. Got yuh. OK, Cap."

"Yuh had better like baseball if yuh wanna be a barnstormer. And one other thing. And this goes fer on the field and off." Garrett pointed his finger into Chester's face. "Watch your back, boy."

Chester glanced outside at a field of green wheat in the early stages of sprouting. He hadn't seen a building or person for miles, only fence posts and scattered herds of livestock, grasslands, and overturned black loam. What had he got himself into in this strange land?

Chester saw the road sign. They passed the state line, and were now in Nebraska. He then asked, "Cap?"

"Yeah, boy?"

"You think we'll ever see white and blacks playing together in the major leagues?"

Garrett grunted, looked straight ahead, and spewed juice into his cup. "Shit, not in our lifetime. My kids probably won't see it neither. Maybe not ever, boy."

"Why not? Aren't we good enough to play with the white boys?"

"What's the matter with yuh?" Garrett snorted. "Yuh been smoking them reefers?"

"I guess I should ask what reefers are?"

"The weed."

"Huh?"

"Yuh know, marijuana."

"Never heard of it."

"Yuh smoke it, boy. Ah, forget it. As long as yuh don't smoke nothing, like you, then yer safe. One of my players in Cuba couldn't lay off the stuff and always had this strange look tuh him. Anyway, where were we?"

"Colored in the majors."

"Oh, yeah. Yeah. For some thirty years now, I've seen enough colored talent tuh fill the majors. I've seen white. Jimmy Foxx. Bob Feller. Rogers Hornsby. All good ballplayers. Real good. But so are them black brothers of ours. They belong alongside the whites. They play against each other in exhibition games. So what's the difference? Not good enough?

It's the Southern white boys who are the trouble. At least a quarter or third of the majors are Southerners. Some are members of the Klan. Once the war is over, teams will train in the South again, like before, where blacks and whites are forbidden by law tuh play together. I'll tell yuh something else, too, black owners don't want integration because it'll wreck their right-handsome profits in the Negro Leagues, not tuh mention their front for their other operations. The rackets, the numbers, and all that. It's our cross tuh bare in life. Welcome tuh raceball. It's here for a long, long time."

Chester was learning fast. Baseball was a game for boys, played by men, and controlled by big-wigs in fancy suits, loyal only to their bank accounts. This was Jim Crow ball. It didn't matter none to Chester. Anything was better than Grambling, Louisiana. He quickly drew an image of his brother. Where was he? Chester remembered the last day he saw Billy. His new duds and his new car. A double-breasted, pin-stripe suit. A shiny 1941 Packard. That day. Oh, that day.

"White owners don't want it," Garrett continued, "because of prejudice, that's all it boils down to, man. Plain, pure prejudice. Nothing's going tuh change. Man, nuthin!" He bent over for the cup full of tobacco juice and chucked the contents out the window. "Shit, caught the side again. And they just washed 'er up. Oh, well."

In ten minutes, Garrett fell into a steady snore.

Chester wanted to sleep, but couldn't even nod off. His mind was drifting too much, and the noisy poker game behind him was keeping him awake. Despite the Horace Jeffries stories, which Chester took to be true, Chester was enjoying himself. So far. Anything new was enjoyable. And he was going to play his first professional game of baseball. He slumped in his seat and looked around the bus. These were all grown men, older than him. Professionals. They were a cast of characters, a fascinating mix of cocksure colored young men and accents, from all parts. There was the mouthy, Pittsburgh-born Flash Barber, the tall, skinny-as-a-pogo-stick shortstop, with the rifle arm from the hole. The Ohioan, Quincy Bell, the ball hawk, patrolled center field. To him, all younger players were simply stud or dummy. He loved to play shallow, run back on balls hit over his head and catch up to them in the gap before they dropped in. And he didn't appreciate another outfielder calling him off. Especially rookie outfielders. Behind the plate, the Southerner from Arkansas, Dingy Smith caught the pitchers. He could throw from his haunches. He was short, but he could hit. Night-train Wilson was the returning slugger on the team, the clean-up hitter and third-baseman. He grew up in Brooklyn within a stone's throw of Ebbets Field. He was slow afoot, but what he lacked in speed he made up for by instinct and anticipation. Second baseman Chick Patterson, from Harlem, hit lead-off and stole bases every chance he got.

Right-hander Francisco "Rabbit" Berenguer was the best pitcher on the team. Due to a childhood accident, his index finger on his pitching hand was sliced down to only two inches long, enabling him to do funny tricks with breaking balls. He was called Rabbit because he was somewhat rare. . . a fast-running pitcher. He was as dark as they came, a Cuban who continually butchered the English language. His only form of communication on the road was Garrett, who spoke and understood enough Spanish to get by. The youngest player—next to Chester—at twenty, Berenguer threw an assortment of screwballs, sandpaper balls, and spitballs, all with blazing velocity. The other pitchers were Manny Mandon, a motor-mouthed Texan who would rather play poker than pitch, and Fred "Popsicle" Jones, from Florida, who acquired his name years ago by sucking on a popsicle given him by a fan between innings of a game he was pitching and going out to the mound with the stick between his lips.

The players were all in a legitimate profession. Baseball. It was going to be fun for Chester because he made up his mind he'd make it fun. The past life. . . Louisiana didn't even exist. Over Garrett's heavy breathing, the road sounds, the engine roar, and the card games, Chester finally dozed off, contented.

Coming up to noon, Flash Barber punched Chester in the arm.

"Hey, Peek, time for yer initiation."

"What?" Chester looked over. "Nobody told me about no initiation."

Garrett yawned. "Come on. Don't be a schmo. Everybody has tuh go through it."

"We're coming up to a car," Barber said. "When we pass it, you gotta hang your bare ass out the window."

Chester glanced over his seat and saw the car. His eyes grew wide. "No, sir. I'm not about to do any such thing."

"Yuh chicken? Yuh wanna be called a yellow-belly chicken?"

Chester shrugged. "Call me a chicken. I don't mind. Honest."

"Yuh gotta do it, boy."

"No, I won't."

"Yuh betta do it, kid," Barber warned the rookie sternly, "or we dump yuh off the bus right now. And yuh can walk tuh our first game. That's Cap's orders."

Garrett nodded. "That's right, boy. Wanna walk and get yer new duds all dusty?"

"No, sir."

"Well?"

Suddenly, the bus load of players fell quiet. Bald-headed Bennie looked to his rear-view mirror, and started to veer off to the side of the road and slow down. The brakes squealed to a full stop. Three of the players began to rise from their seats. Chester could see in their faces that they meant business. They were actually going to give him the heave-ho off the bus.

"OK, I'll do it!" he gulped. "This is crazy."

Grinning, Bennie surged onto the road, and quickly wound the bus up to over seventy miles per hour. In a few minutes, it was forty feet behind the car. Two heads were in the front seat. No other cars were anywhere in sight, behind or ahead.

"Come on!" Flash yelled, "get up tuh the window, boy. Don't be shy."

"Don't you tell my mama, now."

"We won't," Flash laughed. "Over here."

Chester crossed the aisle to the seat vacated by Mandon and Berenguer. The driver swayed out to pass the car. Chester unbuckled his pants and slid them and his boxer shorts down, below his navel, then stood up on the seat, his back to the window. "This is crazy," he repeated.

Barber pushed the window pane up and yelled to the bus driver, "Honk the horn!"

While he braced himself with his arms on the seat, Chester winced, eased down his boxers to his knees, and stuck his bare buttocks through the open window, where he could feel a cool breeze against his skin. After what seemed like eternity, the car driver looked over. . . once. . . twice, then nearly drove off the road.

"Peek-a-boo!" Barber yelled, darting over for a better view of the car occupants and their reactions. "Oh, shit, there's an old lady inside! I think she's having a heart attack. Step on it, Bennie!" he yelled at the bus driver. "Geez, I hope she just fainted."

Bennie changed lanes quickly, sending several players sprawling. The bus sped away from the car and its occupants, while the busload of players roared with laughter.

Chester rushed to tug his pants up. "You guys really are screwy, you know."

"I'll be jiggered," Garrett said to Chester, finding his way back to his seat, and sitting down with him. He slapped his new outfielder on the back. "You actually went and done it."

Chester glanced around at the faces in the bus. Even he had to finally chuckle. He waited for the last of the players to stop laughing, then said, "So, this is what professional ballplayers do on the road."

Ten

Vince Basser produced his pocket identification for the cab driver, a grizzled man near sixty, with a cigarette dangling from his mouth.

"Deputy sheriff, huh?" the driver said through his open car window. "All the way from Louisiana." He snatched the two photographs handed him. "Must be important."

'It is."

"Yeah, that's them," the driver said, quickly.

"You saw them?"

"Hell, yeah. Picked them up right here at the bus depot. At first I thought they were dark whites."

"Where'd yuh take them?"

"One of two places. Either the Peabody or the Prince of Tides. Can't recall which it was. A lot of niggers go to both after coming into town."

"Do you know your way around the black section?"

"I should. Lived here in St. Lou all my life. Been driving hack for twenty years."

"Care to take me there?"

"Maybe. But it'll cost yuh."

"I expected that."

"Get in. Let's go."

"Thanks." Basser climbed into the back, slamming the door.

The driver pulled away from the curb. "So, he's a ballplayer?"

"That's right. Eighteen, almost nineteen."

"Who's the other one? His girl friend?"

"His mother."

"Mother? Kind of young for his mother. On the lam, huh?"

"So it seems."

"How long you been in town?"

"Got in today," Basser answered.

"Welcome to St. Louis."

"Thank you. Do you normally pick up colored?"

"Only when they show me their money first. She had the money. I picked them up. That simple."

The cabbie talked about his two sons all the way to the first hotel. The oldest boy was a tank man in Patton's Third Army. He was alive and unscathed, now in Austria. He had another son in the Eighth Air Force in Great Britain, a B-17 bomber pilot. He too had survived the war in Europe. The Japs were next. They'd be the biggest fight of all, he predicted, puffing away. Basser agreed in his silence.

Fifteen minutes later, the driver screeched to a stop at the front curb of the Peabody.

"There she is, mister. Used to be a nice place at one time. Lookit now. What a dump. I'll wait here. Watch yourself. This is a rough neighborhood."

"Thanks. But I think I can look after myself."

Basser returned to the cab a short time later, his sports jacket over his shoulder.

"Well?"

"Nothing. Let's try the other."

"Right you are, mac. Let's go."

At the Prince of Tides, the slow-moving afternoon desk clerk took his time checking the hotel register and found the names Mona and Chester Logan under May 9. He couldn't recall the two people until Basser slid a five-dollar bill across the counter.

"Yes, siree," the forty-year-old colored man in suspenders and dirty white undershirt said. "They were here fer three days. What yuh coming all the way up here fer?"

"They're wanted for murder in Louisiana."

"Damn. You know, they did seem kinda strange."

"In what sense?"

"They always looked around, like someone was following them. They didn't talk much. When they checked out, I asked them where they was heading and they said maybe west or north."

"That narrows it down to a few states."

"Come tuh think of it now, you said the young fella was a ballplayer. About twenty. Just how good was he?"

"From what I gathered around the town, he was one of the best in his county. Why?"

"Maybe he's playing ball."

Basser gave the man's suggestion serious consideration. "Could be."

"The best colored team I know of in these parts is the Kansas City Monarchs. If yuh can catch 'em. They're always on the road. They came through, stayed overnight here just last week. I heard tell they were looking for players."

Vince Basser wasn't a big sports fan, but even he had heard of the Kansas City Monarchs.

Basser called collect to the Lincoln County sheriff's office in Ruston.

"Ben? It's Vince."

"Where are you?"

"A hotel in St. Louis." Basser undid his necktie and threw his sports jacket on the bed.

"You made it."

"Evidently."

"What's up? Anything?"

"Ramona and Chester have been here, all right. Come and gone. Anything else from the Grambling investigation?"

"They're cooperating. We found something else snooping around. A new wrinkle. The older son, Billy Lee, was in Grambling the day Collins disappeared and he was seen driving a shiny—get this—1941 Packard."

"You don't say? Where's he now?"

"Don't know. Nobody's seen him since."

"That's weird. Nobody's seen him in years. He comes around that particular day, then he's gone. Find him, Ben."

"We're on it. That's it for now. They don't like us much in Grambling, especially the Chief of Police. He didn't have too many kind words for you."

"That doesn't surprise me," Basser said. "The dumb ass."

"The place is still in a buzz over this. People around here don't take cop killing too lightly."

"Nobody does."

"So, where to next?"

"I'm following a lead to Kansas City. First, I'll see how they got out of St. Louis. Train, bus, whatever."

"Good Luck."

"Thanks, Ben."

NORTH PLATTE, NEBRASKA

The Denver Black Sox won the afternoon game at McCook 6-2, then took to the bus. For the second game, the technical foreman, acting for Cap Garrett, offered the $400 to the local white team, the North Platte Tigers, in the morning, and the bait was taken.

The Black Sox bus arrived at the fairgrounds while the midway was still running. Night had covered the country, and it was the bright lights that led the driver to the spot in the middle of town. The players were dressed to play. It was a dry, cool evening in this dusty land of grasshoppers and open highways. Chester was glad he had decided to throw a long sleeve sweatshirt under his uniform. This was not Louisiana.

He was one of the first off the bus, his eyes steady on the high Ferris wheel, drinking in the sight. "Isn't she something," he said, astonished at the fairground sounds. "Let's go for a ride on her?"

"Not now. Later, maybe. Gotta warm up fer the game," said Flash Barber. "Move it, boy."

The North Platte fairgrounds ball park was nothing more than a rough, weedy cow pasture with patches of worn grass, battered boards for outfield fences, tumbledown stands for a few hundred spectators, and open-air benches for dugouts. The portable lights were on, six light standards extended around the playing field, each one with its own gasoline engine motor for power, the engines chugging and sputtering. Chester was amazed. It must've cost Jeffries one awful gas and electrical bill.

Three Sox players began their warm-up with some infield shadow ball, whipping an imaginary ball around, making it look like the real thing. Chester sat and looked across the bench, where he saw

Garrett dipping into a can of paste and lathering Rabbit Berenguer's throwing arm.

"Hey, Flash?" Chester asked the shortstop.

"Yo."

"What's Cap doing?"

Flash glanced down the bench. "The rub down. It all got started when the Rabbit heard 'bout Satchel Paige and his damn snake oil remedy."

Chester made a face. "What?"

"Paige is supposed tuh oil his arm before every game, tuh keep loose."

"So? What does that have to do with Rabbit?"

"In spring training, he told Cap he wanted tuh do the same thing. Cap said OK. Said he had his own special formula. He's been rubbing Rabbit's arm ever since we hit the road."

"Does that... whatever it is, work?"

"Rabbit seems tuh think so. He keeps some on the inside of his belt, too. All he has tuh do is rub it on that cock-eyed hand of his and yuh should see that ball sink. Boom! Like dropping a rock in a puddle."

"Really. Kind of thick stuff, isn't it?"

"Yeah, guess so."

"What is it?"

Flash grinned. "Axle grease."

In the first inning the locals observed Chester's peculiar peek-a-boo batting stance and thought it was part of the act. Chester didn't think it was so funny. In the bottom of the first inning, he jogged out to his new position in right field after striking out with runners on second and third to end the inning.

Rabbit fanned the first Tiger batter on three pitches, the last pitch a wicked grease ball that dropped two feet at the plate. The second batter, a lefty, popped the ball, high and lazy to right field. Chester circled under it, saw a piece of the ball, then lost it in the lights. He froze, looking around frantically. Luckily, Quincy Bell came diving over from center field to grab the ball before it dropped for a base hit.

"Look alive, stud," Bell yelled to him, throwing the ball back to the infield.

"Couldn't see it."

"I could. Why not you?"

"Sorry."

"Forget it."

Chester kicked at the grass with his cleat. This was no picnic. He felt better the next inning when the North Platte second baseman muffed an easy popped ball to his right. The lighting was going to take some getting used to. The noise of the engines, too.

The first two innings was setting the stage for the type of game it was going to be—one of those half-serious, half-fun contests. The fans, all five-hundred of them, seemed to enjoy it, especially when Dingo Smith brought out a milking stool in the second inning and sat on it behind the plate, throwing back every pitch from that position to Berenguer. The pitcher then deliberately walked a batter, and Smith stayed where he was, begging the base runner to steal second. When he did, Smith, still seated, cut him down with a perfect throw. The crowd roared with approval. Bell soon got into the act by wearing his Geronimo feathered headdress and war paint, then caught a pop-up in his pants. Buttonhead Miller, in left field, caught another ball in his cap. Then the tempo shifted in the third inning, when Berenguer accidentally hit a batter who was leaning too close to the plate.

The crowd booed.

In the top of the fourth, Chester, the team's first batter, strolled to the batter's box with his dark-red bat. The boos grew louder and louder. The stinging phrases came in torrents. Snowflake. Jungle bunny. Nigger boy. Chester had heard them all in Louisiana, and tried to drown them out now.

He bolted into his stance. The fans weren't laughing at his batting form this time. They were on the verge of becoming a mob as they pelted the field with half-chewed apples and oranges, pieces of wood, rocks, candy, hats, hot dogs, and carnival prizes. A pop bottle landed at Chester's feet. He looked down and kicked it away.

"Stick it up his ass, Henry!" yelled the shortstop.

The first pitch from the husky right-hander sailed right for Chester's head. He hit the dirt. It was a "duster," thrown to take the edge away from the hitter. He'd been thrown at before, in school, but never so terrifying as it was now, under the dim lights. He staggered to his feet. He looked to the bench. Cap and his players were staring at him. He couldn't blow it now. No longer was this the game of his boyhood dreams. He was a pro, who played to win. Time to be either a man. . . or a mouse.

"Get back in there, boy," the pitcher said calmly from the mound, his mitt under his arm, rubbing both hands on the ball.

The umpire bellowed, "Play ball!"

Chester took two practice swings and slipped into the batter's box as if nothing had happened, smiling awkwardly at the pitcher, twisting the bat in his hands. His eyes centered on the ball in the pitcher's hand, every muscle in his body tensed with determination. His ears ignored the boo-birds' shouts on his ancestry. He was thinking of only one thing. Drive the ball out of there. Pull it. Never mind the lights. Never mind the shouts and the garbage on the field. He waited, poised. The pitcher kicked, cocked his arm, and threw the ball plate ward with all his strength, down the middle, slightly inside, a few inches above the knee. Just where he liked it. Chester saw a streak coming and swung. With a resounding thud, he hit the pitch squarely. . . and watched the speck of white fly. . . high over the right-field wall. . . to the right of the mobile light standard.

It was a blast that left the park in a hurry. Chester's first professional home run put the Black Sox ahead 5-0. The crowd broke into moderate applause. He rounded the bases, stomped on home plate, picked up his bat and ran for the bench. Along the way, he doffed his cap at a pretty white woman in the first row along first base, who had blown a casual kiss at him earlier.

"Nice hit, stud. Lessee that there bat," Quincy Bell said.

Chester handed it over. "Don't get any ideas. It's mine."

Garrett came over to inspect the bat with Bell, and said, "Ain't never heard a sound like that."

Chick Patterson shook his head. "Poor Miller."

"What did he do?" Chester asked, turning his attention to home plate.

"That pitcher is aiming tuh to take his head off."

"Why?" Chester asked.

"First rule of pro ball. A player hits a down towner, the next hitter eats dust. That's not all. Us colored ball players ain't suppose to come back after a knockdown, cause they tell us we're chicken shit." Patterson slapped Chester on the back. "You done good. You sure as hell adiosed that one."

70

Chester was pleased with himself. He hung in there, battled back. Patterson was right. On the first pitch, Miller took a hit, doubled up, and fell to the ground in pain. Chester, Garrett, and three other players ran to his aid. When they got there, Miller was groaning.

"Where'd he get yuh, boy?" Garrett asked the player.

"One guess," he grimaced, looking up.

"Good thing you're wearing a cup." Garrett grinned. "Don't hold nothing, son. There's women and children in the crowd."

The clowning soon returned. Miller remained in the game, although he was a few steps slower, and the Black Sox gave the locals a few runs to make it close. The final score was 8-5 for the Sox. To get on the touring bus after the game, the team was forced to go under the stands and across the far edge of the parking lot. They were going to eat, get some sleep on the bus and head out at sun-up for a game at noon in the next town. Two games in two different towns were on the schedule for tomorrow. Gothenburg and Cozad.

One of the last ones off the field, Chester dodged the steel supports in the darkness, and wound his way into the open lot. He could hear the dance band playing a lively tune. He looked back to the direction of the music. This was some operation Horace Jeffries had. The midway. The ball playing. The band.

Then. . . Chester felt someone grab him and fling him off to the side. Then someone else punched his face and knocked him down to the ground. As his eyes grew accustomed to the darkness, he could see three men standing over him, reeking of whiskey and cigarettes. Groggy, Chester was quickly bound and gagged, dragged across the dirt on his knees, and thrown against one of the steel supports.

"Trying to hustle up my girl, hey tar-ass!" one man snorted.

Chester shook his head, his eyes bugged out of his sockets. He was starting to gag from an oily cloth stuffed in his mouth.

"What should we do with him?"

"Teach him a damn good lesson, Charley."

"Like hell yuh will," barked a voice in the night.

"Who are you?" one man asked, catching a large figure forming under the stands.

"Cool off, boys. Just leave him be and get outta here. I can smell yuh two blocks away."

71

"Why should we? We're just chewing the fat with our new-found friend, here."

"Because I have a pistol." The gun clicked in the clear night air. "And she's loaded. Yuh leave this-here boy alone."

Chester recognized Cap's voice. The three white men threw their hands up.

"Don't be quick on the trigger, now," one of them barked, his voice shaking.

"Yeah, that's right."

"Get! While I'm still in a good mood."

The three men fled into the darkness.

Garrett came up, bent over, and whipped the rags off Chester's hands and mouth. "White rabble, that's what they are. Shit, yuh all right, Peek?"

Chester gasped for air. "Cap, you pulled a gun on a white man!"

"Yeah, guess I did, at that." Garrett helped his player up, then shook him by the shoulders. "Man, yuh gonna learn some lessons the hard way. Yuh wanna end up on some slab? Listen up, boy. Never go anywhere by yerself in white country. There are some nasties out here. Got that, boy?"

Chester licked the blood from around his mouth. "Yeah. Thanks, Cap."

"And don't go fancying no white women."

"I didn't, Cap. Honest! I just tipped my cap at her."

"Well. . . don't even do that anymore. She sure took a shine tuh yuh, though. Kinda cute little thing."

"Where's that gorilla when you need him?"

Garrett's face contorted. "Too busy collecting the loot. He can't be everywhere at once. That's why I carry my own gun."

"Yuh do?"

"Yep. Keep it under my uniform."

Chester was astonished. "You carry a gun on the field?"

"Yep. And loaded."

"Isn't it heavy? Don't it slow you down?"

"Nah, I'm pretty slow as it is at my age." Garrett grinned. "So, what's the difference?"

"How do you carry it around?"

"Keep it strapped to the middle of my chest, in a clipped holster. Yuh never know when yuh might need it. You gotta watch sliding into a base though. I make sure the lock's on. Don't wanna shoot my darn foot off."

"Is it that rough out here?"

"Sure is, kid. Sometimes, anyway."

"I thought we're suppose to take everything the white dish out."

Garrett slapped the gun he returned to the holster under his uniform. "There is a limit, boy. Yuh hungry?"

"I could eat a horse." Chester felt his chin. "I just hope I can chew."

"We hustled up some fresh fried-egg sandwiches and hot coffee on the bus. We living high tonight, boy. Come on. Get yer bag. We gotta get outta here before those rabble-rousers send fer the sheriff and we get turned in."

Eleven

Agnes sat quietly at the Sunday breakfast table before church, picking at her scrambled eggs, listening to Ramona read aloud the most recent multi-paged letter from her son to the captivated audience of six.

Agnes silently treasured these sessions. She pictured Chester's vivid descriptions of the raw Nebraska and Iowa countryside and how he gave a complete game-by-game account of how he had played. To date, he had made only one error, collected three outfield assists, and was hitting over .400. The team was teasing him about the "magic bat" as they were calling it. Some players even seemed to think that it was jammed with cork. Agnes could tell that Chester had writing talent, the result of a good education. His sentence structure was excellent. He was expressive and funny. His accounts of everyday conditions came alive to her and the others at the table. His insight into a few of the players—especially Ted Garrett—were so thorough they were startling.

By now, Agnes felt she knew Chester Henry Parker quite well and this only after a few face-to-face meetings and the third letter home to his mama. Her intuition told her that there was something gentlemanly about Chester that made him a credit to his race. He was a shy, sensitive young man, but full of adventure and ready to take in the world and what it had to offer. He was polite, extremely handsome, and definitely not like the other ballplayers she knew. He had that rare combination of brains and brawn.

* * * *

74

Ramona and her sister followed the after-service crowd out the wide doors of the Baptist church into the bright sunshine, where they talked and mingled with some of the people Anna had met since coming to Denver.

Horace Jeffries attended church that Sunday morning, the first time in months. One of the last ones out, he kept a respectable distance from the others, biding his time, looking for Ramona. He saw her, and his eyes were stuck to watching her every move. Then she saw him. He smiled clumsily and she transferred her attention to an older couple Anna had introduced to her. Jeffries admired Ramona. She was shrewd. He shook his head. Strange that the natural aging process hadn't caught up to her. He knew she was about his age, but she didn't appear a day over thirty-five.

Jeffries ordered Johnson to the car, then waited until the people dispersed before he made a move in her direction.

He removed his hat. "Morning, Mrs. Parker."

"Well, if it isn't our benefactor," replied Ramona, a hint of sarcasm. "Nice morning."

"That it is."

"I didn't know you were a churchgoer."

He cleared his throat and nodded at Anna, ignoring her remark. "Ma'am."

"Mr. Jeffries. How nice. You know my sister, Ramona."

"Of course. We've... ah... met. And I enjoyed every minute of it."

"Funny. You didn't look like it at the time," Ramona said.

Jeffries laughed, his gold teeth glittering. He liked her spunk and her honesty. "How's Chester? Has he written?"

"Oh, you mean Peek-a-boo. As a matter of fact, he has. He hit a home run in his first game."

"He is one talented boy." Jeffries shuffled his feet. "Mrs. Parker, may I speak tuh yuh... ah, in private?"

Anna squeezed her sister's arm. "I'll go see the preacher, honey."

"Thank yuh, ma'am." Jeffries tipped his hat. He waited. Out of earshot from Anna, he turned to Ramona.

"Yes, Mr. Jeffries."

"Mrs. Parker, I must say that is one pretty dress yer wearing."

"Thank you. But I'm sure you didn't want my sister to leave just to inform me of that."

"No, I didn't." He cleared his throat. She was sure pretty. "Ma'am, I can't beat round the bush any longer. How would you like tuh go out tuh dinner with me?"

"Why Mr. Jeffries, I'm surprised at you. I'm a married woman."

"A man yuh running away from? I wouldn't call that a marriage."

"How did you know?"

"I know. Word gets around, ma'am." His eyes stared at her, and she looked away uncomfortably. "Well, I'm waiting."

"Give me one good reason why I should go to dinner with you? I find you rather rude at times."

"That was business. I'm really a nice man once yuh get tuh know me. Truth is," he relented, "I want tuh make it up tuh yuh fer how I acted in the stands. I lost my temper."

"Yes, you did. But come to think of it, I know I wasn't exactly on my best behavior either."

Her smile appeared genuine to him. "Will yuh go out with me?"

"Maybe," she replied.

"That a yes or no?"

"Leaning closer to no. Where would you be taking me, may I ask?"

Jeffries heaved a sigh. "My nightclub."

"Oh, no, I couldn't do that," she declined.

"And why not?"

"I don't drink."

Jeffries tried not to lose his patience. "Yuh don't have tuh drink, ma'am. Just eat. My cooks serve up the meanest barbecued ribs yuh ever tasted this side of the Mississippi."

Ramona looked across at her sister, busy talking with the preacher. "Is that so?"

"Yes, ma'am. God's honest truth."

With some hesitation, she said, "All right, then. I could use a night out. When?"

Jeffries grinned. "This Friday. Pick yuh up at seven."

"Don't be late, now," she said, grinning.

"I won't," he grinned back.

St. Louis, Missouri

He dialed the operator from the phone booth and asked for Ebbets

Field, Brooklyn. He gave the woman the number, which he knew from memory, and waited patiently for the connection to be made.

"Hello."

"Mr. Rickey. That you? This here is Art."

"Yes, Art."

Powell had seen the neutral-site game between the Newark Eagles and the Baltimore Elite Giants, and two players were more than worthy of mention. "I saw the game in St. Louis, sir. Just like yuh asked me to."

"Your evaluation?"

"I'll send them on the wire. Don Newcombe. . . Roy Campanella, both favorable. Campanella is even better than I last saw him. I know Newcombe's a pitcher, but he's a good one. Big and strong and not yet twenty. He can hit, too, sir. You can always use pitchers like him."

"Good job. Send up your reports and head on to Chicago."

"Yes, sir. I'm on my way."

Eastern Nebraska

Manny Mandon jumped on Night-train Wilson's shoulders. The two turned to face the front row of the bus. Waiting for them up the aisle was the team of Popsicle Jones on Dingy Smith's shoulders. The four were stripped to their undershorts. Mandon and Wilson taunted the other two. The rest of the team lined the seats, chanting, cheering, shouting their bets as reminders to the combatants.

"Don't wreck anything, you guys!" Bennie yelled, as he sped to the next town, both hands on the steering wheel.

Smith started the run. Jones hung on, hunched over so he wouldn't scrape the ceiling. They slammed into Mandon and Wilson, and all four ended up in a pile on the floor. Jones and Smith tried to burst free, but were tackled before they could break away to the front.

In a back seat, Garrett shrugged. "Little boys must play."

"Man, anybody ever get killed doing this?" Chester said across the aisle to Garrett.

"Nah. Seen some broken bones, though."

"What did you say it was called?"

"Slammer."

"What exactly is the object of the game?"

The manager smiled, sitting down beside Chester. "Don't rightly know.

I think one team has tuh slug their way past the other. I don't know where they get the energy, what with the road games and everything."

Wilson threw his arms in the air, and pranced in a tight circle. "Pay up, yuh losers! We're the champs!"

Garrett turned to Chester. "I still don't get it."

"What?"

"Where'd yuh say yuh got that bat from?"

"The magic bat?"

"Yeah, the magic bat."

"Some white man in coveralls gave it to me. For nothing. Honest."

"He just up and gave it to yuh, like that?"

"That's right."

"A white man?"

"Yes, sir. Flash saw him. Waiting for me, I mean. My mama saw him, too. The man asked Flash outside the Denver clubhouse to meet me in the parking lot."

Garrett shrugged. "It's strange tuh me."

"Me too. But it sure is one mighty sweet bat."

"If yuh see that fellah again, let him know we'll order a few."

"Sure." Chester waited, then asked, "Do me a favor, Cap?"

"Sure. What?"

"If I ever break it, I want you to grab the pieces for me before any ump does. Just in case it is full of cork."

"Right."

"Oh-oh, looks like trouble," Flash Barber said, going for the window. "Highway patrol."

"Oh, shit. What duh they want now?" Garrett grunted.

Bennie edged the bus to the shoulder of the road, kicking up a cloud of dust on the gravel. A tall, husky Nebraska Highway Policeman quickly emerged from his car, knocked on the bus door, and shuffled up the inside steps once Bennie opened the door.

Garrett sprang to his feet. "Why if it ain't Officer Bream. We meet again. How are yuh, sir?"

"Mr. Garrett. Passing through, are yuh?" The officer removed his sunglasses and put them in the breast pocket of his gray uniform.

"Why, yes, sir, anything wrong, sir?"

"Yeah, as a matter of fact, there is," he said, his eyes intent for a moment on the four men in the front seats in their undershorts. "Our office got a complaint from an elderly white couple that someone in a bus much like this-here one stuck his bare ass out the window at them on the highway."

"Really? That's terrible."

"They were too preoccupied to get the license number, as you could well imagine. You boys wouldn't happen to know anything about this, would you now?"

Garrett looked around at the shaking heads. "Nope. Nothing."

"We don't take too kindly to that sort of thing in Nebraska. Strange, though. This couple swore up and down it was a white ass."

Chester slinked down in his seat and looked at his shoes. The officer paced up and down the aisle, then stopped and stared at Chester.

"It couldn't have been us," Garrett said, deadpan. "My boys wouldn't do anything like that. We're gentlemen. Besides, we're all black."

The officer's eyes were heavy on Chester. "You sure now, Mr. Garrett?"

"Yes, sir. But I got a pretty good idea who it mighta been."

"Yeah, who?" Bream turned to the manager.

"One of them there other colored teams. The Kansas City Monarchs. Heard tell they came through these parts not long ago. They're a rowdy bunch. Worst behaved players I've ever seen."

The officer grunted, walked slowly to the front, and glanced at the driver. Chester sighed a relief. "You keep the speed down now, you hear."

"Yes, sir. I will," Bennie replied.

"I warned you about speeding before."

"Yes, sir. I do remember."

The patrolman twirled around to leave, then turned back. "By the way, what the hell are you boys doing. . . like that?" He pointed to the players in their shorts.

"Playing a game," Garrett answered, sheepishly, walking up to the front.

"What kind of game? You're not some of those. . . funny boys, are you? We don't take too kindly to funny boys around here, neither."

"We ain't no funny boys, Officer Bream," Garrett said. "Honest. We like women."

The officer glared at him. "Do yuh?"

"Oh, yeah, we do. Black women, naturally."

Basser lucked out. The Kansas City Monarchs came to town two days after he arrived. He stayed and watched a game between them and the Memphis Red Sox, then stopped Monarch manager Frank Duncan a few feet from the team bus outside the ballpark.

"Mr. Duncan?"

"Yeah?"

Basser slapped out his identification. "Deputy Sheriff Vince Basser, Lincoln County, Ruston, Louisiana."

"What does a lawman want with me?"

Behind the manager, tired and sweaty Monarch players were filing on the vehicle.

"Have you seen this young man?"

Duncan rubbed his hands on his stained uniform and looked at the two photographs given him. "No, I don't reckon I have."

"Have you played against anybody looking like him?"

"I see a lot of ballplayers. But he don't ring no bell. Why?"

"He's wanted for murder."

"Bad stuff. Who's the woman?"

"His mother. They could be traveling together. She's an accomplice."

"What's his name?"

"Chester Lee. But he might not be going by his real name. He's eighteen, light-skinned, and I hear a very good baseball player. A big boy. Over six feet."

"Light-skinned, yuh say?"

"Yeah. So's she."

"The season's still young yet. I could run across him in my travels. We cover a lot of states, Mr. Basser."

"Here's my card." Basser handed the manager a business card and took the photographs. "Call the office in Ruston. Collect. I wrote the name down. Ask for Ben Hawthorne. He'll find me. There's a small reward out on them."

"How much?"

"A thousand dollars."

"Really?"

"Each."

"No kidding? Who'd they kill for that kinda reward?"

"A cop. One of them. Or both. We don't know."

Duncan read the written name at the bottom of the card. "Ben Hawthorne, huh."

"Tell him who you are and that you were talking with me."

Duncan slid the card in the back pocket of his uniform. "I'll keep my eye open, and let yuh know if I see or hear anything."

"Thanks. I appreciate it."

Twelve

Art Powell got there an hour and a half before the game was scheduled to start at one o'clock, a Friday afternoon contest between a barnstorming colored crew and a decent local semi-pro white bunch said to have a Triple A ringer hurling for them. From the stands along the first-base side, Powell saw the barnstormers step onto the field. To his surprise, he recognized the manager right off, a man he had played with, drunk with, and managed against in the Caribbean and the Mexican winter leagues.

"Cap! Hey, Cap!" Powell called out, leaning over the rusted metal rail.

Ted Garrett turned around and trotted over. His face glowed when he saw his old friend. "Well now, Art Powell. Shit, man. Good to see yuh. How long's it been?"

They shook hands. Garrett spat tobacco juice on the ground.

"Gotta be. . . five years, Cap. Let see. . . Monterey, 1940," Powell said.

"Well, I'll be. What yuh doing here in no-man's land?"

"Looking around," Powell said, carefully. "So, yuh took tuh wearing glasses now."

"Sometimes. Once I hit forty, I went blind."

"Me, too. Use mine tuh read. Still chewing, I see."

"Yeah," Garrett admitted. "Good habits like that never die."

"Little heavier, too."

"You should talk, tubby." They laughed.

"Now, yuh with a team outta Denver, huh? Ain't never been there. Is there black people in Denver?"

"Yeah, some. More all the time." Garrett spit juice on the ground. "She's the best-kept secret in the West. What's with you? What yuh really doing here?"

"Scouting," Powell said, smiling.

"Who fer?"

"The Brooklyn Brown Dodgers."

"That U.S League outfit?"

"That's right."

"You watch it, man. My boys is under contract."

Powell laughed. Everyone knew that no colored contract was ever iron-clad. "Who with, Uncle Sam?"

"Our old friend. Fat Ass," Garrett said, coldly.

Powell's face went limp. "Jeffries?"

"Yep."

"Yuh mean Fat Ass runs you guys?"

"Uh-huh. It's quite the operation. Dance band and midway when we play in Nebraska. Yuh gotta see it, man. There was nothing like this on the islands."

"You lost yer head, or something Cap? Why did yuh get mixed up with the likes of him again, and after what he done tuh some of the players down south?"

Garrett shrugged. "He pays too good. And he pays on time. I'm getting older. The jobs is scarce. You know how it is?"

"Yeah. . . I do," Powell nodded. "Money talks. Unfortunately."

"Shit, man. Gotta live."

"I know, Cap. But why Fat Ass?"

Powell recalled the team he had managed in Mexico before the war, the Mexico City Reds. Fat Ass was a league official and part-owner of the club. He had threatened players into playing better with one hand and with the other was said to have encouraged his players into throwing some games for his own profit, although the latter was never proven. Word was that nobody was supposed to break a contract with him. Jeffries also owned a run of brothels in the city that the players frequented and he had his own protection racket going. Powell couldn't take the conditions anymore. He never knew if his players were on the level or run by bookies. He quit in mid-season and left without a trace for Cuba, staying clear of Jeffries and the Mexican League.

Powell looked around. Fat Ass always had gorillas working for him. It took Powell only seconds to spot one out-of-shape man in a gray suit standing behind the screen. Powell felt uncomfortable. It was not good for his heart.

"That his gorilla over there, yonder, behind the screen?"

"Yeah, that's him," Garrett replied.

"I see he's taking a gander this way," Powell said, concerned.

"Ah, hell with him. We're just old friends talking, that's all."

"Does Jeffries travel with yuh?"

"No. I'm glad he don't. He'd get in the way. His thug is bad enough. The man stays put in Denver and looks after his other investments," Garrett said with special emphasis.

"I see."

"This bunch is a good team. Real good," Garrett said to change the subject.

"Anybody I know."

"Yeah, Berenguer's kid's with us."

"Jose's boy?" Powell smiled. "Francisco?"

"One in the same."

"He used to be our bat boy in Cuba. . . remember?"

"Yeah, sure do, Art. He's our top pitcher, now."

"He always could throw."

"A chip off the ol' block. Just like his old man. Run and throw. The guys call him Rabbit. Can't speak much English either, just like his daddy. But he sure can chuck the marbles with that beaten-up hand and all his grease."

Powell's scouting eye studied the players warming up. "Who's the husky one? Number ten. Yuh gotta a white boy with yuh?"

"Nah, I thought that too at first. Some white blood, but he's black. Comes from Louisiana. Outfielder. Chester Parker. He's only eighteen, fresh outta high school. Never played pro before, till this year." Garrett lowered his voice. "Stick around. This kid's worth watching."

Powell made a mental note. Chester Parker.

"Catch yuh after the game. Good to see yuh again, Art."

"Likewise. Good luck."

"Thanks."

* * * *

84

It didn't take Powell long to discover that Chester Parker did have a lot of raw talent for such a young kid. The stance looked awkward but he smashed a homer and a double off a hard-throwing pitcher who had given up only five hits on the day, and all that with an exotic dark-red bat. In the field, Parker made an excellent diving catch to kill a rally in the fifth inning. In the ninth, the opposing catcher "accidentally" threw dirt on Chester's spikes. Parker was unmoved. He walked, ran like a deer to third on a hit-and-run single, and nearly knocked the catcher cold on a squeeze play at home. Chester Parker reminded Powell of someone else who wasn't afraid to nail catchers—that son-of-a-gun Jackie Robinson. And Parker was fast coming out of the batter's box, too.

Three-point-one seconds.

Later that afternoon Powell took to the street outside the ball park. Suddenly, he was grabbed and spun around by Fat Ass's gorilla.

"Hey, you," he said.

"Yuh talking tuh me, sonny?" Powell answered.

"Yeah. What do yuh think you're doing, pops?"

Powell tried to appear unconcerned. "Who wants tuh know?"

"Me."

"Walking tuh my hotel. There a law against that?"

The man squeezed Powell by his shirt collar, ignoring some bystanders on the sidewalk. "Don't get smart with me, ol' man. I saw you talking with Cap and I saw yuh taking notes. Cap says yuh work fer Branch Rickey and that new-fangled league back east."

"That's right. . . I do."

"Get lost. Yuh won't sign any of our players out from under us."

"I didn't say I was. Just looking."

"They're under contract until the end of the year, unless yuh pay now. Yuh get it!" He released his grip on Powell. "After that Mr. Jeffries makes deals. He don't like no contract jumpers."

"OK."

"What yuh looking at?" the gorilla said to two young white boys, both about ten years old.

"Nothing," one boy said, frightened.

"Then beat it!"

The kids rushed off.

He turned his attention to Powell. "I said, do yuh get it?"

Powell smiled gingerly. "Yeah, I follow."

"Shove in the clutch, pops." He pushed Powell on his way. "Don't call us. We'll call you."

"I'm going."

The Denver Black Sox bus hit the Illinois road, heading west. They were out of uniform for the first time in three days. Supper time was approaching.

Chester stretched his feet out under the seat in front. He was already a veteran of over twenty games. While most of the players were inclined in take everything for granted, Chester, outside the one bad incident in North Platte, was enjoying himself, seeing new parts of the country. Never mind that the team often didn't bother to take off their uniforms for days, eating and sleeping in them until they found a place to wash. Sandwiches, sodas, and coffee was their diet from town to town. The bus was home, locker room, dining room and bed for the night. Chester enjoyed it because he was feeling accepted. This was an opportunity, his first time away from home and his mother. He had a lot to tell her and Aunt Anna that he couldn't put in a letter. Now, he could banter with his teammates. He was an outright Black Sox and a valuable member on the team, already second on the lineup with home runs and outfield assists in the short time he had been playing for them.

"Hey, Peek," Flash Barber said.

"What do you want me to do now?"

"We're hungry."

"So. You guys are always hungry."

"Get us some grub."

"Me again?" Chester folded his arms over his white shirt and tie.

Garrett laughed and turned around. "Come on, boy. You're the lightest one of us. That's why we let yuh join us in the first place."

"OK." Chester grinned. "Pull over at the next place. I can't stand to see grown men beg."

"Neither can we."

"Is there no justice?"

"Not here, boy. This is America."

* * * *

86

Less than a half-hour later, Chester marched down the bus steps and walked through the door of the roadside diner. He was getting used to groups of white folk, and he was getting used to the procedure in dealing with them.

"Yeah, what do you want?" the stooped, pale-faced old man at the counter said, as he gave Chester the hate stare. Cigarette in mouth, ash an inch long, he squinted out at the dusty touring bus through the stained window.

The restaurant crowd grew quiet. A jukebox hummed low in the corner. Eyes bore on Chester, as he cleared his throat. "There's about twenty of us on the bus. Can we come in for something to eat?"

The old man puffed on his smoke, eyeing his five male customers. "I don't think so."

"Well, then, can we order some sandwiches?"

"Depends."

"On what?"

"If you got the money?"

"Yes, sir. We got the money."

"Let's see it."

Chester dug into his back pocket and fluttered his fingers through the bills.

The answer seemed to take forever. "Yeah, I guess so. I can hustle you up some ham and eggs, and roast beef."

"That's just fine."

"How many?"

"Twenty of each."

The counter man called back to his cook, unseen around the corner. "Got that, Junior."

"Yeah, I got it."

"Can we wash up?" Chester asked.

"No."

"Can I ask why?"

"On account of it's out of order," the old man said cagily, finally tapping his ash on the counter, which he picked up and threw in a trash can.

The patrons joined in a quick laugh.

Chester knew the washroom wasn't out of order. That was one of

87

the standard replies. The other answer was Yeah, but hurry up. Don't stay too long.

DENVER, COLORADO

She knew men always took second and third gawks at her, something she had discovered as a teenager. The last thing she wanted tonight was to show too much for any of those wandering eyes. So, when Horace Jeffries knocked at the door of the boarding house, she had on a knee-length, dark green, wool dress, modestly buttoned to the neck.

"Evening, ma'am." Jeffries was clad in a custom black suit with a diamond stick pin, a carnation in the lapel, his hair trimmed short for the occasion.

"Good evening, Mr. Jeffries."

"My, my, Mrs. Parker. You are a sight fer sore eyes," he said to her.

Ramona smiled. "Thank you, Mr. Jeffries." Then she looked oddly at him. "What's that on your upper lip? My goodness, Mr. Jeffries, are you growing a moustache?"

Jeffries rubbed at his thick, five-day growth of gray whiskers. "Yes, ma'am. How do yuh like it?"

"I don't know for sure. Let me think about it."

He grinned. "Shall we."

Stepping inside Jeffries' Cadillac, Ramona sniffed. New leather seats. The car had everything but a toilet and sink. They said very little, as Duke Johnson drove to Jeffries' nightclub, The All-Star Grill, a favorite weekend spot for Denver's partying elite. Ramona walked in beside her date, the muscular bodyguard in tow. The noise of the band on stage hit her first. People were dancing, laughing, having a good time. Glasses clinked. It was a mixed white and black crowd, all dressed to the numbers. The walls were busy with baseball and football photographs, mostly black players. Several were autographed. Jeffries led her up to the second level, overlooking the stage.

Jeffries eyed Johnson. "Go downstairs, Duke. Get yerself a drink. But stay close."

"Sure, boss," Johnson replied, smiling at Ramona. "Ma'am."

Ramona nodded at him. She liked Duke.

A black waiter in bow tie, white shirt, black slacks came up the steps. "Evening, Mr. Jeffries." He bowed to Ramona. "Ma'am. Would you like to start with some wine, perhaps?" he asked, over the band playing a heated dance number.

Ramona shook her head. "No, thank you."

Jeffries lit a cigar. "Me, neither," he said, out of respect for her. "Two barbequed rib dinners."

"Yes, sir."

The waiter retreated as quickly as he had appeared.

Jeffries inhaled his cigar. "Whatta yuh think of Denver?" he asked, trying to keep the conversation going.

"Cool and sometimes hard to breathe this high in the mountains."

Jeffries laughed. "That's what everybody says. So, how's the cleaning business coming?"

Ramona found his stare unsettling. He seemed to know too much about her. "I'm just getting started."

"Maybe I can help. I come across enough people in my travels who will keep yuh busy with contract work. I can give yuh their names. You'll needa vehicle." He passed her one of his All-Star Grill business cards. "Use this at any used car lot round here. Yer credit will be good." Then he signed his name on the back.

"Mr. Jeffries, why are you so nice to me and Chester? You don't even know us."

"Ma'am, you is one direct woman."

"Yes, indeed. I am. Well?"

He waggled his cigar between his wide, gnarled fingers. "Let's say, I like tuh make newcomers welcome."

"Oh."

"And one way of doing that is by being on a first-name basis. Call me Horace. May I call yuh Ramona?"

Before she could utter an answer, Johnson banged up the stairs. "Boss?"

Jeffries turned around. "Yeah, what?"

"Phone call. The road."

"Excuse me, please, Mrs. Parker, or should I say Ramona? I'll be right back. It won't take long."

"Take your time, Horace."

Johnson watched his superior descend the stairs. "Can I get you anything, ma'am?" he said to Ramona.

"No thanks."

"I'll be downstairs if yuh need me. In case someone doesn't know who yer with and all."

"Thanks, Duke."

Jeffries picked up the receiver behind the bar of his luxurious office.

"Yeah?"

"Boss, it's Clem."

"Yeah, Clem." Jeffries kicked the door closed and put his feet up on the desk.

"I thought I better let yuh know there was a scout from that new United States League hanging around at today's game in Rock Island. And he was talking to Cap."

"Did yuh put the screws to him?"

"Yes, sir. He seems to know Cap quite well. Cap said his name is Art Powell."

The owner's feet dropped down with a bang. "Powell! Yuh sure?"

"That's what Cap told me."

"What did he look like?"

"In his fifties. Gray hair. Five-ten or so. Georgia or Carolina accent, I'd say."

"Yeah, that sounds like him. Artie Powell, huh?

"Yuh know him?"

"Yeah. With that new U.S. League, huh?"

"That's right, boss. The Brooklyn Brown Dodgers."

"Who was he looking at? Anyone in particular?"

"The new kid from Louisiana."

"Is that right?" Jeffries drummed his fingers on the desk. "If yuh see him again, let me know. Right away. I have me a score tuh settle with him."

"Got yuh, boss."

Jeffries hung up and considered the call. The Brooklyn Brown Dodgers, he had learned that spring in the newspapers, was being run by Branch Rickey, the president of the white Dodgers. What was coming off here? A white man calls a press conference and tells the news hounds he's taking over a colored team. There had been rumors in the baseball circles since March, and now Jeffries pondered them again. The grapevine from the east spoke of integration coming to white baseball within the year. This he had heard from two writers back east with black newspapers, one with the *Pittsburgh Courier*, the other with the *Chicago Defender*. Did they know something? Or was it just talk? For years, both papers had been campaigning vigorously for the end to Jim Crow in baseball.

Was this finally it? Integration?

This wasn't the first time he had heard such stories. They were going to integrate in 1937, or was in 1938? Buck Leonard and Josh Gibson of the Homestead Grays were supposed to be headed to the Washington Senators, but the deal fell through because somebody chickened out. Either Homestead or Washington. Or both. Then, in 1943, the Pittsburgh Pirates were set to sign Gibson, if it wasn't for the commissioner of baseball interjecting and killing the deal. And it was just last year that Bill Veeck, a white Triple A owner in Milwaukee, was ready to buy the Philadelphia Phillies and stock it full with the best talent of the Negro Leagues. Once again, the commissioner stepped in to keep the majors lily white, the way it had been for sixty years.

The way it would probably be for a long time yet.

Ramona enjoyed the evening out, and Jeffries made sure she was home before one o'clock. She undressed quickly for bed. Once she hit the pillow, she was fast asleep in less than ten minutes. Then two hours into her slumber, she had the dream, again.

Herbie Collins stuck his foot out at the door. . . barged his way in. . . grabbed her. . . clawed at her. Suddenly, she remembered what she used to do as a little girl in New Orleans. Whenever she had a nightmare she would shake her head and wake up.

She tried it.

She came to. It worked. In the darkness, she sat up in her bed for several minutes, her hands over her face.

Thank God it still worked.

Thirteen

Chester waved to the boys on the bus and burst through the door with a large box under his arm. A pleasant aroma wafted from the kitchen where dinner was being served to the packed-house of boarders. He saw his mother come down the hall, and he carefully put the box on the floor.

"Mama!"

"Chester! You're back!"

He gave her a big hug. Aunt Anna looked over from behind the stove.

"Let me look at you, boy," Ramona said. "Oh, my. What happened?"

"What do you mean?" He removed his sunglasses.

"We need to fatten you up some," his aunt cried. "That food on the road made you skinny as a rail."

He shrugged. "I'm not that bad, am I? I lost a couple pounds of fat, but I added some muscle." He was right. He had put on muscle. Everywhere. His arms, his chest. As a joke, he flexed for them in his shirt sleeves.

"Ooh, I guess you did," Ramona admitted.

"Who's Chevy in the driveway?"

"Mine," Ramona answered. "It set me back a whole three hundred dollars."

"Looks in good shape. Can I take it for a ride?"

"Go ahead. Try it out after. Sit yourself down first. Tell me everything." She noticed the gift-wrapped parcel that he picked up. "What's this?"

"Open it. It's for you." Grinning like a little boy, Chester placed the parcel gently on the night stand.

92

"Looks heavy." Ramona removed the wrapping and tore at the tape. She spread back the flaps and cried, "It's a typewriter. For me?"

"Who else? Of course it's for you. You always wanted to be a writer. Now's your chance. You can finish your novel."

Ramona stared at the machine, thunderstruck. It was an Underwood, black, shiny, and new. She had never used a typewriter in her life. Tears came to her eyes, large tears that embarrassed her. She wiped her cheeks, sought her son's powerful arms and chest, and sobbed into his new white shirt. She lifted her head. "You shouldn't have."

"Why not?"

"How much did it cost?"

"Don't matter none."

Someone was coming down the stairs. Chester turned at the sound to see Agnes, classy and pretty as ever. Her hair was different, up on the sides, and she wore slacks.

"Hello there, slugger," she said, her dark eyes locked on him. "Hail the conquering hero."

Chester was tongue-tied once more. "Hello, there," was all he could say, finally, as she strolled by.

BROOKLYN, NEW YORK

Brooklyn was hot and humid for the afternoon National League game between the Brooklyn Dodgers and the Boston Braves at Ebbets Field.

In the privacy of his box under the roof, the Dodgers president puffed on his long cigar, mulling over the scouting reports in his head, paying only scarce attention to the war-time play on the field. There were bigger and better things yet to come. The talent hunt was winding down. There was no new ground to cover. The names were coming in heavy. A certain few kept rising to the surface.

Rickey blew out a smoke ring in the still, heavy air. Something had to be done.

DENVER, COLORADO

After one of Anna's great meals, Chester sat alone in the darkness on a porch chair, pondering the Denver night sky. The temperature had dropped to the mid-sixties. He heard the radio flick on through an open window of the neighbor's house. The blare crackled before it smoothed out. A Count Basie band tune drifted out to him. He also heard the unmistakable slow pound of the typewriter in his mother's room upstairs. She was trying it out. Good for her.

"What you doing out here by your lonesome?"

He didn't expect Agnes to find him. "Well, I. . ." He stood for her.

"Sit down, please," she said, and he did. "That was quite the present you bought your mother. She hasn't left it alone since dinner."

"I know. I can hear her from out here."

She listened. "You're right. I didn't know she had aspirations to be a writer. Bitten, was she?"

"Yes, ma'am. She started a novel, many years ago. It's kind of a family secret. She still has it, written in pen and pencil. Unfinished."

"Really? What's it about? Tell me."

"Oh, a colored Southern family from Louisiana trying to cope with the new South after the Civil War."

Agnes stepped closer, nonchalantly. "Sounds interesting. Now I know where you get your writing talent from."

"Huh?"

"Your mother reads your letters to us at the table."

"She does?"

"Yes. I enjoy them. Your descriptions of the different towns and states and the players are fascinating. Rather poignant, too. I love your funny stories, like playing Slammer. Writing is a talent you have, Chester. A God-given talent. Like baseball."

He was starting to relax with her for the first time. "Thanks. But I guess I never thought much about writing. I just do it. Mama, I know she loves it. She always has."

"It's not too late for her, now that she has a typewriter. Maybe she'll be another great colored writer like. . .oh. . . Richard Wright."

"Who's he?"

"He wrote Native Son."

Chester shrugged. He didn't give a hoot about Richard Wright, unless, of course, he knew how to throw a curve low and outside.

She finally sat in a chair beside him. "What's wrong? Something's bothering you, isn't it?"

He looked ahead. "It's mama."

"What about her?"

"I found out she's been seeing Mr. Jeffries."

"Now don't you think that's your mama's business?"

"He's not the—"

"The right kind of man for her," she answered for him.

"Yeah, that's right. He's not. . . her type."

She folded her arms and stared at two headlights coming down the street. A car went by. "I wouldn't necessarily believe everything you've heard about him."

"Is he married?"

"Divorced, I think. Married some Mexican woman years back. What does that matter? Your mama's married too."

"Hah, only on a document."

She moved closer. He didn't seem to notice.

"I missed you, Chester."

"You did?"

"Of course I did. Especially when your mama would read your letters to us. Those were some swell stories you told your mama and aunt tonight. I was on the stairs, listening," she confessed.

"Why didn't you come in?"

"Oh, I didn't want to embarrass you. You act different when I'm around. It's true, isn't it?

"Well, maybe."

"I don't bite, you know."

"I didn't say you did. Although you have a good set of teeth."

She laughed at his humor. "Are you scared of older women?"

Their eyes met.

"No. I'm not scared of my mama or Aunt Anna."

"I'm not talking about them. What about me? Do you like me?"

"Sure. Yeah. Why not?"

She stood up. "Have you been with a woman before? On a date or anything?"

He shook his head and swallowed. "No."

"You're kidding me. Not ever?"

"No, ma'am. Not ever. That's the God's truth."

"I believe you." She took his hand, and he pulled himself up. "Why, you're shaking."

"Yes, ma'am. That's the God's truth, too."

95

"Why?"

"It's. . . you. . . I guess."

"Me?" She smiled. "You're a good-looking man, Chester Henry. I bet a lot of girls tell you that?"

"No. Maybe. I don't rightly know."

She smiled in the darkness. "I know that song. Can you dance?"

"No, ma'am."

"You've never danced?"

"No."

"What have you been doing all your life?" She put his arms on her waist. "How about I teach you a fox-trot. I'll lead."

Chester didn't think Agnes would be so forward. The smell of her hair and perfume stirred him. She had a slim waist, and firm back. She was not as delicate as he had imagined. She was as solid as an athlete. She was a good fox-trot teacher and he learned quickly.

Then he stopped, too overcome by her to concentrate on his leg work. Goose bumps popped up on his arms. He didn't have to feel them. He knew they were there.

"What is it, Chester?"

"Nothing, ma'am."

"Don't you like bold girls?" she asked him. Her breath smelled sweet at close range. She broke off. Their arms slid away.

"Is that what you are?"

"I know you're too much of a gentleman to come to me. So, I thought I should come to you."

"Well, I. . . uh, getting back to the original question about bold girls, I haven't known that many to compare you with."

She laughed softly. "You're funny, Chester."

Chester glanced away. "I don't try to be. Not intentionally, anyway."

"I suppose we'd better go back in the house," she said. "They might come looking for us."

"Yeah, I don't want my mama to throw a fit."

Their eyes locked for one last time before Chester opened the door for her.

Fourteen

It was the first time Artie Powell had been inside Branch Rickey's office. To one side of the president's desk were framed photographs of retired major leaguers, Honus Wagner, Rogers Hornsby, and the person to Powell's immediate right, fifty-two-year-old George Sisler, a two-time .400 hitter, a Hall of Famer since 1939, and presently one of Rickey's best scouts in the hunt for colored baseball talent.

Rickey had the New York Times open on his desk. He showed honest sympathy when he read aloud the American casualty figures in the war. More than 600,000 men and women had been wounded on all fronts. Over 60,000 were missing in action. Over 75,000 were still listed as prisoners of war. And a quarter of a million were dead. "This is it, gentlemen." Rickey changed gears and jumped from his chair like a jack-in-the-box. "I have narrowed our search down to six players." He looked at Sisler and Powell, the trusted super scouts he had summoned.

They nodded.

Rickey sat on the edge of his desk. He had their attention. He waved his smoldering cigar, and read from a piece of paper. "Roy Campanella of the Baltimore Elite Giants, Piper Davis of the Birmingham Black Barons, Sam Jethroe of the Cleveland Buckeyes. Last but not least, Hank Thompson and Jackie Robinson of the Kansas City Monarchs."

"That's only five, Mr. Rickey," Sisler said quickly. "Who's the sixth?"

Rickey winked a bushy eyebrow at Powell. "Chester Henry Parker."

"Who's he play for?"

97

"This is yours." Rickey motioned to Powell. "You know, Art, you don't look well."

Powell licked his lips. "I'm tired, Mr. Rickey. That's all. I could use a good night's rest before I hit the road."

"You do that. Don't wear yourself out. You're not as young as you used to be."

"So, who's this fellah play for?" Sisler asked.

Powell leaned to his right to face Sisler. "The Denver Black Sox."

"Who are they?"

"A barnstormer outfit." Powell removed a notepad from his suit jacket. "Parker's a rookie. He'll be nineteen in August. Comes from Louisiana."

"A rookie! Nineteen!" Sisler was astonished. "He's too young. And don't you know the weak caliber of competition these barnstormers face. At least the other five players are older, more experienced, and have taken on the big boys."

"Not so. Thompson's only nineteen. And take Robinson. He's a rookie."

"But they're exceptional."

"So's Parker. He can run. . . throw. . . hit. An outfielder. Bats left. Throws left. Put him in that short right field at Ebbets Field. . . and he'll throw out any runner who tries tuh advance on him. His manager said the kid came up a month into the season, and he's already the leader in home runs and outfield assists. The kid's a natural. I clocked him myself at three-point-one seconds. . . running tuh first."

"I'd have to see that to believe it," Sisler said.

"Campy, Jethroe, these others weren't that good in their late teens. No, siree. And this kid Parker. . . is light-colored. All the better fer integration."

"What about pitching?" Sisler argued. "Who's he faced?"

"You heard of Garth Maloney?"

"No. Can't say that I have."

"Judas Priest! I have," Rickey boomed. "The Cardinals were scouting him in 1942, but he signed with the Cubs. Fastball, no curve, good control. Went to Triple A, as I recall."

"Then he enlisted with the Air Force," Powell continued, "and came back in January. He's a couple years older. . . and stronger now. In the game I saw Parker, the Sox only got five hits off Maloney. Parker got a double and a homer. He made a great running catch in the outfield, then nearly knocked the catcher out at home plate in the ninth. A white catcher, too."

"You mean to tell me you saw him in only one game?"

"Yes, sir... Mr. Sisler. I did. But I know the manager, Cap Garrett. He said Chester has more potential than anyone he's seen in twenty years. An Cap has seen and played with some of the best. Josh. Buck. Cool Papa. Satchel."

"Can he hit southpaws?" Sisler asked.

"Cap said he's had his troubles there."

Rickey was obviously pleased with Powell's quality report on Parker. "About the pitching question, Art. I might have to agree with George on this one."

"Mr. Rickey," Powell said. "I know what yer driving at. But I have good friends in Negro ball all over this-here country. As soon as we hear the Sox will play any Negro League teams, I'll be there... rest assured... with yer permission, of course."

"Why don't you keep track of the Sox through your friend, this Garrett?"

"That might not be such a good idea, sir. I know the owner of the team. He's a mobster. Horace Jeffries. Garrett reports to him. I ran a team fer Jeffries down in Mexico once. I had tuh sneak out on him. I don't wish tuh meet up with him no more. If yuh know what I mean?"

"I see." Rickey played with the rim of his glasses. "OK, next. Roy Campanella. I know Art's opinion on him. What about you, George?"

Sisler's glance went from Powell to Rickey. "The best catcher in the game right now. Better than Gibson. He can hit a ton, too."

"But is he the one."

"Maybe. A strong maybe. He's half-white, played on integrated teams. Good attitude."

For the next twenty minutes they discussed Davis, Jethroe, and Thompson in succession. Then Rickey mentioned Jack Roosevelt Robinson.

"He has to be the most uppity, cockiest player around," Sisler perked up. "He's conceited, arrogant, and the best competitor I've ever seen, next to Ty Cobb. Nobody, but nobody today plays with the passion he does. He's got balls, I tell you! Oh, excuse me, Mr. Rickey."

"That's quite all right. I get your drift, George. So, you're saying he has... chutzpah."

"Yeah, that's it, Mr. Rickey. Chutzpah. He can tend to get a little overweight, though. He was pretty chunky the last time I saw him. Well fed, I guess,"

"Lots a grits," Powell cut in.

Sisler chuckled. "But what a gutsy player." His eyes shone. "You know what Robinson did once? In a game with Cincinnati, he was on first. The ball was hit to left field. He rounded second, half-way to third. When the left fielder got to the ball, Robinson faked a dash back to second. The fielder threw the ball to the bag, and Robinson just trotted to third, as easy as could be. Funniest thing I ever saw. They don't run like that in the majors. No, sir. He's smart. He sees something once, and he remembers it. But, he was two glaring weaknesses," the Hall of Famer went on. "Moving to his right and pivoting on the double play."

"Can he overcome these in organized ball?" Rickey asked.

"Maybe. Shortstop is definitely not his position."

"That's what other scouts are saying, too," Rickey said, glancing at Powell. "Including Art, here."

Sisler glanced at Powell, then returned his focus to the Dodger executive. "He could play first base or second base, where he doesn't have to throw too far. If he's weak at going to his right, he could play more in the middle of the field and place the shortstop closer to second. It's been done for other players. As for pivoting and making the double play, I think he could pick it up through practice."

"Art has some concern about his arm."

"So do I. I'd say adequate, not sensational. Maybe he has an injured wing."

Rickey flicked an ash in the empty glass tray. "Is he the one?"

Sisler thought about it. "He has the education, the temperament, when he doesn't lose it, the desire, the maturity, and the talent. As far as being noticeable, he's that all right. He's black. Very black. Outside of a few minor details, I'd go on record as picking either him or Campanella."

A short while later, Sisler withdrew. Rickey was alone with Powell.

"Art, I know you think highly of this Parker kid, but unless he faces some more top-notch pitching, we'll have to take him right off the list."

Powell looked down. He had tried. "I understand, Mr. Rickey."

Powell looked up. "Yuh know, Mr. Rickey, I was thinking."

"What were you thinking, Art, my good friend?"

"If this had been only ten years ago. . . yuh would've had the cream of the crop of colored ball players. Yuh might've had tuh bring up thirty players at once."

Rickey nodded. "Funny you should say that." His voice was soft. "The other scouts have told me that, too, including George."

"Not tuh mention, sir, some who are in the service right now, like Larry Doby and Monte Irvin. There's two that deserve a shot at it."

"Somebody will pick them up, I'm sure."

Denver, Colorado

Chester boarded the bus at dawn and when it drove away, he looked longingly to the second story of the boarding house. Agnes had the curtain pulled back, and she was staring out. She waved. So did his mother from the front steps. He waved back. To both of them. Then he turned away, a sudden sadness in his heart.

It was unfortunate how the men and women at the house had to stay on separate floors. It stopped him seeing Agnes.

One more month. That was too long.

Would one month change things? Would the feelings be the same? He should have kissed her when he had the chances with her. But it would be too embarrassing. He had never kissed a young lady before.

Fifteen

"Are you Mr. Basser?" The hotel clerk asked.

"You got him."

"Phone call came through and a message for you, sir." The clerk handed the deputy sheriff a written note with a name and a number on it.

"Thanks."

Basser hurried to his room, threw his sports coat on the bed, and made the telephone connection to Louisiana. "Ben?"

"That's me."

"It's Vince. I got your note. What's up?"

"It's not good. Billy Lee is dead. His body was found in a ditch outside Mobile, Alabama. Shot twice in the head. And his Packard was gone. Stolen, probably."

"Isn't that great. No other leads there?"

"Not a one, yet. How's about you?"

"Two months and still not any closer," Basser replied. "I'm checking out the ball teams. All I get is the same old thing. 'Try the team that came through here a week ago.' Stuff like that. I got plenty of managers looking for me. Maybe you'll get a call from one of them soon, providing Chester is playing ball somewhere. I'll keep in touch and let you know where I am."

"Do that."

"Anyway, I'll keep at it."

102

"Good luck, Vince."

"Thanks."

DENVER, COLORADO

Chester parked his mother's car in the lot. He and Agnes were finally alone.

The Black Sox were back in town. Another month on the road was beginning to take its toll on young Chester. The excitement of crossing time zones and touring states like the Three Eyes—Iowa, Illinois, and Indiana—had lost its luster. Boredom had set in. Too many gravel and hard clay roads left his bones sore. His right hand showed scars from a collision with a wire outfield fence. His ankles were swollen. The sun had dried his skin, and all the way back to Denver he was spitting out the dust he had collected in the last several weeks that saw only two days of scattered rain. He was looking forward to a break and going out with Agnes on their first date. Besides, he was in a batting slump, hitless in the last three games.

He looked over at Agnes. He had decided on the bus trip back that he'd come right out and say it. "Agnes," he began, "there's one thing I've been dying to do. Just dying."

"What's that, Chester?"

He took a breath. "Kiss you. That's what. Here and now."

She smiled. "What are you waiting for?"

He took Agnes in his arms, and like magic, their lips met. The evening was still sunlit. People could see them in the car. But that didn't bother them. Just the fact that they were together was all that mattered. Chester thought he was going to dissolve. Her smooth, moist lips probed his. She tasted good. His temperature and blood pressure rose together, until he grew unbearably warm. What a kiss for the first time. What a woman.

"I love you, Chester," she said, breaking away, panting.

"You do?"

"From the first moment I saw you. Do you love me?"

He held her in his strong arms. She leaned on his chest. The first kiss seemed to break down whatever barrier he had thought was between them, real or imaginary. "You bet I do. I sure missed you."

"A month seems like eternity."

"Does it ever."

103

Their next kisses were slower, more tender. A car parked beside them, a white couple inside. They glanced over. Agnes and Chester pulled apart.

"We best go in," Agnes said, her voice soft.

"Yeah, guess so."

Horace Jeffries was looking after his boys. It was celebration time. The boss had started it early, at seven o'clock. The midnight wartime curfews on bars, nightclubs, theaters and such that had been made national law in March was strictly enforced from coast to coast, a restriction that Jeffries was subject to. The All-Star Grill was crammed with high-rolling men and women, black and white, the men in top hats, spats, cuff links, ties, shiny shoes, the women in new hairdos and bright dresses. There was a flash of gold and silver jewelry tonight. The wives and girlfriends of the players were easily recognized, the best-dressed, best-looking women in the crowd.

Agnes was no exception.

Chester, in new duds, pin-striped suit, black tie, white fedora and glittering shoes, entered Jeffries' nightclub with Agnes, arm in arm. He was proud to be seen with her. She turned many heads as she entered the room gracefully, as only Agnes could. She was simply beautiful tonight. Chester turned and glowed at the sight of tables stacked with barbequed spare ribs, fried chicken, black-eyed peas, and thick, dark-brown gravy. This was Mardi Gras, Denver style. Food was plentiful, and liquor flowed like a never-ending river, served in crystal glasses by black-tied waiters and waitresses.

Chester ate until he nearly burst, then stood around with the other players, their girlfriends and wives, swapping flattering pleasantries and, of course, baseball stories. He glanced up to the second level and saw his mother at a table with Jeffries. Chester didn't like to see them together. They were laughing. She looked his way, but Chester turned back to his teammates. He saw Agnes talking with Flash Barber, as if they were old friends. Or was Flash trying to move in?

A few minutes later, Horace Jeffries stood by the rail on the second floor, and called for silence. He looked stately in his tuxedo and trimmed, pencil-thin moustache. "Ladies and gentlemen, may I have yer utmost attention." He waited for a moment for the crowd to gather around.

"Thank you. I'm sure you've all been wondering why the gala affair. Me, too." He drew a few laughs. "Many of yuh, especially our players, will be happy tuh know that next month, following the Negro East-West All-Star Game in Chicago, the Kansas City Monarchs have agreed tuh play us in a double-header at Kansas City."

A thunderous roar broke out. Chester stood there. He couldn't believe it. The Monarchs! In Kansas City? Was Jeffries kidding them?

Ted Garrett nudged the rookie. "What's he doing? We can't play those guys."

Chester shrugged. "Why not?"

"Cause they'll kill us, that's why!"

"Look at it this way. Rabbit and Satchel can switch rub-down formulas."

Garrett laughed, lightly. "Yeah, maybe. Shit. The Monarchs! I need a drink."

Chester left his manager's side and roamed through the crowd, suddenly occupied more with the disappearance of Agnes. He scanned the floor for her. He then looked around for Flash Barber. He wasn't there either. Suspicious, Chester took the door to the dimly-lit parking lot outside.

"Chester Parker?"

Chester jumped around quickly, his heart racing. A figure took shape out of the darkness. "Geez, you scared the daylights out of me. What do you want?" Chester's first thought was a detective.

A short man in a dark suit, his hands in his pockets, advanced on the ballplayer, "Can we talk, senor?"

The man was undoubtedly Spanish, that much was certain to Chester. "Who are you?"

He cracked a stiff white envelope. "Eight hundred dollars, senor. Eight crisp one hundred dollar American bills. It's yours if you come to Mexico with me. That's only a bonus."

Chester felt at ease. He had never seen eight one hundred dollars bills at one time. "Let's see," he insisted.

The man flipped open the envelope and snapped his fingers over one edge of the bills, like a professional card dealer in a gambling hall. Then he gave Chester the money to hold. "What do you say?" the man continued. "The Mexican League is the newest big league. They play in the summer. The Pasquel brothers have money to pay you. White players are coming from the majors. Blacks from the Negro Leagues. Mexico is like Denver all year long. Dry, thin air. The ball travels like a rocket. It's a hitter's paradise. The ball doesn't break at all. All the pitchers can throw is fastballs. Big money, too."

"Hey, slow down. You already told me that. Just how big?"

"Four hundred and fifty a month."

Chester liked what he heard. "Can't this season. Maybe next year."

"That can be arranged." The Mexican exchanged the money for a business card. "Call me at that address in the spring, and I'll cable you the bonus."

"Eight hundred?"

"Si, senor."

"Did you come out of there?" Chester pointed at the nightclub.

"Si."

"You better stay away from here. If the owner finds out, there'll be hell to pay. For you and me."

"I know all about Mr. Jeffries. Goodbye, Mr. Parker." The Mexican blended into the darkness. Chester turned and heard a man's voice in one of the cars. Chester walked over to a white sedan and looked in the back seat to find a man on top of a woman.

"Get away! Leave me alone," she said, struggling. "Chester will get you for this."

It was Agnes. Enraged, Chester reached through the open window and grabbed the man by the neck, hauling him part-way through the car window. "Flash!"

"Chester!"

Agnes did her blouse up and got out of the car.

"I'll kill you!" Chester hit his teammate once in the mouth, knocking him to the ground. Then he held back. He couldn't bring himself to hit him again, once he saw that his teammate didn't bother to protect himself. "Come on, fight!"

"No. I don't wanna fight."

"Did he hurt you?" Chester asked Agnes, not taking his eyes off his teammate.

"No," she said. "I'm fine."

Chester stepped back. Flash picked himself up and went inside the grill, dusting himself off as he went.

106

Agnes went for Chester's arms. "Thank you."

"What was that about?"

"He didn't take no for an answer. We used to—" she shrugged.

"Date? You and Flash?"

"For a time. He still thought I was his, but he doesn't now. Thanks to you. My, you have quite the temper. Strong, too. Yanked him clean out through the window."

"Yeah, guess I did." Chester took Agnes back to the grill, where she went to the ladies' room, and he ambled for the bar.

"You all right, Peek? What's the matter, boy?" Garrett said to him.

"Nothing!"

"Shit, man, don't bite my head off."

"Sorry, Cap. Let's have a drink."

"Since when did you start drinking?"

"Just now."

Chester ordered a glass of beer, his first one ever. When it came, he hoisted it in the air. "To the games in Kansas City."

"Here, here," Garrett clinked his glass, full of whisky, water, and ice cubes. He shook his head. "I still say they'll kill us." He saw Flash emerge from the men's room, wiping the blood from the side of his mouth with a tissue. His suit showed dirt stains.

"Lookit?" Garrett said.

"What?"

"Flash. What do yuh suppose happened to him?"

Chester turned to see. A slow satisfying smile warmed his lips. "How should I know?"

Duke Johnson closed the driver's door, leaving Ramona and Jeffries in the back seat of the Cadillac by the curb in front of the boarding house.

"It's getting late, Horace. It's almost one. I really should be going."

"Not until I ask yuh something." He removed a small felt case from his suit jacket and opened it. "Will yuh marry me?"

Ramona stared at the large, gleaming engagement ring. "I can't. I'm still married."

"Then get a divorce. It's not that hard."

"I can't. I mean—"

"Yuh can't?"

"Please, I have to go, Horace. The night's wearing on." She opened the door.

Jeffries grabbed her arm. "Why so fast?"

"Let me go, please." She tried to be tender. "Thanks for the evening."

He watched as she broke away and ran into the house, putting an abrupt foreclosure to the evening. Johnson returned behind the wheel, slamming the door.

"Duke?"

"Yeah, boss."

"I want yuh tuh do something fer me."

The bodyguard looked in the rear-view mirror at his no-nonsense employer. "Sure, boss. What?"

"Check into that there woman."

"Ramona Parker?"

"No, Ella Fitzgerald. Who the hell duh yuh think I mean? Yeah, Ramona. I want tuh know why she left Louisiana. I want tuh know if she's still married. I gotta gut feeling something just don't jive."

"You bet, boss," said the bodyguard, turning the ignition. "Home?"

"Yeah. Home."

Ramona was frantic.

His intention was unmistakable. He had her on the table, his hand over her mouth. He was holding her down with his body, pulling at her underpants, ripping them to shreds. She couldn't do a thing. Not a thing. Too strong for her. She wept into his palm, then closed her eyes, wishing it over.

Ramona shook her head. Once... twice... three times...

She woke up suddenly. The room came into focus. She'd been dreaming. Thank God it was dawn in Denver.

Chester tip-toed down the hall in the morning darkness. He tapped lightly on Agnes's door. Once. Then again. It slid open slowly. Agnes was in a thin nightgown, a bedside lamp on in the corner of the room.

"Chester!" she whispered, rubbing her eyes. "What on earth!"

"I came to say goodbye," he whispered in return. "The bus will be coming soon. Let me in."

"You're not supposed to be up here."

"I know. Just let me in."

Still half-asleep, she opened up with a slight creak of the hinges.

He closed the door, whipped around, and took her in his arms. His awkwardness of the past had vanished. He kissed her hard, and she made no effort to resist. He jammed her towards the wall, but not hard. He was startled to feel her against his chest through the thin nightgown material. He kissed her on the neck, several times. The excitement began to soar in them both.

Agnes was fully awake now. "Oh, Chester!" She put her hands into his open team jacket and around his muscular chest. "You learn fast," she said, her breathing suddenly unsteady. "What brought this on?"

"I love you, Agnes."

She smiled and with her right hand led his face to her chest. He didn't know what to make of it, until she said, "Easy boy. Easy."

The screech of brakes from the street jolted them.

"The bus is here," she said.

"Great!" he grunted. "The one time they come early." He looked in the direction of the window. "OK. Gotta go," he said.

"Yes, you better. Hurry, before Anna or your mother find you."

He kissed her lightly on the lips and released her.

"Write me," she said, opening the door for him. "Get going, before your mother comes."

"So what if she does? She knows about us. I told her."

Agnes was surprised. "Why?"

"I had to."

She swallowed hard. "Go!"

He couldn't. They went for each other's arms, one last time. They kissed long, both caught up in the melting of their mouths.

Agnes finally had to push him off. "Go, please. Don't forget to write me."

"I won't." He headed for the stairs.

And was gone.

Sixteen

Chester took the last gulp of his warm Dr. Pepper, and set the bottle down. He was in the habit now of writing his mother and Agnes every two or three days. It was easy enough to do with all the time the team spent traveling. Today, sitting on the bus steps across from the ball diamond, he caught the moment to start a fresh letter between an afternoon doubleheader, while his teammates lingered about getting ready for the next game in another twenty minutes. His hitting slump had come to an end. Chester was in a groove, and he was enjoying himself again.

This backwoods boy from Louisiana was bitten, and it happened so fast. He was in love. Not a normal love. He was madly, wildly, head-over-heels in love. He sucked on the end of the ball-point pen, mulling over his choice of words. He had put it off long enough. These month-long trips away from Agnes were agony. It couldn't wait until he returned to Denver. She needed to know what was on his mind, or he'd be in torment for weeks. He had to tell her. Trouble was, her return mail probably wouldn't catch up to him until he reached Kansas City.

If he was lucky.

CHICAGO, ILLINOIS

Chicago's Comiskey Park was the place to be this Dog Day in August when the heat and humidity stifled the city. The East-West All-Star Game was the highlight of Negro baseball, the chance for the two

110

leagues, American and National, to showcase their best players, voted in by the fans themselves.

Launched in 1933, only a month after the major leagues began their own all-star game, the East-West Game had attracted as many as 51,000 fans in 1943, its best attendance to date. Half were white it seemed, every year, probably because the whites knew talent when they saw it, too. While colored schedules were so irregular, such as cancellations at the last minute and everything else that went with the bad side of their leagues, the East-West Game was the only consistent part of Blackball. It was the biggest money-maker for the owners. The profits of the game were split by the game's promoters and the teams in both leagues. Meanwhile, the players got the raw end of the deal by collecting a mere fifty dollars each.

For this, the twelfth version of the East-West Game, the entire South side of Chicago was lit up. Hotels and restaurants overflowed. Store sales in the black section skyrocketed. Black entertainers traveled halfway across the country for the event, musicians like Louis Armstrong and Duke Ellington, and sports personalities like Joe Louis. Women came too—dressed seeking to be noticed—among the more than 30,000 fans today.

Jackie Robinson finished infield practice and jogged to the dugout. Looking up and down at his all-star teammates and across the field to the all-stars in the opposing dugout, he was angered by what he saw. So many talented colored ballplayers, all unable to crack the major leagues because of skin color. The game didn't mean anything to Robinson. It didn't bring any extra money outside of the fifty bucks cash. There was no recognition from the white major leagues. So why was he even here?

Who cared that he was hitting .340 to date against some damn fine pitching.

Who really cared?

Taking deep breaths, Powell was feeling the heat. He wiped his forehead with his hand, and scratched in the day's starting lineups on his score book, as announced by the man on the Comiskey Park public address system.

Jesse Williams 2b
Jackie Robinson ss
Lloyd Davenport rf
Neil Robinson cf
Alex Radcliffe 3b
Lester Lockett lf
Archie Ware 1b
Quincy Trouppe c
Verdel Mathis p

Over the course of this year, Powell had either watched or scouted most of these players. But he had come to see Robinson again, under different circumstances, against Blackball's best. He had watched Robinson closely in the warm-up, especially his defensive work. Sisler had it right. Shortstop was definitely not Robinson's position. He wasn't bad mind you, just a little above average. But his hitting shone. He was spraying line drives all over the park, out of a unique hitting style. He had a strange way of kinking his knees, and dropping the barrel of his bat before he cranked one through the infield.

The man on the loudspeaker read off the East's lineup. Powell jotted down the names. Buck Leonard. . . Roy Campanella. . . Willie Wells. . . Martin Dihigo. . . Powell remembered Cuban-born Dihigo who had broken in as a fifteen-year-old first baseman with the Cuban Stars in the 1920s. He was now a veteran of over twenty years of segregated pro ball. In his younger days, he was a star at every position, and he had once led his league in hitting and pitching in the same season. But he was another of those once-great stars who were fading when integration was so close, too damn old at thirty-six.

Powell looked up and to his surprise saw Robinson emerge from the dugout. The scout realized the full measure of Robinson's physical attributes. The West's starting shortstop was an ox-like, well-muscled athlete, thick around the neck and chest, with powerful shoulders and large hands. He stood out, the darkest man in the West's lineup.

"Hey. . .Robinson," Powell called out to get the shortstop's attention, leaning over the rail beside the dugout steps. "How about an autograph?"

Robinson didn't mind. "Here you go," he said, scribbling, giving back the scorecard.

"Thanks. Hot, huh?"

"Shit, yeah."

Robinson signed more autographs, then he ducked back in the dugout.

Denver, Colorado

Agnes heard footsteps in the hall. Then came a knock at her door, and a voice.

"Agnes?"

Agnes opened up for Chester's mother. "Good evening, Mrs. Parker."

"Hi." Ramona gave her a white envelope. "Mail. From Chester."

"Thank you."

"Agnes?"

"Yes."

"Can we talk?"

"Sure, come on in. Anything wrong?"

Ramona chose to stand, while Agnes sat on the bed. "You like Chester, don't you? A lot, I mean."

"Yes, Mrs. Parker, I do. A lot."

"Do you love him?"

Agnes couldn't look away. She couldn't lie either. "Yes, I love him. And he loves me."

Ramona smiled, oddly.

"Don't get me wrong. I'm glad you do. I'm glad for you both. But. . . Chester Henry's just a boy."

"Oh, no. He's not." Agnes thought of the last morning they had together. No boy ever handled her like that.

"He's a boy."

Agnes stood her ground. "I disagree. He's a man."

"You're older than he is. He's your first girlfriend. He's too baseball crazy right now. I'm concerned that he'll never go to college or university. In his letters all he talks about is you and baseball."

"He loves me and he's good at baseball." She fluttered her eyebrows. "What else should he talk about?"

"But where's baseball going to get him? What kind of life is it for you waiting out every month for him?"

Agnes didn't have an answer. Then again, she didn't need one. She wasn't on trial. However, she knew what Ramona was driving at. "So what do you want me to do?"

"Encourage him to go to college. You went to college. He needs to set some goals. Please do that for me."

Ramona's request sounded more like an order to Agnes. She lowered her head.

"Would you?"

Agnes looked up. "Yes, Mrs. Parker. I'll do what I can."

"Much obliged."

"Where does that leave me and Chester?"

Ramona didn't answer. Her heavy face said it all. There was no future for them, it seemed, according to Ramona.

As her hand went to the door knob, Agnes said to her, "I'll take him any way he is, ballplayer or college man, because I love him very much. I hope you understand that, Mrs. Parker."

"Don't do anything that you might regret later. Think of what's best for Chester."

"I am. Maybe it's about high time you did, too, Mrs. Parker."

Ramona left without replying.

Agnes opened the envelope and read the letter from Chester. She only got as far as the first paragraph, before the paper fell to the floor. She put her hand to her mouth to muffle a happy squeal. She was stunned. Chester had asked her to marry him, and just after discussing the subject with his mother.

What was she going to do?

CINCINNATI, OHIO

He was exhausted by the time he arrived at his hotel room in the evening, thankful for the air-conditioning. His jacket and tie were off. His shirt was unbuttoned, and his sleeves rolled up. He brought with him a cold bottle of beer. A casual drinker, he especially enjoyed a cool one on a hot day, the only time that a beer tasted at its best to him.

Lying on his bed, savoring the taste, Basser recalled his day's work. Was this another wild goose chase? He had trudged through the black section of town, showing the pictures of Chester and Ramona Lee to dozens of people, until he met a jovial colored janitor in an apartment building who had claimed to once play in the Negro leagues. The old man had suggested that the boy in the picture could have been from that team out west in Denver, the one owned by that gangster, whatever his name was.

Denver? Basser chuckled to himself, his head resting on the pillow. Now there was a longshot. Hell, Denver!

The telephone rang with a loud shrill.

Basser slowly leaned over and lifted the receiver. "Hello." It was the hotel operator. A call was waiting for him from Louisiana. "Yes, ma'am. Put him on."

Several moments later. . .

"Vince. It's Ben. Are you sitting down?"

"Laying down is more like it, with a beer. What you got?"

"Will you be staying in Cincy there a while?"

"I could. Why?"

"I'll send you something up. Special delivery. The results of the Grambling Police investigation. The cat's out of the bag. Two officers were up to no good."

"Collins one of them?"

"You bet. How'd you guess? A Mark Murphy was the other. Here's the gist of it. They were running guns over the Mexican border. Juggling the books on arrests. Beatings. They even helped to finance the mayor's last election by arranging illegal contributions. And more."

"Send 'er up, Ben."

"You bet. First thing tomorrow."

Seventeen

The Kansas City Monarchs players woke at first light after the all-night ride and came alive with Negro league stories.

As the bus rolled on, one veteran said that Josh Gibson once hit a ball clean out of Yankee Stadium, over the triple deck in left field. Monarchs manager Frank Duncan said he hadn't heard of that one. But he knew that Gibson smashed one to the back wall circling the bleachers in center field, a distance of close to six-hundred feet.

"And I got it from a good source," Duncan went on. "I once saw him hit one over third in New Orleans that cracked a foul pole. But did you hear about the one he hit in Forbes Field, Pittsburgh, when he was with the Crawfords?"

"Which one was that?" a rookie asked.

A few players gathered around. Jackie Robinson remained in his rear-row seat, listening, rubbing his sore right shoulder.

"Well, lessee, it was 1933, or was it '34?" Duncan began the story. "Anyway, Gibson hit one so high and so hard in Pittsburgh that the ball never came down."

"Come on," the rookie said.

"It's true. Managers never lie."

"Oh, yeah, sure," someone shouted.

"Quiet! Well, not usually," Duncan continued. "The umpire looked up tuh the sky, waited awhile, then ruled it a home run. That same umpire followed the Crawfords into Philadelphia, where they played the Stars the next day. Lo and behold, a ball drops outta the sky and is caught by the Stars' center fielder. The umpire runs out, points tuh the Pittsburgh bench and screams, 'Yer out, Gibson—yesterday in Pittsburgh!'"

Pitcher Booker McDaniels laughed. "Like hell, skip."

Duncan grinned. "It's God's honest truth."

Jackie Robinson shook his head. What bullshit!

McDaniels stood up in the aisle. The bus took a turn in the road, and he steadied himself on the seat. "Yeah, well, I once saw Cool Papa Bell go from first to home on a bunt."

Now Robinson perked up. Base-running was his forte. First to home on a bunt!

Duncan waved a hand. "Go ahead. Tell us, Book."

"Well," McDaniels said, arms waving, "Bell was on first. The batter laid down a bunt between the third baseman and the pitcher. The third baseman scooped up the ball and threw tuh first. The runner was out, but Bell took off fer second, rounded the base and was going fer third. Meanwhile, the catcher saw that the third baseman was outta position, and he ran over tuh cover the bag in case of a throw from the first baseman. Bell had already rounded third and ran all the way home as the catcher tried tuh scramble back. There yuh go."

Robinson shook his head. That was the trouble with Blackball. Stories and memories, anything to drown out the miserable lifestyle. Now the team was heading back to Kansas City to play some black barnstorming team from Denver called the Black Sox. How low could they go? He thought of his fiancée, Rae. He wanted to quit and go back to her. Forget baseball. Try something else. Get a real job. But what else paid four-hundred dollars a month?

Not too damn much.

The Monarchs stopped at the neon-signed country gas station that they had gassed-up at at least three of four times every summer for ten years. A middle-aged couple were emerging from the attached diner and got into their car. The players straggled out of the bus to stretch.

A gas jockey, a teenage boy, in torn coveralls and greasy cap sauntered over. "What will it be, boys?"

"Fill 'er up," the driver said.

The jockey grabbed the gas pump and clanked it into the tank.

Robinson saw the tables and chairs through the diner windows. Large hand-lettered signs in the windows displayed the week's specials. The place looked empty. "Wait a sec," he snapped at the boy. "Don't put the gas in."

"Why not?"

"Who's your boss?"

"Henry Watson."

"Who runs the restaurant?"

"He does. Runs everything."

"Where is he?"

"In the kitchen, I reckon. Why?"

"Could you get him?"

"Now? You got a complaint or something?"

Robinson cleared his throat. "No, just get him. Please."

"OK." The boy left the pump in the tank, and headed for the diner.

"What yuh doing here?" Duncan roamed over and asked Robinson. "You'll see."

The boy returned with a man in brush cut and glasses, his sleeves rolled up. "You asking for me?"

Robinson looked at him, hands on his hips. "Yes, sir. Are you Henry Watson, the owner?"

"That's me."

"We'd like a hot meal. We haven't had one in a long time. Can we use the diner?"

"No, 'fraid not," Watson replied, matter-of-factly, adjusting the glasses on the bridge of his nose.

Robinson turned to the gas jockey. "Then take the pump out."

"What did you say?" Watson asked.

No one spoke for seconds. Robinson could feel every eye boring into him. "I said take the pump out. You have your policy, we have ours. No diner, no gas." Robinson's voice was higher than normal. "There's two fifty-gallon gas tanks in this buggy of ours. You want to be out a hundred gallons of gas?"

Manager Duncan cringed. He took Robinson aside, and whispered, "What yuh doing, Jack?"

"What does it look like I'm doing? Trying to get us something to eat and get some gas, too. Look at all the money he's going to lose."

"Oh, yeah. He'll just tell us tuh go and get lost. Why not ask if we can use the washrooms. Why the diner?"

"Why not?"

"He won't go fer that," Duncan said.

"No harm in trying. Back me up, will yuh."

Robinson and Duncan returned to face the owner.

The owner tried to stare Robinson down. "Sorry, boys. Can't do that."

"All right, then," Robinson said. "We won't come back here again. Let's go, men."

"You heard him," Duncan said.

The players began to pile into the bus.

"Hold up!" Watson said. "You boys got the money."

"Yeah, we sure do," Duncan spoke up from the doorstep. "We'll even leave a tip."

The owner considered the ultimatum, glancing at the lettering on the side of the bus. "Well, you boys have been through here enough times."

"That's right. We have," Robinson said. "And we might keep coming back, too. But it depends."

"Oh, what the hell. You boys got the nerve." The owner glanced at the gas jockey. "You gotta sit in one corner, though. Don't want to upset the white folk. Nobody in there right now. Most of them probably won't be coming in for another couple hours. You think you can be in and out before someone comes, just in case?"

Robinson glanced at Duncan. The manager nodded.

"Seems fair," Duncan said.

"We want to use the washroom after, too," Robinson spoke up, his voice shrill. "The white one."

The owner frowned at the audacity of the players, the blackest one in particular. "Yeah, you can, I suppose. Come on in. You boys like roast beef?"

"Yeah!" McDaniels said.

"We got a stack of it. Today's special. Don't forget to eat the carrots. They're good for the eyes. Fill it up, Joey," the owner hand-motioned to the dumbfounded gas jockey.

"But, Mr. Watson!"

"Come on, come on! Do as I say. Who the hell's in charge here?"

* * * *

119

Over roast beef, potatoes, carrots, and coffee, the players ate quietly, a radio in the kitchen turned loud.

The music was interrupted, a special announcement by President Truman. The diner drew quiet.

"Sixteen hours ago an American airplane dropped one bomb on Hiroshima, an important Japanese army base. That bomb had more power than 20,000 tons of TNT. It is an atomic bomb. It is a harnessing of the basic power of the universe. What has been done is the greatest achievement of organized science in history."

Duncan clambered up the bus steps. "An atomic bomb. If that don't beat all. Twenty thousand tons of TNT." He whistled. "Those Japs will give up now."

"Yeah," Robinson said. "We hope."

"Yuh know, that owner wasn't such a bad guy."

"He was OK," Robinson admitted. "Look at the money he made off us."

"Hey, Jack," Duncan called out to Robinson moving to the back. "Where yuh going? You're not sitting back there. Up to the front, mister. You earned it."

"Yeah, get up there," McDaniels urged the shortstop, pushing him gently. Belching, he said, "Thanks fer the meal, Jack. We owe yuh one."

Robinson's face broke into a slow, warm smile. "Ah, no you don't."

Robinson poked his way to the front, moving around some other players in the aisle, who by now were no longer looking at him as the hot-shot college boy from UCLA. They had eaten a meal reserved for whites, in a diner reserved for whites. And they used a washroom reserved for whites.

This Robinson had balls.

KANSAS CITY, MISSOURI

Chester was a bundle of nerves when he entered his manager's room. "Cap?"

"Yo."

"Where are yuh?"

"Try the bathroom."

He found Cap around the corner, unwinding in the filled tub, suds up to his chin, drinking champagne. His eyes were red and he had a cigar in his other hand. His gun and holster were on the floor, near the toilet. It was the first time Chester had seen so clearly the weapon he had heard so much about.

"State yer business, boy." Chester was too startled to speak at first.

"Have a drink," Garrett went on. "She's good fer the rheumatism."

"Yeah, sure it is."

"Shit, this is living, man," Garrett said, sipping his drink, and puffing his lit cigar, his speech slurred from the champagne. "Finally, hot water. Your room OK?"

"Not that bad, I guess," Chester answered, leaning against the door frame. "Once you kill the cockroaches."

"Just don't leave yer clothes on the floor. Unless yuh want something crawling up yer leg in the morning. Hah. Hah. Hey, I here you and Flash ain't getting along. A girl got in the way, huh? He's kinda dumb anyways, like all shortstops, the second dumbest position."

Chester smirked. "You don't mean that."

"Sure, I do. Pitchers are the dumbest."

"Why?"

"All they do is throw the damn ball. Can't do nothing else."

"You've had too much to drink, Cap."

"Oh, contraire, young Chester Henry. I haven't had enough."

"What's the smartest position," Chester asked.

"A tie. First baseman and. . . right fielders, naturally," Garrett laughed.

"Thanks."

"Fighting over Agnes, huh?"

"Yes, sir."

"She's a nice girl, Peek. She's smart, a good-looker. Comes from a good family here in KC. She's the marrying kind. Better hang onto her, boy. Don't let some dummy like Flash snap her up." Garrett lifted his head and saw that Chester's mind seemed elsewhere. "Don't like the advice?"

"It's not that."

"What then?"

"I already asked her. To marry me."

"Got up the nerve, eh? Did she say yes?"

"I don't know. She hasn't written me back."

Garrett rested the back of his head on the tub's edge and roared with laughter. "Son, by chance, did yuh go and propose in a letter?"

"Yeah," Chester admitted, his face flushed.

"Yuh supposed tuh do it face tuh face. Kid, yer a schmo."

"Yeah, I guess I am. I should've asked her in Denver. But I couldn't. I had to think about it."

"Damn right yuh should've asked her back in Colorado." Garrett shook his head. "Forget about taking the plunge, fer now. Get yer mind on tomorrow."

"I'm scared."

"About the games? Shit. Don't let it faze yuh." Garrett dropped his head forward, puffing furiously on his cigar. "Once yer on the field, yuh just play yer game."

Chester sighed. "Yeah, but, we're playing the Monarchs, with Satchel Paige."

"But at least we're facing him in the second game. Better that way." Garrett flicked his ash on the marked-up tiled floor. "Gives us time tuh get used tuh the competition."

"I thought you said they were going to kill us?"

Garrett laughed. "It's not that bad. I've changed my mind about it. As long as we make it close, we've accomplished something. It'll be good fer us."

"Do you think I can hit Paige?" Chester expected a negative answer.

"Oh, hell. Sure you can."

"I can?"

"Sure. Concentration, man. In case yuh didn't know, Satchel Paige isn't the best pitcher around."

"He's not? I thought he was by the way everybody talks about him."

"Hell, no. He's not even the best pitcher in Blackball."

"He's not?"

"Nope. Never was. There's a lot just as good, and a few over the years who were better. Paige just has the biggest mouth. He tends tuh exaggerate his talent. He's a gate attraction. I've seen Chet Brewer, Leon Day, Leroy Matlock, Martin Dihigo. They're all just as good. Before my time there was Smokey Joe Williams, Cannonball Dick Redding, too. I heard Paige couldn't outpitch them two in a month of Sundays." Garrett pulled one foot out of the water and propped it on the side of the tub. Water spilled on the floor. "Yuh ain't got no cause tuh worry. I'll tell yuh a foolproof way tuh hit Paige."

"How?"

"Bunt on him."

"Bunt?"

"Yeah. Yuh got the speed. Or hit them crazy high choppers that take forever tuh come down. Shake him up on the base paths. Rattle him. Outfox him. He don't like that. He's easy tuh steal on with that damn show-off high kick of his. Once he's rattled, then yuh get the hits through the infield off him. Forget about the power and going down-town with the ol' adios ball. The trouble is too many batters try tuh pound him all the time. Nope." He shook his head. "Bear down. Lay down a bunt, or a chop, and take it from there. Shove that bat of yers up his skinny little ass and break it off."

"OK, Cap."

"But, there's one trouble."

"What's that?"

"He's pretty fast. Yuh gotta see the ball first."

"And hit it. Sounds like you don't like Paige that much?"

"I don't. He's a schmo. You can hit him. Remember what I said."

"I will."

"Besides, it's yer birthday tomorrow, ain't it?"

"What does that got to do with it?"

"My mama always said that something real good always happens tuh a person on his birthday. Just give that magic bat of yers a big juicy kiss. I don't get it. You've been using it fer months. And you've still barely put a dent in er. What kinda wood did that carpenter make it outta?"

"Some Colorado tree. That's all I know."

"That fellah could make a bundle in orders. Wherever the hell he is."

"Maybe he was an angel."

Garrett narrowed his eyes. "An angel!"

"That's what my mama said. Look, I'll see yuh."

"Don't lock the door. I'm expecting someone soon."

"What's her name?"

"Grace," Garrett laughed.

"Don't get the clap."

Garrett grunted. "Yuh learn fast, kid."

Chester went around the corner and opened the door to the room. A heavy, busty black woman in a tight blue dress and high heels trotted in, without a word of thanks. "Grace?"

"That's me, sugar. Cap here?" she asked, cigarette in a hard mouth, her eyes appraising him.

Chester thumbed down the hall. "In the tub. Go right in. He's expecting you."

"Thanks, sugar."

"Come on in, Grace," Garrett screamed from the bathroom.

"Tell me something, ma'am," he said, loud enough for Garrett to hear. "You didn't come to play Slammer, by chance?"

"Shit! Tell the whole city, why don't yuh?" Garrett yelled.

The woman giggled, pushing a bony finger into Chester's solid chest. "Yeah, my own version. Yuh wanna play too? There's always room fer one more in the water."

Chester gulped. "Not right now, ma'am, thanks just the same. Ah... I don't think we could all fit in together."

She leaned forward and winked. "But it would sure be fun trying."

Eighteen

Blues Stadium was a single-decked, 17,000-seat hunk of wood and steel. It was built in 1923 at a cost of $400,000 on the corner of 22nd Street and Brooklyn Avenue, two miles from downtown, on what once was a frog pond and ash heap. Considered a pitcher's park with its 350 feet down the lines and 450 feet to straightaway center, the prevailing winds at certain times in the summer heat did however blow towards left field, a great advantage to right-handed power hitters. Home of the New York Yankees' Triple A Kansas City Blues, Blues Stadium was also rented out to the Negro American League Kansas City Monarchs, masters of the winning tradition that made the town of Kansas City and the Monarch team the talk of Blackball all over the United States.

This hot Sunday colored church services were set back an hour to ten o'clock to accommodate the Monarch fans heading to the park by game time, and the New York Yankee policy of segregated seating for the Blues' games was dropped for the sake of the enthusiastic colored fans.

Today the park was wide open.

The sun hung like an orange fireball over the grandstand roof. It was going to be a hot one.

Art Powell got there early and sat with a congregation of Monarch fans behind the team's third-base dugout. He was surrounded by the smells associated with a colored double-header—popcorn, sandwiches, fried chicken, pork chops, hot dogs and beer. Here, melted in with a crowd, was the best place not to be seen by a Jeffries gorilla. This was a rare opportunity for the super-scout. He had a chance to see the two prospects, Jackie Robinson and Chester Parker, oppose each other on the same field. Powell still felt that he had to keep his trained eye on Parker. There was something about the kid that he liked. Facing the mighty Monarchs would be a true test of the kid's guts.

Two hours before game time, Chester stepped onto the field, glove tucked under his throwing arm. His nose caught the sweet scent of freshly-mowed grass, the smell of baseball. Several hundred fans were already in the stands, the majority behind the Monarchs dugout along third base. Like the other Sox players, he was awed by the stadium and the sight of the Kansas City players across the field in their red, blue, and gray uniforms.

Blues Stadium was another Kramer Park in neatness, only bigger, and more spectacular to Chester's rookie eyes. He was impressed by the outfield walls containing colorful signs advertising Coca-Cola, shoes, double-breasted suits, soap, cigarettes, beer, whiskey, boot polish, used cars, and war bonds. He quickly realized that the park was built on the edge of a ravine, where the right and center-field fences took on the illusion of growing clean out of the hillside.

"Ooowee," Manny Mandon said. "This is one fine place tuh play. Beats them cow pastures we've been twisting our ankles on."

"I'll say."

"Take a gander over there, Peek. Ain't that Satchel Paige?"

Chester picked out the tall pitcher signing autographs. It had been nine years since Shreveport. April 9, 1936. Paige seemed taller and thinner. This was the great Satchel Paige? He sure was one skinny fellow.

"Listen up, men," Garrett said to his forces, waving them into the dugout. "Get yer butts over here."

Chester made sure he found a spot furthest away from Flash Barber. He looked to the field. Some of the Monarchs players began loosening up, bending and stretching. Not Paige. He continued signing autographs.

"This. . . well, this is it, men," Garrett started, stumbling with his unprepared speech. He yawned and rubbed his two-day growth of whiskers. "Our biggest two games of the two years the Black Sox have been together. We've all heard of the Kansas City Monarchs. Well, dammit, don't be frightened by them. They have tuh pull their pants down tuh shit, like the rest of the us." He spat tobacco juice on the ground and waited for a few laughs to die down.

"Who's pitching fer us?" Mandon asked.

"I'll get tuh that," Garrett said. "They're going with a strong lineup, most of their regulars will be playing. Booker McDaniels will be facing yuh for the first game. They call him Cannonball for obvious reasons. He throws smoke, boys. Real smoke. Then it's Satchel Paige fer the second game. Don't let him fool yuh with all his fancy-ass deliveries and high kick, and all that shit. Don't try tuh overpower him. We're going tuh bunt on him, and hit choppers, get men on base, and rattle him. Manny, you'll pitch the first game." He tapped Berenguer on the shoulder. "Rabbit, the second."

Dingy Smith leaned toward Chester and whispered, "Snake oil verse axle-grease."

Chester nodded. "Yeah."

"These Monarchs think we're a buncha chumps," Garrett continued. "Well, my daddy used tuh say, 'if yuh wanna hang around with the big dogs, then yuh have tuh piss in the tall grass.' They're the big dogs. So go get them." Garrett then read off the lineup. Chester was hitting fifth, playing right field, his usual spot.

In batting practice, Chester sent two balls deep over the fence in right. He stopped to watch the second, then turned his attention across the infield. Heads jerked in the Kansas City dugout. Even Satchel took note at the sound of the bat.

Powell remained several rows behind the Monarchs dugout in the shade. The stands started to fill. Then he spied him, walking down the aisle to the right of the Denver dugout. Powell lifted his binoculars to his eyes. Even from across the field, he could tell who it was. Fat Ass had a moustache now. He was with somebody—a gorilla. It had been five years. A chill gripped Powell's body.

It was five years too soon.

It was a customary Sunday Monarchs crowd. They cheered every pitch and every good play by the home team. Booker McDaniels struck out the first three Denver batters on eleven pitches. The Denver bench was stunned. They had yet to face such a fast pitcher before so many fans.

Garrett shook his head. It was a brutal awakening. "We've had it too good on the road, meeting all those amateur and semi-pro teams. The Monarchs are the real thing." He clapped his hands together. "Get out there, men."

Chester ran out to right field, knowing that his team had their work cut out for them today. The first batter singled through Flash Barber at short. The second batter, Hank Thompson, homered over the left field fence. It was already 2-0, with none out. The third batter walked on five pitches. Chester felt bad for Manny, who was fidgeting on the mound. But he struck out the next batter, and got the following man to ground into a double play initiated by Barber.

Chester ran to his dugout. He saw Horace Jeffries in the stands. He looked around for his mother, and was glad he couldn't see her. At least she wasn't traveling with him. He hoped.

"Guess who's out here?" Chester said to Garrett on the bench.

Garrett lowered his voice. "Who? Grace?"

"No. Mr. Jeffries."

"Oh, shit. What does he want?"

"I dunno."

"Grab a bat. Yer on deck, boy," Garrett said, poking his head from the dugout. He saw Jeffries looking at him.

Jeffries mouthed, "See me after the first game."

Garrett nodded.

On one knee in the on-deck circle, Chester watched McDaniels firing into Night-train Wilson, and thought if McDaniels was that fast, then just how fast was Paige?

Wilson popped up to the third baseman. Chester strode to the plate, taking three swings along the way. He stepped to the side of the batter's box.

McDaniels stared at Chester. "Get in, kid. And take your medicine."

"I saw yuh in batting practice," the catcher said to Chester, smiling through his mask.

"Good for you."

"Where'd you get a half-ass stance like that, boy, leg out, looking over yer shoulder?"

"My mama showed me it. She's big and she's tough."

"Yeah? Just how big is yer mama?"

"Six-foot-five. And she's sitting behind your dugout."

"Go on. Hey, I thought this Denver team was supposed tuh be colored."

"It is."

"What you doing in it? You look white tuh me. Trying tuh sneak into a black team, are yuh?"

"Maybe I'm not as black as you. But I'm still black." Chester got ready, bat cocked high. He could hear a few chuckles in the stands. The pitcher stood on the mound, shaking his head. He went into his wind-up, and threw. The first pitch sailed right for Chester's head. He dove for the dirt.

"Ball one!" the umpire barked.

Chester picked himself up, reaching for his hat and bat.

"Happy Birthday, Peek-a-boo Parker," the catcher said, throwing the ball to McDaniels. "Nineteen, huh? This is a man's game, boy."

"All right, you had your fun," Chester said, glancing down at the catcher in his crouch. "Now pitch to me."

"Smart-ass little rookie, ain't yuh."

"Yeah, I learned a few things on the road."

"Don't worry, boy, we'll pitch tuh yuh. Ol' Cannonball will turn yuh inside-out. You and the rest of this-here team of yers from Denver. Yuh ain't on no barnstorming trail no more. If yuh think he's good, just wait till Ol' Satch comes along." He waited for Chester to back in. "Yer too close to the plate. Plan tuh pull the ball, do yuh?"

Chester lined the next pitch past the first baseman, who stabbed at the hopper unsuccessfully as it bounced foul.

"Yeah, I guess yuh do." The catcher smacked his lips. "Right nice swing, boy. A little too early, though. How heavy is that goofy bat of yers? Looks illegal tuh me. Must be all full of cork."

Chester glared down at the catcher. "Would you kindly zip it."

"Ooh, testy, huh." The catcher gave the sign and banged his mitt with his hand. "Come on, Book! Let's have it! He can't hit!"

Chester thought low and away, because the first two were in tight. He was wrong. The ball came in knee high, then the bottom dropped out of it. It was a spitter the likes Chester had never seen before. All he could do was watch in awe.

"Stree-ike!"

"What yuh think of that one, Peek-a-boo? Bet yuh they don't throw pitches like that in Colorado."

The umpire chuckled with the catcher.

Another curve hummed his way. This one Chester got wood on, and drove it to over the second baseman's head. It looked like it was going to drop in, but the speedy center fielder came out of nowhere to haul it in off his shoe straps.

"Better luck next time!" the catcher shouted to Chester, as he rounded first. "Here's your bat! Catch!"

"Don't let that catcher bother yuh," Garrett said to Chester, coming to the dugout, bat in hand.

"I know. He's just a loud-mouth schmo."

"Yeah, that's right."

In the second inning, Kansas City scored another run when Chester muffed a hard ground ball that shot through the infield, and rolled all the way to the right field fence.

Garrett let Chester have it after the inning was over. "Wake up, Peek. Yuh should a had that one."

"I know," Chester admitted. "Went right off my glove."

The Sox went down one-two-three in the third and fourth innings, while Kansas City scored again to make it 4-0 in their bottom half of the fourth.

Powell slid his reading glasses down and fished for his binoculars as Robinson made his way to the plate. After taking Mandon to a three-and-two count, Robinson cracked a pitch between first and second that appeared to be a sure double.

Powell watched Parker closely. The ball bounced and curved to the foul line. Robinson rounded first, heading for second, full steam. His cap falling off, Parker ran over, grabbed the ball on the third bounce, spun completely around, and gunned Robinson out at second by a full two steps.

Powell was amazed.

"Whatta play!" someone gasped behind the scout. "Did yuh see that? He threw Robinson out!"

"Nobody does that," another colored man said. "The kid turned right around and threw without breaking stride."

Robinson stood up and brushed himself. He didn't argue the call. Instead, he tipped his cap at Parker.

Powell smiled. Parker was still his boy.

When Chester came to bat in the fifth, Wilson stood on first with a walk. The Sox still hadn't collected a base hit.

"Right nice throw kid," the catcher admitted.

"Thanks."

"But yuh were lucky."

Chester laughed. "You don't quit, do you."

"Yuh know who yuh threw out?"

Chester whacked the dirt off his cleats with his bat outside the batter's box. "No. Who?"

"Jackie Robinson."

"Who's he?"

"The college man from California. UCLA. The fastest man on the team. He told me tuh tell yuh that was one helluva throw."

"Jackie Robinson, huh? Never heard of him. But tell him thanks."

"I will, kid."

Chester slid into the box and pounded the first pitch off the right-center wall. He flew around first, second, and slid into third, as if shot from a cannon, while Wilson crossed home. It was Denver's first hit and first run.

Hitching his belt, Chester was proud of himself. Garrett clapped his hands in the dugout, now alive with enthusiasm. Then Chester saw the shortstop, Robinson, in a jawing discussion with the second base umpire.

He pointed to the bag, as the umpire looked down. Now it was the umpire's turn to point. His finger went from Chester to second base to the sky.

"Yer out!" the umpire yelled.

The crowd screamed and jumped to their feet.

"What's going on?" Chester asked his third-base coach, Quincy Bell.

"I think yuh missed second base."

What the hell was the umpire doing out there? Powell wondered. The Kid touched the bag. A blind man could see it.

131

Powell flipped the stopwatch towards him, to check the time he had clicked in the split-second Parker's right foot pounced on first base.

It wasn't possible. Three-point-zero from home to first!

From the Kansas City dugout, opposite third base, Frank Duncan got a good look at the Denver youngster chugging into third.

The manager recalled his conversation with the Louisiana detective in Kansas City two months ago. He still had the business card. The kid was named Chester—and so was this kid Parker—and his mother was. . . He couldn't remember if he was told her name.

Chester "Peek-a-boo" Parker was a dead-ringer for the kid in the photo.

Nineteen

As soon as he plodded to the mound under the steamy, overhead sun to pitch the second game for the Kansas City Monarchs, the fans came to their feet and cheered.

He was the drawing card of Negro ball, a cult hero, a pro for twenty years of the segregated game. He had played year-round since 1929. Spring, summer, fall, and winter, answering the alluring call of the almighty dollar throughout the United States, Canada, Cuba, Puerto Rico, Mexico, and South America. He was the richest colored player, commanding a salary better than most white major leaguers. An odd physical specimen, he was built like a broom, six-foot-three and one hundred and fifty pounds. He wore size fourteen shoes. He had an assortment of pitches that mesmerized fans and players. He was brash. He was a loudmouth. He was an entertainer. And he thought he was God's gift to Blackball and to the women—black and white—who followed the game.

Some said Paige was forty. Others said he was forty-five or perhaps fifty. No one seemed to know for sure. Whether he even knew his true age or not, he never let on.

Regardless of how old he was, Satchel Paige could still hurl a fast-ball at blinding speed. He had names for his storehouse of pitches. A Bee Ball was a straight fastball, his fingers on the smooth of the ball. A Jump Ball was a fastball with his fingers on the seams. When he threw the latter, the ball headed straight to the plate, then rose half a foot. He also had a blooper, a looper, a drooper, a hurry-up ball, a nuthin ball, and a bat dodger.

Satchel Paige was a man revived. Seven years earlier, he had developed a sore arm in Mexico and was told by doctors he'd never pitch again. The owner of the Kansas City Monarchs came to the rescue and offered Paige a job as a part-time pitcher and gate attraction. Paige accepted. He played first base and pitched an occasional inning for the Monarch B team that barnstormed through the American Mid-West and Canada. Then one day on the road outside Winnipeg, Manitoba, the strength miraculously came back to his arm. He was quickly moved up to the big club. He was now stronger than ever, and at the same time very grateful. Before the arm trouble, he had a nasty habit of jumping from team to team, leaving many owners in the lurch. Since the comeback, he had decided to stick with the team that had given him his second chance.

The leather-lunged Kansas City Monarchs faithful showed their gratitude, cheering him every time he took to the turf at Blues Stadium.

Chester was still defending himself by the time the first game ended 6-2 for Kansas City.

"Don't let it bother yuh, kid." Garrett spat tobacco juice on the dugout steps, while he rubbed Rabbit's arm from shoulder to fingers with axle grease.

"I did touch the bag. I caught the edge. Honest. I felt it."

"The ump's a schmo. He lives here in KC. What yuh expect? Sit still, Rabbit, yuh little bugger."

"Si."

"Besides, yer not why we lost. Just get yer mind on the big guy out there." He gestured at Paige throwing warm-up pitches on the mound, then lowered his voice. "This is what I want yuh tuh do, kid. Stick tuh the strategy that we talked about 'til I say otherwise. There's some money riding on yuh."

"Me?"

"Yeah. You. Yuh gotta come through, boy. Jeffries put up five hundred bucks against some favorable odds with a bookie in town. Hit a home run and he collects."

"What if I don't hit one?"

"We're dead."

"Huh?"

"Dead. Like a door nail. Like a post. Get it?"

"Yeah, unfortunately."

"Just be glad he's not betting against us."

"Yeah, I guess so." Chester looked away to Jeffries in the stands. Five hundred dollars! He sniffed. "That stuff sure stinks."

"I know. Watch out for his hesitation pitch." Garrett slapped his pitcher's arm for good luck. "There yuh go. Beat it."

Berenguer smiled and walked away.

"His what?" Chester asked.

"Hesitation pitch. He goes into his wind-up, plants his foot, hesitates a second or two, then throws the ball." Garrett poured a few drops of kerosene on his hands, wiped them on a rag, then grabbed his first baseman's mitt. He was going to start the second game at first. "Most of the time the batter has already swung once Paige plants his foot. It destroys the batter's timing. Don't be fooled."

"Got yuh."

The second game kicked off with Paige striking out the first four batters with ease. He had his speed today.

"Batter up!" the umpire yelled.

Chester walked to the plate in the top of the second. He was about to face the old soldier, Satchel Paige, waiting, calmly flipping the ball in his hand. The situation reminded him of the Bible. David verse Goliath. But no slingshot here.

"If it ain't Peek-a-boo Parker, the kid who missed second base," the catcher said.

"You got iron legs or something? I was hoping you weren't going to catch the second game, too."

"Yuh kidding? I wouldn't miss this fer anything. Besides, the other catcher has the shits from some bad food. Ol' Satch is gonna make mincemeat of yuh, boy. He's going tuh hog-tie yuh all and send yuh packing to Denver. By the way, Mr. Robinson sends his regards, and better luck next time."

"You can tell Mr. Robinson from me to. . . to go and. . . ah, forget it."

"Get in."

"I will. Don't rush me." Chester stepped into the batter's box and readied himself.

"Here comes that high-tone kid with the big ol' shiny bat!" Paige yelled from the mound. "Yuh think yuh can hit me, boy?"

Chester licked his lips, salty from his sweaty face. He looked to Popsicle Jones, now coaching at third. Cap, arm, elbow. The indicator—the elbow. The cap. The bunt.

"Yuh shaking boy," the catcher laughed. "Stop it, will yuh. The ground's moving."

"Yuh won't hit nothing with that stance, boy!" Paige yelled, bending over for the rosin bag. "All I can see is yer eyes."

"Just pitch, Mr. Paige," Chester whispered.

"What kind of pitch do yuh want to miss?" Paige called out, his white teeth gleaming.

"Is he joking?" Chester said out of the side of his mouth to the catcher.

"No. What do yuh want and where duh yuh want it?"

"Fastball at my knees."

Paige dropped the rosin bag and looked for the catcher's signal, who offered his round mitt as the target. All boney arms and legs, Paige cranked into his wind-up, kicked high and loosed a throw. The ball snapped into the catcher's mitt like a bullet.

Knee high. Strike one.

Chester erased any doubts of Paige's speed. Maybe his body was somewhere around forty or more, but his arm was a healthy twenty. He could bring it on home. Chester looked to his bench. Garrett threw up his arms. Chester knew what his manager was thinking. Stick out the bat. Bunt, kid. Bunt.

"Bear down!" Garrett cupped his hands to his mouth, and yelled over the crowd. He looked back to Jeffries.

"Why didn't yuh swing, there, Peek-a-boo?" the catcher wanted to know. "Maybe yuh can't hit what yuh can't see, eh, boy? Where duh yuh want the next one?"

"The same."

"OK."

Chester had to talk himself into the box. What was he doing here?

"What yuh mumbling, boy?" asked the catcher.

"Nothing." Chester glanced at Popsicle. The bunt was still on.

Paige reeled back, and planted his left foot into the mound.

"Here she comes, kid."

It was the hesitation pitch. Chester brought his bat to his waist and dropped a bunt to the left of the plate. But it went foul.

"Trying tuh bunt are yuh?" the catcher said. He retrieved the ball and whipped it to Paige. "Now what? Can't bunt again. Not with two strikes. So, where duh yuh want this one?"

"Fastball at the waist."

"OK, kid."

Chester studied Popsicle's signals. He couldn't believe it. The bunt was still on. With two strikes? Bunt it foul and he'd be out. He shot a glance at Garrett. Garrett nodded, smiling. Yeah, it was bunt. What nerve.

"Here she comes, kid," the catcher said.

Chester got off a perfect tap of the ball, between Paige and the first baseman. Both were too surprised to move in time. Chester raced to first safely. The Denver dugout erupted.

Paige walked towards first base and stopped part-way to shrug at Chester. "Why you cocky little high-tone. I give yuh the pitches yuh want, then yuh go and bunt with two strikes. Satch don't like that."

Chester smiled. He remembered what Garrett had told him. Shake him up on the base paths. Shove that bat up his skinny little ass and break it off. He now took a long lead off first, and bent over slightly. There was a spring to his knees. The first baseman hugged the bag. They were going to hold him on. He watched for Popsicle's signs to the next batter, Buttonhead Miller, and picked up the steal sign.

Paige glanced over at Chester and threw to the first baseman. Chester got back easy. Then he took a bigger lead. He wiggled his arms and legs. Paige wasn't impressed. He went to the plate. Chester broke for second. In a quick move, the catcher pulled out to the side of the plate. It was a pitch out! But it didn't matter. Chester had such a good jump on Paige that he belly-slid headfirst under the tag at second as Robinson applied the tag too late.

Chester popped up. "Did I touch the bag that time, Mr. Robinson?"

"Gutsy move, kid," Robinson said. He pretended to throw the ball to the mound. The old hidden-ball trick.

"Thanks. Now give Mr. Paige the ball. You're not going to make a fool of me twice."

Robinson grinned and threw the ball over to Paige.

Chester took a wider-than-normal lead off second. Paige looked behind him. Robinson darted for the bag, and Paige threw the ball into center field. Chester ran for third, chuckling to himself. Garrett, the old master, was right about Paige.

Paige took the ball back. Miffed, he checked Chester leaning off third in foul territory. The so-called greatest pitcher who ever lived was so upset that he threw the next pitch a bit too down the middle in the strike zone, and Miller got under it with a hard upper cut. The ball sailed high and far to left field, helped along by the prevailing wind blowing out. Chester waited and tagged up. Instead, the ball flew three feet over the leaping Monarchs left fielder for a two-run adios ball. Chester jumped and leaped his way to home plate, waited for Miller, then slapped him on the back. The two of them jogged for the dugout.

Garrett punched Chester in the shoulder. "What did I tell yuh."

Dingy Smith headed to the batter's box.

"He's going down, I bet," Chester said.

"Yep," Garrett smirked with satisfaction. "Satch is hotter than hell now."

They watched as Smith leaped out of the way of Paige's first pitch, a chin-high fastball, in tight.

In the second inning, Garrett came to the plate and ran out a ground ball and stumbled on the bag at first. Down he went in a clump. The Sox team crowded around, but he got up and walked to the dugout on his own.

"You OK, Cap?" Chester asked.

The manager held his ribs. "Damn. I fell on my gun."

"That'll teach you."

"Yeah. At least it didn't fall outta the holster." Garrett threw his mitt to Chester.

"What's this?"

"Yuh gonna play first."

"Me! I've never played first before."

"Nothing to it. I'll put Manny in right."

Chester shrugged. "You say so."

In the bottom of the inning, Berenguer became uncommonly wild, walking the first two batters, the second one on four pitches. Garrett called time and walked out, wincing at the pain in his ribs. He waved for Dingy to come over. Chick Patterson at second and Flash Barber at short join him at the mound. Chester ran up to see what was the trouble.

Garrett asked Berenguer something in Spanish. The pitcher answered in his native tongue, jerking his head towards home plate. The two bantered back and forth.

"What's up?" Chester leaned to Chick, who knew bits of Spanish.

"As near as I can make out, there's some dolly behind home who keeps turning round and pointing her rear end at Rabbit. Says he can't concentrate."

Berenguer jerked his head towards home plate. Garrett and the players looked. A chubby colored woman in a bright red dress waved and smiled. The fans around her laughed.

"Lookit that! She's bending over and showing her bloomers!" Patterson cried.

"You-who! Hi yuh, sugar!" the woman yelled, sitting down.

"Hey," Chester said, "that's Grace."

"Who?" the other players piped in unison.

"Grace. She was hanging around the hotel."

"Shut up, yuh guys. Never mind her." Garrett frowned, and spat tobacco juice. He turned to Berenguer, took his palm in his and slapped the ball in it. "Forget her and pitch!"

Rabbit understood. "Si, senor Cap."

The Monarchs tied the score in the third inning, then leaped ahead in the fifth, only to have Denver tie it up in the seventh. Going into the ninth, the game stood at 4-4. Berenguer kept pace with Paige, amazing the players and the fans with his assortment of snapping fastballs, gooey sinkers, and arching curves. Both pitchers had recorded ten strikeouts each.

At the top of the ninth, Jeffries leaned over the dugout roof and said to Garrett in a low voice, "What yuh waiting fer, Cap?"

"The time wasn't right before, Mr. Jeffries. I said I'd do it my way."

"It's the ninth now. That's my money yer playing with, mister."

"I know."

"Get on with it."

139

Chester led off the ninth. He had gained some confidence by now. He was two-for-three against Paige, two stolen bases, two runs. He had struck out his second time, admiring the third strike, but managed a bleeder single his previous trip, that fell between three Monarch players.

"Fake a bunt, then hit away," Garrett told Chester at the dugout steps. "Now's the time, kid."

Chester nodded and sauntered to the batter's box.

But Garrett called him back. "Remember, kid. Swing hard, just in case yuh hit something."

Chester tried to laugh. He couldn't. He glanced back at Jeffries' steady eyes. He was dead if he didn't come through. Five hundred dollars. All on one at bat. Drenched in sweat from the day's heat, he met the catcher at the plate. Chester's jockstrap stuck to him. It felt weird. He was itchy, but he knew he couldn't scratch himself in front of a packed house. "Do I get to call my pitches again?" he wanted to know.

"No!" the catcher said flatly.

"OK."

Chester faked two bunts, one a strike, the other a ball. Both times the Monarch infield edged in close before the pitch came. Garrett clapped his hands. The Sox players joined in, shouting encouragement. Calculating Paige's release point, Chester geared up for a fastball down the middle.

Concentrate. Stay loose.

He balanced on the balls of his feet. Paige kicked high and uncorked, the chords in his neck bulging. Pulling himself together, Chester snapped his wrists and swung with a heave of strength at a pitch that was dropping into the dirt. The sound of the bat meeting the ball sent a chill through his body. The sound meant everything. Foul tips always sounded weak. Pop-ups were no better. Bunts and chops were mushy. This sound was heard for blocks. Paige's body snapped around to follow the flight of the ball. He stood motionless, mouth gaped open.

The ball cleared the first baseman's head by several times his height. Chester knew it was well hit, whether it would be fair or foul was what really counted. He started a trot to first, eyes fixed ahead. The Sunday crowd rose as one powerful wave, with eyes converging on the foul pole and the ball. The right fielder was in the best position. But he never made a move towards the fence. He turned his back to the plate and stared hopelessly as a white streak flashed overtop him, still rising, two feet inside and five feet higher than the top of the pole. The ball climbed and climbed, until it landed on the street above the playing field, and bounced over a fence and into a yard.

As far as the fans knew, no one had ever hit Paige quite like that. Or anybody else like that in this park.

Art Powell was so excited that he was on the phone to Branch Rickey from a colored phone booth near the ball park within minutes after the game.

"Mr. Rickey, sir, this is Art in Kansas City. It's hot here." He wiped his brow with a hanky. "You'll never believe what I just saw. Never." Powell was speaking quickly, unlike his usual drawl. He slid the door to the booth closed for complete privacy.

"What is it, Art?"

"The Parker kid, sir. I saw him and Robinson play in a double-header here this afternoon. In the first game, Parker threw Robinson out at second trying for a double. In the second game, he went three-for-four against Satchel Paige. Satchel Paige, sir! He stole two bases off him, one on a pitch out. This kid can run. I clocked him at three-point-zero to first. In the ninth, he homered off Paige that went clear outta the park and into the next county! I'm not kidding yuh, sir. The people round here are saying it was the longest ball ever hit in this park. We're crazy if we don't sign this kid. The Sox beat the Monarchs 5-4 with Paige pitching! They beat Satchel Paige!"

"Slow down, Art. Where are the Black Sox going next? Back on the road?"

"Heading up tuh Detroit tuh play in some newspaper tournament. White and black teams. There's a couple of lefties, I here, pitching up there."

"Follow them."

"Yes, sir. I was hoping you might say that." Powell caught his breath.

"What about Robinson? What did he do today?"

"Oh, yeah. . . him. I almost forgot. Yeah, he done pretty good, too."

"How good?"

"He went four-fer-four and he stole home to boot."

* * * *

Frank Duncan waited outside the Denver clubhouse, under the stands. "Hey, Parker!" he said to Chester, seeing him coming out in a suit, his hair wet from the shower. The Sox players were so rowdy that Duncan had to raise his voice above the clamor.

"Yo."

Duncan held out his hand. "I'm manager Frank Duncan. Great game."

Chester shook his hand. "Thanks."

"Yuh from the South ain't yuh?"

"Yes, sir."

"Where from?"

"Louisiana. Why do you ask?"

"Oh, no reason in particular."

A roar from the clubhouse made the two turn to the half-open door. "What's going on?"

Chester smiled. "Just a friendly game of Slammer."

"Not you guys too!"

Powell phoned for a colored cab, then took to the street outside. A dusty Cadillac pulled up instead, and the front passenger quickly got out.

"Hi yuh, pops. Remember me."

Powell recognized Fat Ass's gorilla from the ball park in Rock Island, Illinois. "Yeah." He wanted to turn and run.

"In the car, ol' man."

"What if I. . . don't want tuh?"

"Get in!"

Clem Rowe grabbed Powell by the lapel, opened the back door, and pushed him inside before any bystanders noticed anything. Powell fell to the floorboards. The interior smelled of cigar smoke and expensive cologne. When he looked up, Fat Ass was staring down at him. The door banged closed, and Rowe slid into the front, with the driver, Duke Johnson.

"Well, well, well, if it ain't my old buddy, Artie Powell." With his polished shoe, Jeffries crunched Powell's right hand until he winced, then grabbed him by his short, gray hair. "I thought yuh were warned tuh stay far away from my Denver players," he said. "Leave Parker alone. He ain't about tuh go east till I say so."

"Who said I'm scouting yer players? I'm looking at the Monarchs."

"Get up. Sit down."

Powell slid up to the seat.

Jeffries checked inside Powell's suit jacket and found three things. "I do declare. A stopwatch and binoculars, just small enough tuh tuck away. Only serious scouts carry this stuff around."

Keeping the reading glasses, the Black Sox owner flipped the two other items to Rowe. Powell said nothing, until Jeffries crushed the glasses under his shoe.

"Hey!"

"Shut up! I've been hearing some stories this year, Artie. Some rumors back east. I've heard tell integration is coming tuh the white leagues. I was wondering if yuh could shed some light on the situation?"

Powell stiffened. "Why me?"

"Have yuh heard anything, boy?" Jeffries watched Powell's reaction.

"I hear that integration stuff every year."

"I thought yer working fer Branch Rickey in Brooklyn?"

"I am. . . fer the Brooklyn Brown Dodgers. . . the United States League."

"Sticking tuh that line, are yuh, Artie? Well, I know fer a fact that two years ago Branch Rickey told the Dodgers front office that the team will start scouting colored players."

Powell nodded his head. "Yes. . . that's true. But only fer the Brown Dodgers. The white Dodgers have a financial interest in this new colored league too. They're the ones springing the loot for Rickey."

"Yuh sure about that?"

"Yes. . . sir."

Jeffries reached over and squeezed the scout by the throat, then slapped him across the face with the other hand.

"What did yuh go and do that fer, Mr. Jeffries?" Powell asked, holding his hand to his mouth, then checking it for blood.

"I was owing yuh one fer ducking out on me in Mexico. This is two warnings now. The next time I'm gonna hang yer family jewels from a telephone wire." Jeffries shot a glance at Rowe. "Get him outta here."

Rowe got out to the sidewalk, reached in the car, and ripped Powell from his seat in one motion, throwing him to the street. The Cadillac drove off, spinning its tires in Powell's face.

Powell propped himself up on one elbow, dust on his face. "Some days it just don't pay to be a scout."

Frank Duncan held the business card and dialed the operator from his Kansas City home.

"Ma'am, I'd like tuh make a collect call tuh Ruston, Louisiana." Within two minutes, the connection was made. "Mr. Ben Hawthorne, please."

"This is Ben Hawthorne."

"My name is Frank Duncan, from Kansas City. I'm the manager of the Kansas City Monarchs colored baseball team."

"Yes, Mr. Duncan."

"I was talking with someone from yer office, two months back here in KC. His name was Vince Basser."

"Oh, yes. Go on, Mr. Duncan."

"He said that I should call you if I come across a young man about nineteen and his mother. The boy's name was Chester Lee."

"Yes, that's right."

"Well, I think I saw the young man."

"Where?" The voice was interested.

"Here in KC, playing for a colored baseball team from Denver. He fits the description. Light-skin, nineteen or so, big boy, over six feet, and a good baseball player."

"Sounds like him."

"Goes by the first name of Chester. This boy calls himself Chester Parker."

"Sounds like it could be our boy. Where can we find him?"

"He left on the team bus tonight. Heading fer Detroit."

Then the Louisiana voice said, "Vince hasn't checked in for a couple days now. He's in Pennsylvania somewhere. But I'll get him. Thanks for everything, Mr. Duncan."

"Mr. Hawthorne, I sure as hell hope y'all wrong about this kid being some murderer."

"Why?"

"Cause that Chester boy is one helluva ballplayer. Wish I had him on my team."

144

Twenty

The Dodgers president leaned back in his chair, telephone receiver in hand. "Clyde?"

"Yes, Mr. Rickey."

"How's the weather in Chicago?"

"It's sunny today. Has been for a few days, now. Though, I heard there were some hit-and-miss storms around."

"Did you catch the game today?"

"No, sir. The train was late."

"Too bad." Rickey blew out cigar smoke before giving scout Clyde Sukeforth some instructions. "I want you to go out to Comiskey Park, tomorrow. Early. See Jackie Robinson. I want you to pay particular attention to his arm. There is some discussion among the other scouts about his defense. Then I want you to bring him to me. Identify yourself as with the Brown Dodgers. Do you understand, Clyde?"

There was a pause at the other end. "Yes, sir. I do."

"Goodbye, Clyde. Good luck."

Rickey hung up.

He paced the floor, the cigar stuck to his lips. He couldn't get Art Powell out of his mind. Was he still serious about this boy, Chester Parker? If he was, then Rickey knew he had better run a thorough check on Parker, as thorough as the one on Robinson, Campanella, Davis, and Thompson.

She left the one-floor office complex and ventured to the dead-end street, a slowness to her step. The weekend could not have come any sooner. It was another long cleaning day this Friday. Four buildings, ten hours, and she was tired. Her arms ached. But she was busy six days a week, and that's what mattered.

Her writing was keeping her going each day. The second day with the typewriter, Ramona had started to transfer her old hand-written novel to typed pages. She quickly surprised herself at how enthused she was about her project. She had made several changes that took weeks. Her speed on the keys picked up. She was creating new scenes, new chapters. She had taken out books from a library on the post-Civil War period. Ramona was staying up late at night to work on her novel, sore bones and all. Now what she feared most was sending it off to a publisher. Would she do it under an assumed name? A pen name?

Ramona came to an abrupt stop. One look at the Cadillac parked next to her Chevy sedan in the near-vacant lot told her that Horace Jeffries had returned from Kansas City. Ramona still didn't know what to make of Jeffries. No other colored man she ever knew lived that well. He seemed a decent sort of man at times, polite when he wanted to be, although rough around the edges, lacking many social graces. He was an uneducated hick. She often wondered how he had gotten as far as he had here in Denver. He was easy to know, but hard to really like. Twice, already, he had asked her to marry him. Both times she rebuffed him. How many more times would he try? He had money. Was that everything? Marrying into his money wasn't right. To her, that was no way to get ahead. Especially how he made it, if all the stories about him carrying on were true. Moreover, she didn't love him. She didn't trust him either, and more often than not, he gave her the heebie-jeebies.

The rear window rolled down slowly. Jeffries tugged at the brim of his new Panama hat. "Ramona. Nice tuh see yuh again."

The smell of cigar drifted out, catching Ramona in the face. She smiled, waving the smoke away with her hand. "Horace. How was your trip to Kansas City?"

He stepped out. "Thanks tuh yuh son, it turned out quite well. We beat the Monarchs. Yer boy socked a homer off Satchel Paige tuh win 'er."

"That's my boy."

Jeffries handed her two sealed, unstamped letters from Chester, marked 'Agnes' and 'Mother'. "It's all in there probably. Told yer son I'd beat the post office back here."

"Thank you. I'll give the other to Agnes when I see her. She went to visit her family in Kansas City."

"She's a right nice girl, that Agnes."

"Yes, I suppose she is. At least, Chester seems to think so."

"Chester has a future, Ramona. I was wondering if we could talk about it?"

"Now?"

"There's no time like the present."

"I'm hardly appropriate, in my work dress."

"Sorry. It can't wait."

The manner in which it was put to her, she knew she couldn't refuse. She dropped the letters in her purse. "If it's that important to you."

"It is. Have yuh ever seen a Colorado sunset? I know a viewing spot on the edge of town that's breathtaking. Will yuh join me? She's just down the road apiece."

"Lead the way, Horace."

The bodyguard had pointed the car north and left the city at high speed. After fifteen minutes, he stopped at a lookout point, and got out for a cigarette and a walk.

"Let's get out here," Jeffries insisted.

They were standing by a rail, against a fifty-foot drop to some bushes. The sky over the mountains burned a brilliant sun-setting orange. A breeze stirred the evergreen trees along the road.

"How's the novel coming along, Ramona?"

"You know about that, too?"

"Of course. There's hardly a thing I don't know that goes on in this here town."

"It's, well, progressing. Anything else you wish to know or discuss?"

"Yeah, now that yuh mention it. That offer of marriage still stands."

If there was one thing Ramona admired about Jeffries, it was his persistence. "What about the sunset? And I thought we were going to talk about Chester's future?"

"Chester has something tuh do with it, in a way. I want tuh know. Will yuh marry me?"

147

"No. For the third time. No. I am still married, at least in the sight of the law."

"That's a whole lotta double-talk. Laws are made tuh be broken. All yuh have tuh do is get a divorce."

Obtaining an official divorce was the last thing she wanted. Any attempt at that would bring the Louisiana authorities down on her and Chester. "But Horace, I don't love you."

He didn't seem to care. "What does that have tuh do with it?"

"Didn't you hear me?"

"Yeah, I heard yuh. Well. . . yuh could learn tuh love me."

Her lips were set. "Horace, you are one blunt person."

He sucked on his cigar. "We're two peas in a pod, the two of us. Both blunt."

She laughed. "You think it's that easy, do you? Get married just like that?"

"Sure thing. It'll be fun."

"Fun, you say."

"I can give yuh anything yuh want. I'll take care of yuh. We can winter in Mexico. Yuh'll have the best of everything, dresses, food, good house."

"I can't."

"Oh, yuh will," he said slowly, displaying a smile.

"I beg your pardon?"

He grabbed her by the arm. "Lookit, woman."

"Ow! That hurts!"

"Too damn bad."

Jeffries's reaction stunned her. It all came back, flooding her subconscious, dark as it was. Grambling, Louisiana. Sergeant Collins at her front door, bursting his way inside, forcing himself on her, then taking her to the kitchen and propping her on the table. . . "Leave me be. What's gotten into you?"

"You'll marry me, Mrs. Ramona Lee. If yuh know what's good fer yuh." He squeezed tighter. There was fire burning in his eyes. "That's yuh last name, isn't it? Lee."

She felt her muscles stiffen. Her worst fears had come true. Someone knew. "What are you talking about? My name is Parker."

"Like hell it is, woman. One of my boys took some time digging up the information down there in Louisiana. But he got it. That name

Parker threw him off. Until he did some checking at Beckford High in Grambling, yer son's school. Then all the pieces came together. Yuh husband's some white trash. I wondered why Chester's so light. And yuh have French white blood. Chester Lee. Ramona Lee. On the lam. Both left town suddenly, whereabouts unknown, as they say. It seems you two is murder suspects, wanted fer questioning in the death of a Grambling policeman, name of Herbie Collins. The Lincoln County Sheriff's office in Ruston is looking fer you two. They've had a deputy on yer trail fer months." Jeffries waved his cigar triumphantly. "One phone call will tell them where you two are hiding out."

He let her go with a jerk.

Ramona knew it was no use denying now. What could she do? "I commend you for your resourcefulness."

"Thank yuh, ma'am."

"So, if I marry you, then you'll keep silent."

"That's kinda the picture, yes, indeed."

"I'll think about it."

"Oh, yeah?" He slapped her across the mouth with the back of his hand.

It took her breath away. "Horace!"

"Don't Horace me. I'm sick of yer high-and-mighty attitude, woman! Yuh have thirty seconds tuh decide. Me or a murder trial? Yuh'll probably hang, you and Chester. Those are yer choices, me or the rope, or the chair, whatever they do down there in Louisiana."

She promised herself she wouldn't cry. She had to be strong. Was he capable of this? Of course he was. People had warned her of Jeffries' temper. She was seeing that vicious side to him that others had experienced. He was scary. "Why would I marry you now? You're just another woman beater. One was enough for me."

"Then I'll make myself a phone call down tuh Ruston. Is that what yuh want?"

"No."

"Then yuh will marry me?" He glanced at his gold wrist watch. "Fifteen seconds tuh go. Say the word, Ramona. Yes is what I want tuh hear."

"All right," she choked a reply. "I'll marry you."

"Now that's a good girl."

"Why me? You could have anybody else. Some younger woman, perhaps."

Jeffries tromped on his cigar butt. "Because you'll make me look real good."

"I'd be good for business, would I?"

"Yes, ma'am."

"More money in the long run."

"That, too." He nodded. "You're educated and damn fine looking, too. Come here." He wrapped his arms around her, his big stomach poking her. "What do yuh say we go into the back seat fer a spell? It folds out tuh a bed."

"What about your driver?"

"He's gone fer a long walk, my dear."

She tried to spring loose. It was just like Collins. The more she wiggled, the tighter he held her. "Not until we're married."

He threw her to the ground. She landed on her side, and felt a terrible pain in her shoulder.

"I call the shots now, woman. Get up, and get in there!"

Ramona looked around, groping to sit up. She was aware of a ringing in her ears. Jeffries shed his jacket and held it in his hand. She searched his face for any sign of sympathy. There was none. Her only immediate option was to submit, silently, humbly, like the others under his control. . . his cooks, his bodyguards, his players, his girls. If only she could shake her head and emerge unscathed from this nightmare.

"Yes, boss," she said, lifting her head, the words falling out of her without meaning. Jeffries grabbed her by the arm and yanked her to her feet.

WESTERN MICHIGAN

Dusk had settled upon the Michigan countryside. It was a long trip and the Black Sox bus was only a few miles from its destination. The only food the players had that day was sandwiches five hours ago. A hot meal loomed welcome in Detroit for those awake after six games in two days since leaving Kansas City.

Four men were playing cards in the rear of the bus, beneath a weak overhead light, rummy at ten cents a round. Garrett was the first to give up. "I've had it, boys." He slid in beside Chester near the front.

A farm house streaked by in the moonlight. Chester paid no heed to

Garrett. He was deep in thought. He was going to marry Agnes, if she said yes. A spring wedding would be perfect. Not a day went by that Chester hadn't remembered the taste of her mouth, the smell of her perfume, the feel of her against him in her bedroom. Only one thing was taking those longing aches for her away—stepping onto a baseball diamond.

"Peek? You awake?" Garrett asked.

"Yeah."

"How would yuh like tuh meet Josh Gibson?"

"Very funny," Chester replied.

"I'm serious. There's a change of plans. I phoned ahead at the last stop tuh the booking agent in Detroit. There won't be no tournament."

"Yeah, why not?"

"Two of the white teams backed out. They refuse to play us. One team said we're too professional."

"What did the other say?"

"We're too black."

Chester chuckled. "They didn't know that beforehand?"

"Guess not. Or maybe they didn't think we'd show. One team wants tuh meet us, though. They got a humdinger of a lefty."

"Whoopee. I love lefties."

"They call themselves the Michigan Spiders. A pick-up team. Mostly college kids. Some is property of them Detroit Tigers."

"What's this about Gibson?"

"Two teams in the Negro Leagues, the Cleveland Buckeyes and the Homestead Grays will play an exhibition game before our own game, on Sunday."

"Sunday. You mean we don't play tomorrow?"

"Yuh got it."

"Then we have a day off?"

"You bet yuh. I thought that might cheer yuh up. Saturday night in Detroit City. I hear Count Basie's in town. We can raise some more cane. Make Kansas City look like—"

"Hey, maybe I can call Agnes and get this whole thing straightened out with her."

"Yuh better. I told yuh she's one nice girl."

"Cap, I could kiss you."

"Wait a minute." Garrett pulled back. "Yuh think I'm some funny boy."

Twenty-one

Duke Johnson wheeled the Cadillac to the boarding house curb. He peeked into the rear-view mirror at Ramona Parker adjusting her dress and sliding out the back passenger door. Tears filled her eyes, as she walked on unsteady legs to the front door as if in a trance. Neither she nor Jeffries said a word in parting.

Duke knew what had transpired when he had gone for a walk in the country before the sun went down. It was the same thing that happened the other times that Jeffries took a woman to the same deserted road. Duke knew what it was all about tonight. The boss had the goods on Ramona, based on what Duke had discovered through a detective friend in Georgia.

Duke watched her stumble up the steps in the darkness to the door, seeing the pain in her every movement.

"Anything wrong?" Jeffries said to Johnson. "What yuh looking at?"

"Nothing, boss. Nothing at all."

"What yuh waiting for? Drive on."

"Yes, sir."

PITTSBURGH, PENNSYLVANIA

Vince Basser arrived at the hotel lobby, his second night at The Royal in downtown Pittsburgh and headed straight for the phone booth.

"Long distance, please," he said to the operator, who transferred his call to Louisiana. He waited, then said, "Ben?"

152

"You got him."

"It's Vince, checking in."

"Glad you called. We hit pay dirt," Ben Hawthorne said, his voice crackling over the wire. It was a bad connection tonight. "Finally. I know where the Lees are, at least Chester, for sure. You remember speaking with a Frank Duncan?"

"Duncan? Let's see. Yeah, I remember. The Kansas City Monarchs manager, a month or two ago?"

"He called the office and said Chester Lee goes by the name of Chester Parker. He's been playing for some barnstorming ball team out in Denver, called the Black Sox. He fits the physical description. They're expected to play in Detroit this weekend. Briggs Stadium."

Basser looked at his watch. Midnight in a few minutes. "Thanks, Ben. I'll get there as soon as I can."

"That's not all. Listen to this. Some black fellow was hanging around Grambling asking about Ramona and Chester Parker."

"Really?"

"Uh-huh. Told a local hotel owner he was a detective from Atlanta, Georgia. When we went to check on him, he disappeared. The name and the private agency using his surname he gave was phony. Said his name was Gilbert. Turns out, no such detective agency by that name."

"So, someone else is looking for the Lees."

"Seems so."

"Thanks for everything."

By the time he had hung up the receiver, Basser had his plan laid out before him. Detroit was too far to drive and get there in time. Besides, renting a car would cost a fortune and buses were too slow. He would have to get aboard the first airplane to Detroit, and that probably wouldn't be until the morning.

DETROIT, MICHIGAN

It was a warm, breezy night in the war plant metropolis of two million people, known as the Motor City in peace time before the war plants came along. It was expected to resume its title as the car capital once the troops got home and everything returned to business as usual in the city that Henry Ford built.

Inside the Claymore Hotel, near Briggs Stadium, Garrett slapped a white envelope at the bar in front of Chester. Count Basie had just finished a piano solo and the band behind him took over with a dance number.

"Here yuh go, boy."

Chester spun his stool to face his manager. Garrett had a colored woman under each arm.

"What's this?" Chester took the envelope handed him.

"Open it." Garrett turned to the girls. "Go take a seat. Be right with yuh."

"Sure, honey," one of the women said.

Over the blast of the band and the jitterbugging couples on the nearby dance floor, Chester peeled out two fifty-dollar bills.

"The boss wants yuh tuh have a damn good time. Just a little reward fer winning the game fer us in Kansas City."

Chester looked at the money strangely. "Thanks."

"Don't thank me."

"Then thank the boss from me."

"Sure will. He can afford it. The odds were four-tuh-one. So he took home two thousand bucks. I made fifty on the deal myself. There's more good news. He wants yuh batting clean-up, too. I agree. Peek, yuh might find yerself in the Negro big leagues by next year."

"You really think so?"

"I do."

"But I like Denver."

"Piss on Denver. Did you call Agnes?" Garrett wanted to know.

"Yeah, but she wasn't there. My mama said she went home to Kansas City for a few days to see her family. Just when we left town too." He looked dejected. "She probably never got the letter."

"Or maybe she ran home tuh get ma and pa's advice."

"Could be. Hadn't thought of that."

"Now, kid, let me give you some advice?"

"What's that?"

"Try some winter ball tuh sharpen up yer skills. There's Cuba, South America, Mexico. The boss will encourage yuh tuh try Mexico. But don't listen to him. It's too dry and dusty, and the roads is bad. Hard on yer bones riding them crummy buses."

"But I thought the ball carries better there."

"It does, but that ain't everything. Living conditions aren't the best. The food stinks. Too spicy. Rotten water, too. I know one player who had the shits all season. Couldn't keep his asshole shut for months. My favorite is Puerto Rico. I know somebody who can help. I'm going there myself in the fall. Wanna come?"

"Maybe. Why there?" Chester asked.

"Shit. Yuh kidding? It's beautiful. Bluest water yuh've ever lay yer sore eyes on. Swimming. Sitting in the sun. Ocean breezes keep the heat down. Average temperature is seventy degrees in January. Great hotels. Nice looking women with some zip, starving for affection." He chuckled. "Oh, sorry, forgot about Agnes. Hell, you can take her with yuh!"

"Sounds good."

"She'll keep yuh outta trouble. There's eight teams in eight cities. Lemme see. . . San Juan, Santurce, Ponce. The island's only a hundred miles across. So there's your longest road trip. A measly one hundred miles. Sure beats the hell outta driving 500 miles fer a doubleheader," Garrett laughed.

"Yeah. You're right."

"They only play on weekends. Saturday and Sunday. Four months, forty games. During the rest of the week yuh can practice and work on yer weaknesses, or take some correspondence courses. Yuh mama will like that. Yuh get the best of both worlds. Like I said, yuh can marry Agnes and bring 'er with yuh."

"If she'll take me."

"Hell, boy. She will. Don't yuh worry none."

"Anyway, thanks, Cap. Sounds great. Isn't Puerto Rico kind of far, though?"

"Big deal. Five-hour flight from Miami tuh San Juan."

"Five hours in a plane! I've never been in a plane before."

"Nothing to it. Jes keep a vomit bag handy. Better yet, don't eat before yuh get on. Nice place, Puerto Rico. Blacks are more equal there than here. Got some other news fer yuh. When we get back tuh Denver, we're gonna play the House of David."

"That bearded team? The Mormons? I heard they're good."

"Hey, Peek, look who's coming. The man himself."

"Who?"

"Josh Gibson."

155

"Where?" Then Chester saw a round-faced, powerfully-built man wearing a gray suit.

"Josh!" Garrett called out.

Gibson turned and stared at Garrett through glassy, pathetic eyes. His right eyelid drooped. He had been drinking. Then a thin smile came to his lips. Gibson was a big man, muscles everywhere, but bordering on overweight. "Cap. It's been a long time."

The two shook hands. Two teammates, long ago, more than a thousand miles away in Puerto Rico.

"What yuh doing here?"

"We're playing tomorrow," answered Garrett. "After you guys."

"Yer not that team from Denver, are yuh?"

"That's us. I was just telling this boy here about playing down in Puerto Rico. Kid," Garrett said to Chester, "Josh, here, was the batting champ, the homer king, and the MVP in the Puerto Rican League in 1941."

Gibson grinned, slowly, sadly. "I was right proud of that one. Who's the youngster? One of yers?"

"Yep. Chester Parker meet Josh Gibson."

Gibson stuck out his hand, and Chester found himself shaking it. The slugger's grip was strong. "Mr. Gibson," Chester said, trying to find the words that were stuck in his throat, "my daddy took me to see you play nine years ago, down in Shreveport, Louisiana. I remember the date. April 9, 1936. Still got the ticket stub. The Pittsburgh Crawfords won 8-0. Satchel Paige struck out fourteen and you hit two homers, one of them flew over the left field roof."

It took Gibson several seconds to answer. "I remember. And yer the big, bad boy who homered offa Satch in KC."

Chester was startled. "How did you hear about that, Mr. Gibson?"

"Word travels fast when something like that happens. I would a liked to a been there tuh see it."

Chester quickly felt comfortable in the presence of such ball-diamond nobility. "Will you join us for a drink?"

"Sorry," the slugger said to the two Black Sox. "I'm meeting someone. Maybe we'll see each other again. Both of yuh. So long, Cap." Then he lumbered away.

"There goes the greatest of them all," Garrett said, Gibson's back to them.

"Yeah. Got that right."

"A helluva ballplayer at one time. He's sure put on the pork. I told yuh he was a nice feller. But he's not the same man. Not by a long shot." Garrett showed Chester a hand-to-mouth gesture, imitating a man smoking.

"You don't mean reefers?"

Garrett nodded. "Uh-huh. He's got that look."

Twenty-two

Denver, Colorado

He cried out with agony into her face, then fell headfirst to the floor, a knife in his back.

She slid off the kitchen table. "Billy! Chester!" she screamed.

Ramona woke up.

She was dreaming again.

The door was ajar. Anna knocked and entered Ramona's room. "Mr. Jeffries is waiting outside," she said to Ramona.

"I know. I saw his Caddy out the window."

"You're kinda. . . flushed. What's the matter, honey?"

"Nothing. Why should anything be the matter?" Ramona snapped, slipping into her green dress in front of the mirror.

Anna shrugged. She was already in her Sunday service attire of beige hat, white blouse, and pale blue skirt. "Yuh don't look yourself. Yuh had a nightmare last night, didn't yuh? I heard yuh yelling out Chester's name."

"I did?"

"Yes, yuh did, honey."

"Well, just, don't worry about me, sis."

"Yuh were out pretty late last night."

Ramona flicked at her hair, turning to her sister. "I know."

"Mr. Jeffries?"

"Yes. That's right."

158

"Yuh been seeing him again, then?"

"Why all the questions, anyway?" Ramona turned her body to the right and to the left before the mirror. "There."

"Just asking."

"Well, for your information, Horace asked me to marry him."

"Again?"

"And I said yes."

"Yuh don't look that happy about it, honey."

The words sliced through Ramona. "See you at church," she said to Anna, trotting out of the room and taking the stairs down.

"Morning, ma'am," Duke Johnson said, outside, opening the car door for Ramona. It was a bright, sunny day. Johnson had his sunglasses on.

Ramona smiled. "Good morning, Duke. Thank you."

"Yer welcome, ma'am."

"Come back in twenty minutes," Jeffries mumbled to Johnson.

"Sure, boss." Johnson climbed out of the Cadillac, leaving Ramona and Jeffries alone in the back seat on the country road.

Ramona watched Johnson, hoping to prolong the inevitable. She knew now that Jeffries had no intention of going to church.

"Take it off," he demanded. "All of it. Be right quick about it, too."

"What? While you watch."

"Uh-huh. Why not?"

She frowned at him. "It's Sunday morning. My sister's expecting us at church."

"So? Don't get pure on me now, woman."

She saw his hand start to go up. Not another slap. She started undoing her dress. "Well, I never. I'm not some hussy."

"Come on, come on. Hurry up."

"The zipper's stuck."

"Here, I'll do it!"

"Careful. Don't rip the material. It's new."

Together, they managed to get the dress over her head.

"How romantic," she said.

"The slip, too," he said.

She wiggled the slip off. She was down to her underclothes and shivering. He removed his suit jacket, and began unbuttoning his monogrammed shirt. That was as far as he got. They watched as a Ford sedan pulled alongside the Cadillac and screeched to a stop in the middle of the road. Two white men lumbered out. One of them grabbed open Jeffries' door.

"Get out!" the other man shouted, shoving a shotgun into Jeffries's temple. "Move! Now!"

They dragged him out to the ditch and forced him to kneel in the grass.

"Who are yuh?"

"Duke! Duke! Where are yuh?" one man shouted.

The other man advanced upon the Cadillac and looked at the slim, shapely woman through the open door. "What do we have here?"

Ramona reached for her slip and braced herself. "Leave me alone!"

"Back off, you two!" Duke Johnson yelled from a distance.

Ramona glanced to the side of the road. Johnson ran up from the bushes.

"Duke!" she cried through the open window.

"Yuh heard the lady. Leave 'er alone. You got yer man," Duke said.

"Watch it, boy."

"She doesn't come with the deal."

"Too bad."

"Duke? What yuh doing?" demanded Jeffries. "Stop em!"

"Not this time, boss," Duke said.

"Why yuh filthy piece of nigger trash." Jeffries stared into a gun barrel pointed at his head. "I paid yuh all these years. If it wasn't fer me, yuh'd still be in the gutter, a washed-up boxer."

"That's enough," said the white man with the shotgun. "Say yer prayers, Jeffries." Then he shot Jeffries twice in the head. The sound echoed in the morning air.

Ramona froze in the back seat, unable to move or even breathe, as the two threw Jeffries's deadweight body into the car trunk. She had just witnessed a murder, only a few feet away, in the bright, morning sunshine. So quick. So unemotional. So drastic. And on a Sunday! Now what were they going to do with her and Duke? The same? But the men proceeded to drive away as if nothing had happened.

"Duke! My God, Duke!" She held the slip to her, trembling. "What was that all about?"

"Put on yer clothes, ma'am," Duke said to her. "You have nothing to fear from me."

She gulped. "Promise you won't stare."

He smiled. "I'll try not to, ma'am."

He turned away, until she was done and got out, then he helped her to the Cadillac's bumper. There, sitting, soaked with perspiration, she tried to unwind.

Johnson had the good sense to not move too close. He put one foot on the bumper four feet from her. "Ma'am, it was a long time coming. Mr. Jeffries overstepped his boundary. He gotta little too big fer his britches, yuh might say. He was operating a reign of terror on blacks and whites. The white people of Denver were, well, upset. He had debts he couldn't pay. Business debts. Gambling debts. Big loans he couldn't pay. He had threatened people, influential white people, the same whites who were using his houses. Some white men prefer black women. If yuh know what I mean?"

"I think I do." Ramona thought of her own husband.

"The mayor was one of his customers. He and the boss had a squabble over something, a piece of property, I think it was. One thing led tuh another, and the boss was going tuh tell the mayor's wife. . . Anyway, the details are not important. I was asked tuh help. Forced to, actually. I didn't mind. I had a bellyful too. I knew the boss's schedule and his habits. Out here was perfect. I'm sure they'll come up with some story on how he died. White people can do that, yuh know."

"Yes, they can," Ramona nodded.

"White people don't take that kinda stuff from black men. They came tuh settle up. There's colored, ma'am, then there's niggers like Jeffries. A little ways back, he asked me tuh get some information on yuh. A detective agency in Atlanta ran a check on yuh down in Louisiana. That's how he blackmailed yuh into—" He stopped short of saying what had occurred the night before in the back seat, and dug into his suit jacket for several folded sheets of paper. "Here's the file my friend found on yuh, ma'am. It's yers tuh do with how yuh please." He handed it to her and she took it, slowly.

"Thank you. I didn't kill anybody, Duke. Neither did Chester. You have to believe me."

"As far as I'm concerned, those papers don't exist. No one else knows about them. I'm sorry we couldn't have done anything before last night, ma'am, before he, yuh know," he said apologetically.

She smiled. She was touched by his concern for her. Her eyes filled with a mist, and a strange peace swept over her. "You are a good man, Duke. Bless you."

He worked his face muscles into something that resembled a smile. "Don't let that get around, though, ma'am. I might be outta a job. My bodyguard business in Denver has taken a sudden turn fer the worse."

She smiled, again. "Yes, apparently it has."

"May I drive yuh home, ma'am?"

"Yes, Duke," she answered slowly. "Please."

He opened the door for her. She cast her eyes to the road before she got in and saw blood on the asphalt. Horace's blood. Now that he was dead, she pitied him. Live by the sword, die by the sword. It was in the Bible.

"By the way," she said, "what about his newspaper, his grill, the team and the rest? Who's going to run his operations?"

"Everything will continue, probably under white control now. The whole kit-an-caboodle. Including the cat houses."

"Figures. Whites do what they want. Blacks do what they're told."

"That's right, ma'am. Don't matter if it's the South or here in Denver."

Detroit, Michigan

Powell knocked.

Garrett opened his hotel room door.

"Morning, Cap."

"Art! What yuh doing here? Yuh following me or something?"

"No. Can I come in?" He removed his new glasses and slid them into his suit jacket.

"Sure, be my guest."

"I thought I'd. . . better get yuh before breakfast."

"Good thinking. I was just about tuh leave." Garrett slammed the door. The Denver manager looked awful. His eyelids were swollen and dark, and he was unsteady on his feet.

"I gotta talk tuh yuh, Cap."

"So, talk."

"We want yer boy. . . Parker."

162

"Who's we? The Brown Dodgers?"

"Not exactly."

"Who then?"

Powell was burning inside. He couldn't tell Garrett the truth, not yet. He'd have to find out for himself. At a later date. He looked around the room and saw an empty whisky bottle on the floor. "I can't say. I can't go to yer game, either. Our friend, Fat Ass, said that if he saw me round yer team again, he'd hang my nuts offa a post."

Garrett laughed. "Shit, don't worry about it, now. Fat Ass is now dearly departed."

"What!"

"He's dead."

"He is?"

"Yep."

"Since when?"

"Since somebody shot him in Denver. So, yuh don't have tuh worry about his gorilla anymore. He high-tailed it, without the loot. I got it."

"So, Fat Ass is dead. What a relief. That makes things a whole lot easier."

"Yeah, somebody shot the dumb bastard. Gonna miss his money though. Shit, nobody paid like him. We have tuh head back tuh Denver right after the game, meet up with our new owners. Hope we don't get a cut in pay. So, yuh coming tuh the game?"

"I wouldn't miss it." Powell turned to leave, then swung back around to face his old friend. He thought more about it. Should he or shouldn't he? Cap was an old friend, a trusted friend.

"Cap?"

"Yeah, what? Yuh OK? Looks like yuh got yer boxer shorts wound too tight. What's the matter?"

"Cap. . . I gotta tell yuh something. I can't hold it in any longer. Yuh better. . . sit down."

"Will it take long? I'm hungry."

"Forget yer stomach, Cap. . . fer a change. Yuh might even lose yer appetite after this."

"What is it?" Garrett sat in the only chair in the room.

Powell stood over him. "It's here, Cap."

"What's here?"

"What we've been waiting tuh see fer years?"

"What the hell yuh talking about?"

"The Dodgers want Parker."

"Yeah, so? The Brown Dodgers, right? The US League. Well, do they or don't they? What yuh looking at me like that fer?"

Powell shook his head. "No. Not the Brown Dodgers."

"Who then?"

"The white Dodgers want Parker," Powell said, selecting his words carefully. "The Brooklyn Dodgers of the National League. The majors. The white majors."

"The hell you say!"

"You heard me. The Dodgers been using the US League as a shadow tuh scout colored."

The Black Sox manager steadied his arm on the nearby window sill. Something in him touched a nerve. "Yuh been into the booze?"

"This is integration, my friend." Powell remembered how hard hit he was when Rickey informed him in April, and wondered if he looked as stunned as Garrett did at this moment.

Garrett was speechless. Five full seconds of awful silence weighed on the manager. He was barely conscious of cars driving past the open window. A horn. A curse. His mind was too fogged. This was more than he had ever hoped for in his lifetime. "You want the kid, don't yuh? Chester Parker?"

"We sure as hell do."

"This has tuh be a gag."

"No gag, Cap. It's the truth. Cross my heart an hope tuh die."

Garrett looked into Powell's eyes. "Yeah, yuh was never one fer tricks and stuff. I believe yuh."

"I saw the game in Kansas City."

"Did yuh?"

"Yuh bet I did. I got myself onto the phone tuh Branch Rickey after it. And he told me tuh come up here. Cap, if he can hit off a lefty, he's in. He's in. Anything tuh tell the Dodgers brass. That's how close it is."

Garrett smiled thinly. "Wasn't that something, that homer in KC. And offa Satchel Paige, too. He hit it six miles, didn't he?"

"He did. Maybe seven."

"I ain't never seen a long ball like that. Ever! I was so proud of him.

Really proud. Like a father. He's a one-man Murderer's Row. And I've seen guys like Gibson, Leonard, and Suttles."

"The kid has almost everything tuh make it, Cap. Run, throw, hit. He can hit the inside pitch... pull it over that short right wall at Ebbets Field."

"Yeah, I've played there."

"How's the boy's attitude?"

"None better. He's a good boy. He's learning and getting stronger all the time. He's one of those well-spoken colored. He don't sound colored. He's educated. That helps, don't it, Art? Don't it?"

Powell nodded. "Does it ever. Does he have the heart? Can he take the coming abuse?"

Garrett thought hard. "Yeah, hell yeah, he can take it, Art."

"Please listen carefully, Cap. This is what I want... yuh tuh do fer me. Get Chester by himself. Are yuh still gonna face that lefty today?"

Cap nodded. "As far as I know, yeah."

"Tell him that if he plays well that somebody big is after him tuh sign a contract that he won't believe. But, fer heaven's sake... don't say a thing about integration. Got that? Don't tell anybody. I'll... get skinned alive! The press can't know yet. I wasn't supposed tuh tell yuh... or... anybody, yuh here me?"

Cap nodded again, dazed. "My boy, Chester. A Brooklyn Dodger in the majors."

"He has a good chance. Real... good chance. Let's face it... Cap. We're no fools."

"Huh?"

"There's big money in New York backing this up. Forget this civil rights issue that we hear about in the papers, our right tuh play alongside the whites... and all that crap. The name of the game is money. The Dodgers want pennants. And they want tuh make money. Colored players will... provide both. Yuh see?"

Garrett nodded. "I get yuh. I ain't stupid. Chester Parker, huh? How long have yuh known about this, Art?"

"About Parker?"

"No, that the Dodgers want tuh bring up colored players."

"Since April," Powell replied. "But the Dodgers have been scouting fer two years."

"Two years!"

"Uh-huh. The biggest talent hunt yuh ever seen."

"Who else did they have in mind?"

"I don't know if I should say?"

"Come on, you led me up tuh this so far. Who else? Come on!"

Powell paused. "Jackie Robinson. . . Sam Jethroe. . . Roy Campanella. . . Piper Davis. Hank Thompson, too."

Garrett had seen them all play. They were all exceptional. "Robinson and Thompson, huh? We just played them boys in KC."

"Yeah. Robinson is a front runner."

"That hothead? Did yuh see how he kicked up a stink about Chester missing second?"

"Yeah. I got news fer yuh. Parker didn't miss second. He caught the edge. I saw 'er from the stands."

"That so. That Robinson, he's pretty smart fer a shortstop."

"If Chester does well today, he'll be in the running right with Robinson."

Garrett stood, wearing a proud expression. A black man in the majors. Finally. "One of my players, huh. Leave it with me, Art."

"Remember," warned Powell. "Please, don't tell a soul. I'll be cooked."

Garrett waved it off. "Yuh kidding? They wouldn't believe me, anyway."

"Yeah," Powell chuckled. "Probably not."

Twenty-three

Chester had been awed by Denver's Kramer Park, and overwhelmed by Kansas City's Blues Stadium. But Detroit's Briggs Stadium was in a class by itself. Home of the 1945 pennant contending Detroit Tigers, Briggs Stadium was a monster monument of steel and concrete three times the seating capacity of Blues Stadium.

This was the big time. A real major league park.

Briggs Stadium was double-decked all around. The roof down the right field soared skyward, one hundred feet high, and the facade came out a few feet over the playing field. This was a hitter's park. The foul lines were close for pull hitters like himself. As a backdrop in straight-away center field, the scoreboard was the largest Chester had ever laid eyes on.

The expanse of grass was an even green. The Tigers had often filled this place, but few Negro League teams could do the same. There were barely 2,000 people in the stands today to see two of Blackball's best, the Cleveland Buckeyes and the Homestead Grays square off, with most of those fans in the lower deck between first and third.

Chester knew that the weather had to be responsible for the poor showing. It had rained earlier that morning. The papers were saying the skies would be cloudy at game time. They were right. Eighty degrees for the predicted high, seventy-two for the low, and rain a heavy possibility by late afternoon.

Chester had an aisle seat, sitting with six other Sox players behind home plate when the public address announcer barked, "Ladies and gentlemen. Please rise for the National Anthem."

Springing to his feet, Chester felt a tug on the sleeve of his jacket. He turned... and there was Agnes, adorned in a white, loose-fitting blouse, with green slacks that snugged her slim waist and hips. A thin jacket draped over her arm, she had a gray suitcase tucked by her feet. She was devoid of makeup, but pretty enough without it, anyway. She always was.

"Hi there, slugger."

Chester searched for something to say. "Agnes?" was all he could utter. "What the—"

"It's me."

There she was, in person, only two feet away. She smelled good too. He saw something pleasant in her eyes, a certain excitement not there before. He glanced up at the top of the stands in the lower deck. "Let's go... up there," he said, finding the words. "Let me have your suitcase."

Hand in hand, they sprang up the wide concrete steps, two at a time, until they were behind the spectators, where they pulled into two seats in the very last row. The anthem went on.

"What are you doing here?" he asked.

"I had to see you."

"Then you didn't go to Kansas City to see your family."

"No. That was just a story I had to use to get away. I took a bus up to see you. Whew! What a trip. The thing broke down twice."

"Does my mama know you're here?"

"No."

"Did you get the letter?"

"Yes. That's why I tracked you down. We agreed before that a month away from each other is too long." She took his hand and held it to her. "You scoundrel, you. Proposing by mail. I must say, though, it's different."

"I couldn't wait. Honest. When I think back, it was kind of shallow. I should have asked you to your face."

She leaned to his ear, and purred, "Well, I think it's... original and... romantic."

"You do?"

Their faces touched.

"Ask me now."

168

"Will you marry me?"

"Yes."

"You will!"

"Certainly. I'd be a fool not to."

He kissed her. Her lips were soft and warm. "When?" he whispered in her ear.

"As soon as you want," she whispered back.

He pulled away. He held her eyes with his. "In that case, how about after the game? Cap should give me some time off. I hope."

They continued kissing. The anthem finished.

CHICAGO, ILLINOIS

He rose slowly from the Comiskey Park dugout, his team in town for the third of three league games against the Chicago American Giants.

"Robinson. Hey, Robinson!"

Jackie Robinson looked and saw a tall, skinny man in his forties, his fedora flipped back on his head. Cautiously, the shortstop trudged over to the rail. "You talking to me?"

"Yeah. I'm Clyde Sukeforth, a scout for the Brooklyn Brown Dodgers. The United States League. Have you heard of us?"

Robinson definitely had heard of the Brown Dodgers and the new so-called super league. "Yes, I have," he replied.

"Are you playing today?"

"No."

"Why not?"

"I have a bad shoulder."

"How bad?"

"Just some soreness. It'll be fine."

The scout looked troubled. "Too bad. I wanted to see your throwing arm."

"Why did you want to see my throwing arm?"

Sukeforth glanced at the sky, avoiding the question. "I'm glad that storm missed us. I heard it's moving east."

Robinson could care less about the weather. "What do you want with me, Mr. Sukeforth?"

"Can we talk somewhere after the game?"

"Suppose so. What for?"

"Mr. Branch Rickey wants to know a few things about you. Can you come to my hotel room?"

"Where are you staying?"

"Steven Hotel. Do you know where it is?"

Robinson shook his head. "No, sir. I don't."

Sukeforth wrote down the directions and room number on a pad of paper. "Here."

Robinson took the paper and shoved it in the back pocket of his Kansas City Monarch uniform. "Thanks."

"Can you at least take some batting practice?"

"Sure," Robinson shrugged. "I can do that, I guess."

Detroit, Michigan

Josh Gibson disappointed Chester by going hitless in three trips to the plate, then was taken out in the eighth for another catcher. Twice Gibson went down swinging, fooled both times on off-speed pitches.

While he got dressed and took to the field to warm his throwing arm up, Chester still thought about Gibson. Garrett was right. If today was any indication, Gibson was a washed up memory. Chester saw Agnes in the first row behind the Black Sox dugout, and waved. She waved back, smiling.

They were happy. And why not?

Garrett walked up and steered Chester away from the other ball-players. "Got some news fer yuh, Peek," he said, spitting tobacco juice on the ground.

"What?" Chester pounded his glove.

"There's a scout in the stands and he's after yuh, kid."

"Yeah? Who's he with?"

"A team back east. A good team. You do something against this southpaw today and you'll make more money than yuh are now. With Jeffries gone, yuh can now bust out on yer own. Take the highest bid."

"You think this scout's on the level?"

Garrett glanced around. "Yeah, I do. He's a good friend of mine."

"But I haven't gotten too many hits off lefties all year. And this white boy today is pretty good. Word is he's headed to the Tigers next year."

"Concentrate, kid. Yuh hit off Paige. Yuh haven't faced that many lefties, that's all. Yuh can get tuh this boy, too. Use yer head up there.

Bear down. Impress yer girl." Garrett winked and slapped Chester on the back. "Your turn in the cage. Go get 'em."

"You bet."

In the batting cage, with Mandon throwing the balls, Chester knocked several pitches into the upper deck in right field. He had his timing down. Each time the ball sailed higher and farther back in the stands. Then he undercut one just right, and watched the flight of the ball. It was that sound again. He stood and watched the ball disappear in a hurry over the roof. Everyone in the park—players and fans—stopped what they were doing.

That one hundred feet to the top facade didn't look so high now.

Garrett saw the blast from the dugout. He caught the eye of Powell in the stands. They nodded at each other. Powell gave the thumbs-up. But could he do it in the game against the southpaw?

The lefty's name was Hank "Jo-Jo" Riggins, a blonde, six-foot-six, twenty-two-year-old with thick legs and an exceptionally long reach, said to be eighty inches. He possessed a killer curve to go along with a wicked change of pace, and a flaming fastball that he usually had difficult controlling in early innings.

In the first, he struck out Chick Patterson and Flash Barber in succession, then walked Dingy Smith. Chester dragged his magic bat to the plate, leaving a line in the dirt. The wind picked up, blowing the pennants on the roof towards right field. The sky blackened to the west. The rain that was forecast to come later in the afternoon had started, lightly, not enough to call the game. But there was no doubt in his mind that this game would be at least delayed or even canceled altogether within a short time.

The Michigan Spiders' pitcher twirled the ball in his hands. He knew who he was facing—the kid who hit the ball over the roof in batting practice. But that was batting practice, when the ball was lobbed in, big as a basketball. Riggins squinted through the rain drops for the catcher's signals. He shook off the first two, then nodded, staring at the black boy with the comical peek-a-boo stance. He stretched, kicked, and threw with all his might.

Chester hit the first pitch foul. Overanxious, he swung and missed the next offering, a major-league-style curve out of the strike zone, twisting his legs up like a piece of chain in the process. Worse, he fell to the ground. Embarrassed, Chester stepped out of the box.

Garrett's unsympathetic eyes bore into him. His manager was not one to baby any player. Chester slid back in. The rain didn't let up. The next pitch was a sinker in the dirt, getting through the catcher. Dingy Smith took off for second and danced off the bag, considering third base too, had the catcher not retrieved the ball in time.

Riggins received the ball and wiped it on his uniform. It was raining a little harder now.

The umpire looked to the sky. "Hurry up. Finish this batter!" he yelled.

Vince Basser descended the ramp of the twin-engine prop airplane with his suitcase, and headed inside the air terminal with the passengers on his flight. It had been a smooth ride, until they neared Detroit. There, they met turbulence, and a funnel cloud was spotted to the west.

Basser sprinted through the terminal hall that emptied into the street. He was in luck. Cabs everywhere. He ran to the first one, a green Plymouth.

"Taxi!"

"Where to, pal?" asked the balding, pipe-smoking man behind the wheel.

"Briggs Stadium. Have to catch a ball game."

"You're joking? See a ball game today? It's started to raining."

"Just go. How far is it?"

"A good twenty minutes this time of day."

"Get there in fifteen minutes and I'll pay you double."

"You're on! Get in!"

The count went to two balls, two strikes. It was getting difficult to see now, due to the darkness and the rain. The temperature had dropped drastically. Chester was beginning to wonder if he'd even finish his at-bat. The rain felt cool on his arms and face. He squinted, licking the drops that landed on his lips.

Then he remembered what Cap had said to him. A scout in the stands. He tried to charge himself and stay loose, not tighten up, as he usually did when he took on lefties. But he couldn't find the adrenaline that he needed. Ah, why go east anyway? He liked Denver. He liked

172

barnstorming. The road life was tedious, but fun. It would be so easy just to strike out and get this over with, and get out of the rain.

The umpire called the next pitch a ball, low and outside. A full count, three-and-two.

Now Chester was thinking fastball.

Most of the fans by now had retreated for the overhead roof protection, Agnes with them. She could see from a glance that many had gone home. The ones that remained, a mere five hundred or so, saw her fiancée take a viscous swing with ox-like strength at a sinker destined for the dirt for ball four.

Crack.

Chester met it squarely. The ball shot off the bat, straight as a ruler on a rising trajectory, and got caught up in the wind coming over the roof. It sliced a swift path through the downpour. It soared. . . and soared. . . climbing. . . until it struck the scoreboard in center field, and ricocheted into the bleachers directly below.

Agnes gasped. She had only heard about Chester's homer off Satchel Paige. But if it compared to anything like this one, then it was a scorcher.

Chester didn't know the distance to the scoreboard. Five hundred feet, at least. He wouldn't want to guess, though. It didn't matter for the moment. All he cared about was that he nailed it. Off a southpaw.

Where's that scout?

As he came around second base, the pitcher ran up, following him to third. "That was my best pitch, boy."

Chester laughed, tapped third base, and doffed his cap. "And that was my best hit."

"Uppity nigger."

"You say so."

Two infielders jumped in to hold their pitcher back. "Easy, Hank. Easy," the shortstop said. "Let the smoke go."

Then the sky opened up with a crack of thunder that buzzed the ground and rolled across the field, echoing for several moments through the grandstand like a cannon shot.

"See you around," Chester said to Riggins, stomping on home plate.

"Yeah, after the game, nigger."

"I'll be waiting."

Lightning and another crack of thunder broke overhead.

"Clear the field!" the umpire called out, glancing at the furious sky overhead. "Before someone gets killed!"

Art Powell shook Chester Parker's outstretched hand under the stands.

"This is my boy," Garrett said. "And this is his fiancée, Agnes Hudson."

"Pleased tuh meet yuh both." Powell nodded at Agnes. "Ma'am."

"How do you do?" Agnes said.

"Just fine." The scout turned his attention to Chester. "My name is Art Powell. I'm a scout fer the Brooklyn Brown Dodgers of the United States League. So, sonny, yuh got power like I ain't seen since. . . I don't know who," he said. "Maybe since Babe Ruth. How would yuh like tuh come back east with me. . . and. . . play fer Branch Rickey at Ebbets Field? He wants tuh meet yuh in person. This new US League could use a power hitter like you. . . sonny."

Chester wiped his face on his uniform. He looked to Garrett for confirmation. "I dunno."

"Go, Peek. Yuh got my blessings."

"But I'd be walking out on you and the team."

Garrett shook his head. His voice broke when he said, "Oh, no. Believe me. Yuh wouldn't."

"There's a cab coming fer us," Powell informed Chester. "We gotta hurry. Get dressed. We gotta. . . plane tuh catch."

"Plane!" Chester blurted. "Look at the thunderstorm out there."

"Just a shower, that's all. She'll run 'er course."

"Agnes is coming. I can't go without her."

"Fine."

"I have to shower," Chester said, unbuttoning his uniform. "They won't let us use hot water here. How about the hotel?"

"No time."

"Forget it, kid," Garrett said. "Yuh only played an inning. Yuh hardly worked up a sweat."

"Oh, yeah?" Chester countered. Then he retreated to change into his civilian clothes and grab his gear. He came back a few minutes later.

Garrett held out his hand. His eyes went glassy. "Goodbye, Chester. Give it to them fer me in New York. Kid, yer the best player I ever managed. Thanks fer the great summer."

Chester shook his manager's hand. Was it over with like that? A mere handshake? "Thanks, Cap. For everything."

"Remember to touch second."

"Oh, yeah." Chester chuckled. "Could you tell Riggins I'll take a rain check on our fist fight?"

"Sure thing. While I'm at it, I'll knock the shit outta him fer yuh. Oh, excuse me, ma'am."

"That's all right," Agnes said. "I've heard worse. Much worse."

The cab skidded to a wet stop by the Michigan Avenue entrance to Briggs Stadium.

Glancing at his meter, the driver said, "That'll be seven-fifty, doubled. That comes to fifteen dollars." He eyed his wristwatch. "I made it in thirteen minutes."

"So you did." Basser reached into his pocket and thumbed a bill to the driver. "Here. Keep the change."

"Twenty bucks! Thanks, pal."

Basser got out. "Don't mention it."

"Wait, mister," the driver said through the window. "You forgot your suitcase."

"Yeah. Thanks." Basser reached in the passenger door and pulled the case out.

The driver cracked his knuckles, and relit his pipe. Dispatch told him to stay where he was and take two men back to the airport. Moments later, someone tapped on his window. He lifted his head at a black man with white hair and a young black couple, the collars of their coats up to keep their hair dry. He rolled down the window. "Sorry, I'm waiting for someone."

"We're them," Art Powell said.

"Yeah? Well. . . I don't take colored."

Powell removed a twenty-dollar bill and flashed it at the man. "Here's yer bonus. Up front."

The driver didn't want to pass up another twenty. What was with people today? "OK," he crouched and scanned the curb, front and back. "Get in. But keep down, damn it."

Powell slid into the front and Chester and Agnes jumped in the back seat. The three of them squatted on the floor, luggage by their sides.

The driver flicked his signal light on, and waited for the traffic to clear on Michigan Avenue. "You know, I just dropped someone off at the stadium who had just come from the airport."

"Is that right?" Powell said.

Basser pounded on the Sox dressing room door, until one of the players appeared.

"Can I speak to the manager, please."

The player turned to his side. "Cap!"

"Yeah."

"Somebody wants yuh."

Garrett showed his face at the door.

"You the manager?" Basser asked.

"That's me."

"Can we talk outside?"

"Don't see why not." Garrett shut the door. "Yeah?"

"Do you have a player on your team named Chester Parker?"

"Used to. Not no more."

"Where is he?"

"Who are yuh? A scout I bet?"

"Yeah, that's what I am. A scout."

"Yer too late. He just left a few minutes ago."

"Where to?"

"Brooklyn."

"Was he with anybody?"

"Yeah, another scout. And a black woman."

"Why Brooklyn? Who are they going to see?"

"Why do yuh wanna know that?"

"Tell me!"

"Branch Rickey of the Brooklyn Brown Dodgers."

"How are they going to Brooklyn?"

"Why do yuh wanna know all this?"

"Tell me!" The deputy sheriff grabbed the manager by his uniform collar.

Garrett pushed him away. "Get yer hands off me."

"Sorry. Tell me, please! This is life or death!"

Garrett was puzzled. The man was persistent.

"All right, all right. Airplane."

"Thanks."

Basser turned and ran with his suitcase for the exit. He flew into the rainy street, just as the same cab that had brought him to the park pulled away from the curb, thirty feet away, with no one apparently in it.

Blasted all to hell! There were no other cabs around.

Twenty-four

Powell nestled into the aft section of the DC-3 passenger plane with Chester and Agnes. It didn't matter to Powell that blacks sat at the back. The scout was happy enough to catch the last three seats on the flight to New York without being bumped by some whites with money. He glanced out at the dreary rain falling on the city. The sky was beginning to clear to the west.

One starboard prop spun slowly, and the engine fired up.

"Relax, folks," Powell said to Agnes and Chester in the seats behind him. "This is going tuh be a new adventure for all of us. I've. . . never flown neither."

Then the other prop started spinning.

Basser frantically checked the passenger lists of all the airlines.

"Here they are, Mr. Basser," the counter woman at Mid-Eastern Airlines said. She pointed to the register book with a ball-point pen, then turned it around for him to view. "Powell and Parker. Gate four. It's ready to depart."

"You've got to stop it."

"I don't think we can do that."

"Here," said Basser, giving the startled woman his suitcase. "Keep it till I get back."

"But you can't—"

Basser rushed through the crowd of people in the main area, while the loudspeaker blasted above him, "Mid-Eastern Airlines, Flight 118 now departing for Cleveland, Buffalo, and New York City."

Basser made it to Gate Four, and glanced through the large windows to see the ramp being pulled away from the side door on the DC-3. The engines revved and the aircraft pulled away. Basser charged at the terminal doors.

But they were locked.

Thirty minutes in the air, Chester was fixed to his seat. His breathing came in heavy pants, and his hands gripped the hand rests. "I don't like this," he said to Agnes, breaking into a sweat. "I don't like this at all."

"Everything's fine," Agnes said, calmly, from her aisle seat, next to him. She seemed to be enjoying herself. "Relax. Look out there."

"I can't."

She pointed. "It's pretty. The sun's shining. We're above the clouds. Make's you feel so small, doesn't it?"

Chester didn't dare glance out. He exhaled slowly, erratically. The DC-3 hit an air pocket and bounced. Then the right engine sputtered.

"What's that?" Chester asked.

Powell got out of his seat for a look at the wing. He saw the right prop spinning very slowly. "Gosh. We're down to one engine."

"What!" Chester said.

"Settle down. These pilots know what to do."

Chester closed his eyes and prayed. What if the plane suddenly nose-dived to earth? The only place he wanted to be was on the ground. Alive and well. And married. He looked over at Agnes.

Eyes shut, she was praying too.

Chicago, Illinois

Clyde Sukeforth and Branch Rickey had two things in common. They were mediocre catchers in their formative major league careers, and they were now involved in the most organized talent hunt in history. But Sukeforth had one jump on Rickey. The scout had already conversed with Jackie Robinson, one of the front runners in the hunt.

Rickey hadn't. Yet.

A knock. Sukeforth went to the door of his Steven Hotel room. "Hi, Robinson."

"Hello, Mr. Sukeforth."

They shook hands.

"Did you have any trouble getting here?" Sukeforth asked the player.

"No. Your directions were easy to follow." The player looked around. "I like the air-conditioning."

"Yeah, nice huh. Have a seat, Robinson."

"Thanks."

Robinson walked proudly, his shoulders back, a sense of determination written on his face. He sat on one of the wooden chairs opposite the bed. Sukeforth parked himself in the other chair. He was impressed by the dark-skinned Kansas City Monarchs shortstop who wore a gray sports jacket, and gray slacks.

"How's the shoulder?"

"It's still sore," answered Robinson. "You said you wanted to ask me some questions?"

"Yes, I did. The owner of the Brown Dodgers, Mr. Branch Rickey, wants to know a few things about you."

"Like what?"

"Your army discharge to start with. There seems to have been some trouble with the authorities."

Robinson's face went sour. "Oh that."

"Mr. Rickey would like your side of it."

Robinson shrugged. "I was at Fort Hood, Texas. I had taken over a platoon of the 761st Tank Battalion. I was asked to go overseas with the unit but I was told by the officer in charge of the battalion that I couldn't because of an ankle injury I had from my college days. He said everything would be cleared as long as I would go to the nearest army hospital and sign a waiver relieving the army of any responsibility should anything happen to me overseas. I said sure. I'll do that.

"So," he paused, "I hopped the army bus to go to the hospital. On the way there I sat near the front with the white wife of one of the lieutenants in my platoon and we talked. The driver—who happened to be white—stopped the bus and ordered me to the rear. I ignored him and kept talking. He returned to his seat and was about to drive off, but noticed I hadn't moved. He then came storming back and yelled at me this time that if I didn't move there would be plenty of trouble. I told him I didn't care what he did. He drove on, but before we got through the gates of the post, where I would transfer to the city bus, he got off, then returned with the dispatcher and a few other drivers. He screamed at me and pointed. He said, 'There's the nigger who's been causing the trouble.' I put my finger in his face and told him to get the hell off my back."

"What then?"

"I turned my back to him and escorted the woman to the city bus. All of a sudden, a jeep pulled up and military police carted me off to go see their captain and what looked like his secretary, although she was dressed in civilian clothes. She did the talking. She told me I had no right sitting at the front of the bus. Every time I tried to answer her questions, she would interrupt me with more questions. She wouldn't let me answer properly. She said one of my answers didn't make sense. I told her they would make more sense if she would keep quiet long enough to listen to me. That's when the captain shouted at me, told me I was an uppity nigger and that I had no respect for women. In short, I was escorted to the hospital. There was talk of a court-martial."

"Then came the trial," Sukeforth said.

There was a fire in Robinson's eyes. "You mean frame-up."

"But you got off. That's what counts. Then you were given an honorable discharge."

"That's right."

"I hear you have quite the temper."

Robinson said nothing.

"How about that white gas attendant you punched on a road trip?"

Robinson licked his lips. "How did you know about that?"

"We've been checking into you."

"Yes, I did lose my temper," Robinson admitted. "After he filled up the bus tank, I wanted to use the washroom and he showed me the colored washroom. He was laughing at me. So, I used the nearest one, the white washroom. When I came out, he screamed at me, and he gave me a shove. So I hauled off and hit him."

Sukeforth shook his head. "Pretty serious stuff. You knocked him out cold."

Robinson smiled through his anger. "Yeah, but we left the money beside him."

"How's your ankle now?"

"It aches a bit, sometimes, after double-headers mostly. I'll get by."

"Apparently, it doesn't bother your running."

"Not really."

"What's your ambition in life, Robinson?"

Robinson's eyes wandered. "I don't know for sure at this point."

Sukeforth knew what it might be. Help integrate the majors. After that. . . who knows. The more the scout talked with Robinson the more he was awed by his intelligence, his aggressiveness, his determination to stand on his own two feet. Rickey would like him. "Look, I know you're laid up for a while. Why not ask your team if you can take a few days off?"

"Why?"

"Mr. Rickey would like to meet you in person."

"I don't know if the Monarchs will let me do that."

"They will, if you ask them."

"I'm sure the Brown Dodgers scouts don't go through all this trouble with every player." Robinson waited for Sukeforth to answer.

"No, I must admit, we don't."

"So, why me?"

"I'll leave that up to Mr. Rickey to tell you, OK?"

Robinson shrugged. He still didn't know what to make of the fuss over him. "OK."

"Good, because I've already made some telephone calls for train connections. An overnight sleeper. Can you meet me in Toledo at noon, no later?"

"I suppose I can. Sure."

"Good man. There's a train leaving from there that will take us into Brooklyn."

CLEVELAND, OHIO

The three of them waited in the terminal with the other Flight 118 passengers for two hours for another aircraft to take them east. Night had arrived and they were tired. A baby was crying in her mother's arms. Others chatted and grumbled, until a clerk with Mid-Eastern Airlines approached the group.

"We are sorry for the delay," he began.

Chester didn't hear the words of the apology or the offer of compensation that followed. He turned to Powell, before the clerk had finished his spiel, and said, "If you want me to go to Brooklyn with you, then we will take the train. Forget this flying. I'm not getting on another plane for the rest of my life."

"Me neither," said Agnes, her hand in Chester's.

Powell sighed. His plan to get to Brooklyn as soon as he could was not such a smart idea after all. "OK. Maybe we can. . . catch one of them there overnight trains."

"Fine with me."

"Me, too," Agnes nodded.

Twenty-five

When Powell and Chester entered Branch Rickey's office at Ebbets Field ten minutes early on Tuesday, they were surprised to find that the Dodgers president had visitors. Two men. One white. One black.

"Art." A smoking cigar in his fingers, Rickey greeted Powell with a handshake. "I see you brought your young man."

"Yes, sir, Mr. Rickey."

"Everybody sit down. Please." Rickey waited for them to take a seat, the players closest to the Dodgers executive in his swivel chair. "Gentlemen, as far as I know, only two of you have met so far, Robinson and Parker." Rickey didn't wait for any acknowledgment. "Art, this is Clyde Sukeforth, one of my scouts. Clyde, say hello to Art Powell."

The scouts shook hands.

Rickey studied the two black players, Jackie Robinson and Chester Parker. The contrast in the two was more than evident. One was ink-black, the other younger, light-skinned, almost like a well-tanned white man. Both were well-dressed in suits and ties. "You two are the reason for this meeting. Chester Parker of the Denver Black Sox meet Jackie Robinson of the Kansas City Monarchs."

Chester looked over at Robinson. "I did touch second base," he said.

Robinson laughed, lightly. "I know you did. I just thought that if I kicked up a big enough stink, the umpire would see it my way."

"I guess he did."

Rickey glared at the Kansas City shortstop. "Robinson?"

184

"Yes, sir?"

"You got a girl?"

"I think so," Robinson answered weakly, amazed at such a question.

"What do you mean, you think so? Don't you know?"

"We're engaged, so far."

"So far? Would you mind explaining yourself, young man?"

Robinson went into the plans for him and his fiancée, Rachael, the problems with distance, and the difference in upbringing. Chester listened, wondering what all that had to do with playing for the Brooklyn Brown Dodgers. Then Rickey turned to him.

"What about you, Parker? Got a girl?"

Chester thought of Agnes in the other room. "Yes, sir." Unlike Robinson, Chester's answer was full of confidence.

"When you get through today, you could use a woman by your side. Turned nineteen this month, eh?"

"Yes, sir."

"What's your girl's name, son?"

"Agnes Hudson."

"What does she do?"

"She's a pharmacist."

Rickey seemed impressed. "She must be university educated, then."

"Yes, sir."

"Sounds like a smart woman."

"She certainly is."

"Does she live in Denver?"

"Yes, sir. I don't see her too often. Or as often as I'd like to. But I asked her to marry me. She's in the waiting area. We want to get married while we're in New York."

"What's she doing out there? Bring her in, I'd like to meet her."

"Yes, sir." Chester went off to get her. When she walked in, Rickey asked her to sit down. She chose a place beside Chester, in a chair provided by the secretary, who was now out of the room.

"So, Miss Hudson, you want to marry this fellah, do you?"

"Yes, sir, Mr. Rickey," she answered warmly.

"Do you have any idea what you're in for?"

She flashed her eyes at Chester. "A pretty fair idea."

Rickey shook his head. "Oh, no you don't. Not by a long shot."

She looked puzzled.

"Both of you—Robinson, Parker—are going to need a source of strength to draw from when the times get tough. And believe me, times will be tough. Do either of you know why you're here?"

"To sign up with the Brooklyn Brown Dodgers," Robinson said. Chester confirmed the statement with a nod of agreement.

"That's what you were supposed to be told. The fact is, neither of you are candidates for the Brown Dodgers. Instead, I want you both to play for the Brooklyn Dodgers of the National League. I think you can play in the major leagues, with the best of the white boys. Perhaps, start you off in Montreal, our top farm team in the International League. What do you think of that?"

Chester sat very still, while the room seemed to spin around him. He and Agnes stared at each other. Nothing had prepared him for this. His heart beat so loud that he feared Rickey could hear it. He looked to his side, directly at Powell. The scout's eyebrows went up, as if he already knew. Was Chester hearing right? He felt Agnes squeezing his hand tight.

The majors!

Many things went through Chester's mind at once. Garrett saying that blacks wouldn't play in the majors in his lifetime. Did this mean no more sleeping on the bus, or at ball parks or at third-rate hotels? And no more wolfing down crummy cold meals at slop joints and breakfasts of pop and candy bars? No more Jim Crow Blackball? No more raceball?

Then Rickey talked with the scouts for two minutes as if the players weren't there. Did they have the talent? Could they make the grade? It made Chester uncomfortable. Did Garrett have something to do with all this?

"I know you're both good ballplayers," Rickey's voice rose at the players, his face red, "but do you have the guts!"

"What do you mean by guts, Mr. Rickey?" Chester wanted to know. "Isn't talent enough? Isn't talent and ability all that we need to make the grade?"

"Let me explain," said Rickey, backing off. "You two are not just two athletes hired by a ball club. No, sir. We are playing for big stakes. Our search has been exhaustive. It's been going on for two years, with the major part of it this year. Dodger scouts have gone to Mexico, South

America, Puerto Rico, Cuba, and from coast to coast in the United States. We narrowed it down to five candidates, and finally you two! We have a complete file on you, Robinson. We've investigated your life to dig out your character, your habits, and your reputation." He turned to Chester. "But you, Parker, are the mystery man. Our man, Art Powell here, has compiled a favorable report on you and your character and attitude from your manager. However, for some strange reason, you don't exist back in Louisiana. Would you mind explaining why?"

Chester's pulse hammered in his throat. "We had to change our last name, my mama and me."

"Why?"

"My daddy had threatened to kill us," Chester lied. "We left for Denver, where my mama has a sister. My daddy is not a good man, Mr. Rickey. We changed our last name, so we wouldn't be traced. My. . . my real name is Chester Lee."

Rickey sighed. "I'm glad that's straightened out." He drummed his fingers on the desk top, dragging on his cigar. "This isn't going to be easy. Do you realize just how tough it will be for two black boys to make the majors? Do you have an inkling? On the management side of things, we can't fight this for you. We have no army. Nobody's on our side. Not the umpires, the players, the newspapermen, the other owners, nor the fans. You have to win them over to you by your play and your attitude. But those aren't the only things. It's unfortunate we can't count on only runs, hits, and errors, what we see in a box score. You know, a box score is a very democratic thing. It doesn't say how tall you are, what church you attend, what color you are, or how your daddy voted in the last election. It only states how a ballplayer performed that particular day."

"Isn't that all that counts?" Robinson said, staring at Rickey.

"It should be, but isn't, Robinson," Rickey replied. "One day soon it will. For now it won't. From this point on, you and Chester are going to need courage beyond what most men can endure. Do you young men have the courage and the guts to play the game no matter what happens?"

Robinson answered with a slow, "Yes, I think I can."

"And you, Parker?"

"I'd like to be given the chance," answered Chester. He glanced at Agnes, who nodded.

"Pitchers will throw at you. At your head!"

"I've been thrown at before, Mr. Rickey," Robinson said.

"So have I," Chester added.

"It will be different in the future. Opposing pitchers and players will call you names. You'll hear bench jockeying like you've never heard before. As far as they're concerned, you two are just a couple of no-good niggers! Pardon the expression."

Chester felt a prickly heat build up in his face. "Is that right?"

"Yes, that's right! Does that make you angry, Parker? Of course it will. But you will have to hold your temper when they use every name in the book. Snowflake. Jungle-bunny. Sambo. Spear-chucker. Nigger! Tar-ass! Hey, shine my shoes, nigger boy! How many white women have you slept with in the last week? You can't let them get to you. If you can show them that you came to play, they will stop saying such things. It won't happen overnight. It could take years. They might attack you physically. Will you stay loyal to your aim, through all this? Can you do it?"

Rickey jumped from his swivel chair like a man possessed and came charging directly at Chester, knocking into him, pushing him back a few feet, chair and all, enough so that Agnes's hand-grip on Chester snapped loose. "I'm a hot-headed first baseman from Alabama, and I just elbowed you as you came running down the line to beat out a bunt." He pushed Chester, trying to make him mad. "I scream in your face, you black bastard, you filthy sonavabitch, go back to Africa, boy! What do you do, Parker?"

Rickey's face stopped mere inches away from Chester.

"I know what I'd like to do."

"But you won't!" Rickey stomped his foot. "Judas Priest! You can't! You mustn't!"

Chester slowly moved his chair up to Agnes.

Rickey turned to the muscled Monarchs shortstop. "You, Robinson, you're on the bag at second taking the throw from your infielder. It's a double play ball. You go to throw to first and the runner comes in and spikes you. He gets up and all he sees is that black face of yours. Your black face! He hates your guts. He sees you only as just a dumb nigger. A tar-ass. He takes a swing at you, like this." Rickey's fist barely missed Robinson's face. "What do you do, Robinson? What do you do?"

Robinson took a breath and glared up at the wide-eyed Rickey baring

188

down on him. "Mr. Rickey, are you looking for a colored man who's afraid to fight back?"

"No!" Rickey exploded. "I'm looking for a colored ballplayer who has the guts enough not to fight back. Don't you get it?" he asked the players. He heaved a sigh. "I want to read you something."

Rickey reached over his desk and picked up a book. "This is taken from Giovanni Papini's *The Life of Christ*. Listen to this."

Rickey read a passage that was particularly relevant to the two ball-players. According to Papini there were three ways a man could answer violence—revenge, run, or turn the other cheek. In the white leagues, revenge was out of the question. Running wasn't any better—it would only invite pursuit. Turning the other cheek meant taking the second blow. The adversary wouldn't be ready for anything like that. It was what the author called moral courage, the highest form of bravery. The one who could conquer himself could conquer his enemies.

Rickey slammed the book shut and looked at the players. "Can you do it? Have you conquered yourselves?"

"I think we get you now, Mr. Rickey," Robinson relented.

"Do you? We'll see about that."

"Here it is, Parker," Rickey said. "A Southern teammate of yours—a white man—finds out his friend has been sent down to the minors to make room for you on the roster. If looks could kill. Opposing players will taunt you. They could provoke a race riot in the stands. You will get hate mail. They will hate your guts, and do anything to get you to fight."

With a burst of energy, despite the already long session, Rickey moved towards Robinson and grabbed the player by the lapel. "What if I knock into you at second and slap your face or punch you? What will you do?"

Robinson's muscles were as tight as guitar strings, his fists clenched. "I've got two cheeks, Mr. Rickey."

The Dodger executive returned to his swivel chair, contented. "Another thing. You will have to play better than the whites. Not just as good. Better! You have to make yourself known out there. Forget hitting .200 or .250. That won't do. You will face good pitching every day, especially when the service boys return. You must play real good ball. Run, hit, and throw. Well, do you two still want to go through with this?"

Neither player answered quickly.

"If you have this much faith in me, sir," Chester said, "then I promise you there will be no incidents."

"You'll have to be there for him," Rickey encouraged Agnes. "He'll need you."

"I will. I'll be there," she said, playing with Chester's hand.

"Robinson?"

Robinson stared at Rickey. "There won't be any incidents."

"You promise?"

"Yes, sir."

"Our plan is to send you both to Montreal for 1946, and perhaps bring you up in the same year, or in 1947." Rickey paused. "Do you have any idea where this is going to lead your race? Making the majors will help to break down other barriers. In years to come black people will be able to book into the best white hotels and eat in the best white restaurants, and be called sir instead of boy. Retaliate once, on or off the field," Rickey waved his arm across his chest, "and everything will go for nought. Do you understand?"

Robinson and Chester nodded.

"Our offer to each of you for 1946 is a signing bonus of 3,500 dollars and 600 dollars a month salary. None of this will be made official until a press conference is called in Montreal sometime in the fall. What do you say to that?"

For Chester, 1945 was one shell shock after another. The money kept getting better and better.

He could see a new way of life open to him as a married man. Baseball would do it. He'd play as long as he could, then start a business or go to college or both. He'd raise a family with Agnes. His mother could write full-time.

"For the time being," Rickey explained, "go back to your teams as if nothing has happened. Only girlfriends and parents should know about this meeting."

After the two players, Agnes, and Sukeforth were dismissed, Powell felt drained, although he had hardly been spoken to during the meeting. He was surprised at the language Rickey used on the players. Rickey was a devout Christian man, and for him to use such words must have been difficult. But they had to come out to show Robinson and Chester

190

what they would be up against in organized ball. Rickey stole the show. He should have been an actor.

Rickey said to Powell, "I want a thorough check made on Chester Lee, now that we know his name."

"But Mr. Rickey. You said yuh were. . . gonna sign him."

"Not necessarily. Where did you say he was from?"

"Grambling, Louisiana."

"Get down there and look into his background."

"Yes, sir."

Rickey smiled to reassure his scout. "Don't worry, Art, it's just a formality. He looks like a decent enough young man. She seems nice too."

Twenty-six

Two men had seen Chester, the black woman, and the white-haired black man go through the entrance to Ebbets Field. They had no choice but to wait it out in the squad car.

Two hours later, Vince Basser leaned forward from the passenger seat. "That's him."

"There's only two of them," said the Brooklyn cop. "Where'd the old guy go?"

"Search me. He doesn't matter, anyway. It's the kid I want."

The stale street air greeted the couple. Chester was still in a daze from the Rickey interview. Montreal! The top Dodgers farm team! A bonus of over three thousand dollars! The majors was only two years off for him and Robinson! It was too good to be true.

Agnes and Chester settled into a slow stroll through the busy Brooklyn street in the direction of the tunnel that would take them under the East River to New York City, back to the zoo of people he had seen coming into Brooklyn. Chester couldn't stop talking, unable to hide his enthusiasm. This was an adventure for them. He and Agnes were excited and scared at the same time. But they'd go through it together. Presently, the most important thing on their mind was finding a justice of the peace, and spending the night in a hotel. Then for the honeymoon they'd see the sights around New York and catch a train to Denver in time to play the House of David on the weekend. Chester couldn't wait to tell his mother. Cap would be surprised to have him back. Or would he? What did he really know?

He and Agnes would be happy. He was going to marry her. He loved her. He was never so sure of anything in his life. She was the woman for him. His heart shuddered just thinking about their future together. Then he stopped along the sidewalk and thought of something that had never occurred to him, and it scared him half to death. What if the press found out who he really was? It was inevitable, once the news broke of the signing with Robinson.

Agnes squeezed his hand. "Chester, what's the matter? You look like you've seen a ghost."

"Chester!"

Chester turned around. A man in tie and shirtsleeves advanced on him, flashing identification.

"Vince Basser. Deputy Sheriff, Lincoln County, Louisiana."

Chester's body stiffened. "What do you want with me?"

"Are you Chester Lee?"

"My name is Parker. Chester Parker."

Basser stood steady as a rock. "I got the first name right. You fit the description. Come with me. We have to talk." Basser rushed Chester and Agnes to an alleyway.

"What do you want us for?"

"It's you I want, Chester. Not her. I know who you are. You're Chester Lee. I've been trailing you across the country for four months. Chester Lee, you are wanted for questioning in the murder of a Grambling policeman, Sergeant Herbie Collins."

Agnes glared at the detective. "You must have the wrong man."

Chester didn't see a gun. It had to be concealed. He figured the possibilities. They could run. Or he could fight for the gun, if there was one. Or they could go with the deputy sheriff, and everything would be all over—his baseball career and his coming marriage to the most wonderful woman in the world. "I don't know any Herbie Collins."

"Then why was his body found buried in your vegetable garden? Why was his car found down the road in a creek? Why did you and your mother leave Grambling so suddenly with no forwarding address before your final senior high year?"

"We didn't do anything!"

193

"What happened? You've got to tell me what happened, Chester."

Chester suddenly relived the kitchen scene. He could see the knife again. "He was raping my mama!"

"Sergeant Collins?"

"Yes, Collins."

"Come back to Louisiana and testify."

Chester stepped back. "What chance would we have in one of your Southern white courts?"

"A good chance. Collins had a record for assaulting white and black women. The Grambling police force were a bad bunch. We've got the records to prove it. We've been investigating them for months. You can help us. Did you kill Collins?"

"No."

"Did your mother?"

"No!"

"Do you know who?"

"Yeah. My brother."

"Billy?"

Chester recalled that day. Why did Collins have to do it? "He was raping my mother when we got home and. . . and Billy stabbed him in the back to get him off."

"You saw him raping your mother?"

"Yes."

"Why did you run?"

"We had to."

"Who buried the body?"

"Billy."

"He didn't bury it deep enough. I have something else to tell you. Your brother's dead, Chester. Come back with me. It can all get straightened out."

"Billy's dead? How?"

"Shot in the head. We don't know who did it. Come back with me, please. I don't want any trouble."

"I'd like to believe you." Chester looked to Agnes for support, but she couldn't speak.

Then a police car skidded around the corner, turned up the alley, and slid to a stop, blocking any retreat that way. When Chester saw

194

the policeman in uniform step out, he was suddenly aware of an ill feeling. He didn't believe the deputy. He was lying. He had to be. He'd say anything to get him to go peacefully back to Louisiana. Black cop killers wouldn't survive ten minutes back home. Forget a trial. He'd be lynched by the Klan. Chester looked up the alley, once, twice, towards a set of garbage cans. A voice inside him whispered—run, you fool. Run. Where the alley ended, he didn't know, hopefully on the street. If not, a door would do fine. Any door.

"Yeah, I'll come with you," Chester said. There was no time to think about the possibilities anymore. All he could do was react. He grabbed Agnes by the arm, and yanked her. "Come on!"

She shrieked as they broke into a run up the alley.

"Stop!" the policeman yelled, reaching for his gun and firing once, at the same time as Basser tried to pull the pistol away.

"No!" Basser screamed, taking the bullet. "I want him alive!" He slumped, holding his chest.

"What did you do that for? I could've had him," the policeman said, looking down at the deputy sheriff falling to his knees, blood spurting to the ground in front of him. "Basser!" The policeman grabbed the deputy before he fell on his face.

"You shot. . . me, dammit," Basser said, gasping. "Don't stand there. Forget me. Go after them! But bring them in alive!"

Chester and Agnes flinched at the gunfire behind them, but didn't dare look back. Hand in hand, they took off to the right and ran through the alley, around the garbage cans and a delivery truck, to the edge of the street. Then they composed themselves and walked slowly. They saw some people move towards the opening to the alleyway they had just left, curious at the sound of a gunshot. They couldn't go that way. So, they walked off in the opposite direction, falling into the jungle of Brooklyn pedestrians.

Chester saw a taxi driving towards them and checked to see if it was colored. It wasn't. He let it go by. They walked a block, turned left, then walked two more blocks at a brisk pace, not saying a word. Finally, he stopped by a street lamp and looked back. No one was following them that they could see.

"Listen to me," he said to Agnes, shaking her, holding her firmly by her arms, pinning her to the street lamp. There were tears in his eyes and hers.

"Chester, you're hurting me."

He eased up on her. "Agnes, you don't have to marry me. You don't! You don't owe me anything. I took you out of there, but it was wrong of me. You're an accomplice, now. You have to make up your own mind. Now you have a choice." He lowered his voice. "Yes, my mama and me are running. But we didn't kill anybody. Honest. The whole thing is a long story. If you stick with me, there could be trouble. I can't go back to Louisiana. I want to see my twentieth birthday. And lots more after that."

She gulped, but didn't say a word.

Chester spied a black cab out of the corner of his eye, parked down the street. "Well?"

"You couldn't kill anybody. Back in Detroit, I said I'd marry you, didn't I." She wiped her tears. "You're stuck with me."

"I love you, Agnes."

She kissed him hard on the mouth. "Same here, slugger," she whispered in his ear. "Let's get the hell out of here."

Rickey took the long distance phone call in his office.

"Mr. Rickey. . . sir. . . this is Art Powell. . . in Grambling, Louisiana. I have. . . some bad news fer yuh." Powell's voice sounded older and slower in the four days since their last meeting.

"Go ahead, Art," Rickey said, although he knew what Powell had called for. It was unfortunate that the scout hadn't checked in partway on his trip.

"Chester Lee. . . and his mother are wanted fer questioning in the mysterious murder of a policeman here in town. . . sometime back in April. No one had seen them since then. I had. . . no choice but tuh tell the local police I been scouting Chester, but I didn't tell them who I was really. . . working fer. I told them I was with a. . . team down in Cuba. I didn't want tuh involve yuh. . . or. . . the Dodgers, sir."

"Thank you, Art. That was fast thinking."

"What. . . do. . . we do now, Mr. Rickey."

"We go with Robinson. He'll go alone. Art, you're not sounding well."

"I'm just fine, Mr. Rickey. Really."

"Another thing, Art. From here on in, our boy never existed."

"Why, sir?"

"There's been a deputy sheriff from Chester's home county on his

196

trail since April. He was shot just a few blocks from here a half-hour after our meeting with Robinson and Chester. I was questioned about it. They promised to keep it out of the news. Chester and his girl are wanted for the shooting. No one seems to know where they are. I put a detective on his mother in Denver. She's gone too."

"It's a damn shame, sir. Chester was the best young talent I've seen in years. Years! It just ain't fair."

"Life's not fair, Art. Come on back."

GRAMBLING, LOUISIANA

Powell had lied to Rickey. He was not fine. Pains in his chest had been bothering him all day, and his breathing was irregular. He picked up the receiver—a chore in itself—and dialed the colored cab company in town.

In minutes, the cab was on the way to the train station, the scout in the back seat. Now Powell's pains were stronger, more piercing.

"You okay back there?" the colored driver asked, glancing in his mirror.

"Get me. . . ah. . . doctor. Please."

"Hey, old man. What's the matter?" the driver glanced again in the rear-view. The old man wasn't there.

He had fallen to the floorboards.

Twenty-seven

Rickey stood in the light rain with the other mourners at the grave site, oblivious to the fact that he was the only white person among the more than sixty people. The preacher uttered the final words of his eulogy and the casket was slowly positioned by the six pall bearers into the fresh hole in the ground.

The widow, in black, was escorted by a handsome young man about twenty-five to the waiting limousine at the front of the procession of cars. Rickey arrived at the vehicle, as the young man slammed the door, the widow disappearing behind metal and tinted glass.

"Douglas?" Rickey asked, rain dripping off his umbrella.

"Yes."

Rickey held out his hand to the bareheaded man. "I'm Branch Rickey."

The man's eyes beamed a greeting. "Ah, yes. This is a pleasure, sir. A real pleasure. My father has talked about you. Thank you for looking after the funeral arrangements. I would introduce you to mother, but she's not herself."

"I understand. It was the least the organization could do for your family. He passed away working for us."

"Yes, he had heart problems for about five years. He didn't tell many people."

"Douglas, your father did a great service for us. In another month, you and everyone will know just how great his service was."

Rickey tipped his hat and bade Art Powell's son goodbye.

198

Flashbulbs popped in Jackie Robinson's face at the Montreal Royals' press conference held inside the Delorimier Downs ball park. The white-haired president of the team, Hector Racine, announced that Robinson, a colored shortstop from the Kansas City Monarchs, had signed a contract to play for Montreal in 1946.

"I am confident Montreal ball fans and the fans in the rest of the International League will judge Robinson on his playing ability only, and not on the color of his skin," Racine said.

The dozen reporters dashed for the phones like madmen to relay the information to their daily newspapers.

When they returned, Robinson smiled and tried to be at ease with the writers. But he felt strained. The director in charge of Brooklyn Dodgers farm clubs, and son of the Dodgers president, Branch Rickey, Jr., tapped Robinson on the shoulder. "Don't worry," he whispered. "We'll handle them."

"Mr. Rickey, how long was this decision in the making?" a reporter asked.

"As soon as my father went to Brooklyn in late 1942 he received permission from the board of directors to scout Negro talent. Since then, the Dodgers employed black and white scouts and proceeded with an intense search during that period, with most of the work conducted this year. We narrowed our list down to less than ten players and from there, one. Jackie Robinson."

Hands shot up in the crowd. "How much did it cost?" shouted another reporter, over the others.

"I don't have the complete figures on hand," Rickey Jr. said. "But I can tell you that the Dodgers spent twenty-five-thousand dollars employing two scouts in the Caribbean countries and Mexico, only to discover that the greatest Negro players were here, in our own country."

"What kind of reaction do you think Robinson will receive?"

"There will be some negative reaction in certain parts of the country, I'm sure."

Robinson chuckled to himself. That was an understatement, if he had ever heard one.

"Do you think you're inviting trouble?"

Rickey Jr. smiled. "No. But we won't avoid it when it comes. Jackie

Robinson is a fine young man, intelligent and college bred, and I think he can make it, too."

"What about Southerners within the Dodgers organization?"

Rickey Jr. took a long time to answer, looking around at the faces. "If you're asking me if some players would rather leave the Dodgers because Robinson is on the roster, then I suppose that's up to them. Some of them who are with us now might choose to quit. But they'll be back in baseball after they work a year or two in a cotton mill."

Robinson's eyes went glassy. The fight for acceptance in white baseball would have been a whole lot easier had that kid Chester Parker or Lee—whatever his name—been here too to take the load off. Where did he go? Robinson knew the next years would be tough. Some war vets had returned to the States during the end of the 1945 season. Hank Greenberg had led his Detroit Tigers to an American pennant and a World Series win over the Chicago Cubs. Bob Feller had drawn the biggest three-year crowd at Cleveland's Municipal Stadium his first time back. He had struck out twelve Detroit Tigers and beat them 4-2.

Many more vets would follow, including pitchers. And some of those would be bean ball pitchers from the South.

Twenty-eight

Robinson was the biggest star in the International League. With only a few days left to go in the season, he had helped his team clinch a first place finish, and he was leading the league in batting average and stolen bases. His presence set attendance records around the league.

He stood in the street outside the clubhouse, under a sign that read NO ADMITTANCE. There, he saw a young face in dark sunglasses in the throng of autograph seekers. He was a husky, light-skinned black man, about twenty, with tight dark hair.

Robinson wanted to sign as many pieces of paper as he could. He went through the people, slowly, politely. The fans didn't know how he had suffered that season—the abuse, the near nervous breakdown, and the stomach disorders. But he had hung in there, for the good of his race, despite the oppressive bench-jockeying, the screams of nigger and other choice names, the spikes at second base, the bean balls, the unfair umpire decisions, and the nasty looks from players, some from his own teammates. Branch Rickey wasn't wrong about any of it.

"Can you sign it to Tommy," a parent asked. "He's my boy."

"Sure," Robinson said.

"Thanks."

A scorecard slid in front of Robinson. He looked up at the young black man, as he removed his sunglasses.

It's him, Robinson thought. "How do you want me to sign it?"

"To Chester."

201

"The last name?"

"That's not important."

Robinson rested the scorecard up on his belt. This autograph was for the one person in the crowd who had some kind of inkling what Robinson had felt during the year. He wrote,

To Chester, wish you were here.
Jackie Robinson.

"Here you go."

Their eyes locked.

The colored man took it back and stared at the inscription, his thoughts to himself. "Good job, college boy," he said, then left.

Robinson soon lost all concentration. He signed some more autographs, but there were still so many scorecards and sheets of papers. He finally had to shake his head. "Sorry, I can't sign them all. I have to go."

Robinson wove his way through the fans towards the street, using his hands, trying to find him. It was too late. It was the last he ever saw of Chester Lee.

Epilogue

MONTREAL, CANADA—OCTOBER, 1947
Chester accompanied his wife and his mother on the downtown city bus. For two years, they had been using the last name of Hinton.

It was Saturday, a day off from the monotony of their jobs. Time to shop. Ramona Hinton cleaned houses on her own, and worked part-time in a bakery to help out a neighbor friend whose husband owned the business. And she continued to write for her own amusement. Chester Hinton labored in a sheet metal factory, a basic job that paid well. At night he was taking an accounting class. He had always been good with numbers. Agnes Hinton held a job as a lab technician for a large pharmaceutical company, specializing in chemical analysis. The three of them rented a clean apartment in the middle-class section of Montreal, where many races lived together, and where their color was less of a novelty.

"This is our stop," Chester said to the women, tugging down on his fedora.

Ramona nodded, buttoned up her coat, and slipped off the bus with her son and his wife. It was a windy day. The autumn chills were heavy on them, the whisper of winter was gearing up. The cool weather came early in Montreal, too early for the Hintons. Canada was colder than Denver, as they had discovered the first winters here in 1945 and 1946. But they were doing their best to make Montreal home, where the color of a person's skin wasn't what it was south of the border. Montreal was a favorable city to hide away in, far from anyone who was still looking for them in the United States. Montreal was a place where they could use their Southern backgrounds as the perfect cover, giving the excuse—if the occasion arose—that colored births and family names had been ill-kept for decades going back to slavery. No one could prove whether their last name was Hinton or not.

They walked two blocks, looking at the store fronts as they went, until Ramona saw the Italian delicatessen that she often frequented.

"Go ahead, mama," Chester urged her, adjusting his sunglasses. "We'll wait for you."

"I'll be right out."

"Sure." He looked across the street traffic to see a group of young boys and men in front of a store that looked interesting. He knew what they were probably watching. "Take your time. Catch us over there," he said.

"Where?"

"By the television sets."

"Forget about buying one. They're too expensive. Besides, they're just a fad."

"I don't want to buy one, mama."

"The game's on," Agnes informed her mother-in-law.

Ramona saw the intent in her son's eyes. "Oh. Go ahead, you two."

Chester and Agnes walked off to the corner traffic light, arm in arm. Nearing the television store, they saw that all eyes were glued to the only working screen on the other side of the window, a bulky, wood-consoled unit, placed in between other sets.

It was the fourth game of the World Series between the New York Yankees and the Brooklyn Dodgers. Chester had seen this new-fangled television before, once in another store. But this was a first for him. Baseball on a television set. He had been following the Series in the papers. The Yankees won the first two games in New York, but the Dodgers took the third game in Brooklyn.

"What's the score, boys?" Agnes asked, a Brooklyn player at bat.

A small boy squinted and said, "One-nothing for the Yanks, lady."

"What inning?" Chester asked. The wind gusted and he flipped up the collar of his greatcoat.

"The third."

"How's Robinson doing?"

"Went out the first time up. Flied out, I think," one of the adult men said, a French accent, keeping his eye on the screen. "The Dodgers don't have a hit yet."

Chester leaned forward when the next batter strode to the plate. It was Jackie Robinson.

"Here he comes," a boy said, excited.

Chester's heart sank. He thought it odd. He didn't see Robinson. Instead, he saw himself striding to the plate in a Dodger uniform, the way it should have been, the way he used to stand. . . bat high. . . leg out. . . eyes over his shoulder. The major leagues could have been his stage. But he was denied his chance for the limelight and to represent his race. They were fading memories, now. Two years ago. It might as well have been twenty, or thirty.

Few would remember Chester Henry "Peek-a-boo" Parker. He had to remind himself not to be bitter. His mother too wasn't resentful at not sending her finished novel off to a publisher for fear of the authorities tracking her down. The two of them were partners in crushed dreams. It would have been much more difficult for Chester had Agnes not come north. He thought of the Black Sox, disbanded that autumn, according to a phone call he had made to Denver. Where was the carpenter who made the magic bat? Who was he? Where was Garrett, Chester's mentor? Down South, in the Caribbean for the winter? Or was he at home in Florida with his wife, three daughters, two dachshunds and tanks of tropical fish. He missed Garrett. He missed the team. He smiled, thinking of Slammer on the bus. . . Berenguer and the axle grease. . . Cap in the bathtub smoking a cigar and drinking champagne. . . Two, sometimes three games a day. . .

And the open road.

He pictured the grass of Kramer Park, the colorful outfield fences of Blues Stadium, the vastness of Briggs Stadium, and the hundreds of cow pastures and rock-hard ball diamonds in the Mid-West. The year 1945 seemed to blend into one, a precious summer for a wide-eyed, teenage youngster from the Deep South. There was a harsh torment to such pleasurable memories, now locked in his own tunnel of time. He remembered one of Garrett's sayings: "Baseball will always break your heart." How right Cap was. How did he know? But, of course, Cap knew everything.

Chester closed his eyes for a moment, then opened them when his wife tapped his elbow. She seemed to know what he was thinking. She was a good woman. The best.

"There it goes!"

Chester held his breath. Robinson had gotten hold of one and drove it to the outfield. It looked like it was going to drop in, except the Yankee left fielder snapped it on the fly with a great running catch. The street crowd groaned. Chester showed no expression. He could've caught that, too.

A few in the group dispersed. One young boy, eight or nine, his hand in his father's, turned around to look at Chester. "You're like him, aren't you, mister?"

"Who?" Chester asked.

"Jackie Robinson. You're one of those colored people."

"Quiet, Bradley," the father scolded the boy.

Chester smiled. "I don't mind, mister. Honest. Yes, I am colored, Bradley. So's my wife."

The boy looked up at Agnes. "Do you play baseball, mister? My daddy says all black people can play baseball."

"You'll have to excuse the boy," the father said. "I didn't quite say it that way."

"I know. Yes, I. . . used to play. I haven't in a while, though."

"Did you play professional?"

Chester hesitated, then nodded. "I played against Robinson once. Far from here."

"Could you hit like Robinson?" the boy then asked.

Chester stared at the boy. He thought of Sergeant Collins. If he and his mama had notified the police right away, would he be wearing a Dodger uniform in the World Series today? He'd never know. He pictured the scoreboard in Detroit, the blast into the pouring rain, and the roof-shot in practice. Then the hill at Blues Stadium, and Satchel Paige came to mind. Such efforts would only live in the minds of those who saw Chester play. He turned back to the television.

Agnes followed her husband's stare and knew what he was thinking deep in his wonderful heart. She would never, to her dying day, forget the straightaway upper-deck homer in Detroit.

"Bradley," she said, glancing down at the boy, "Robinson is pretty good. But you should have seen my husband. He was. . . really something."

Afterword

Many names of the characters in the novel are fictional, including Chester Lee, Ramona Lee, Agnes Hudson, Ted Garrett, Art Powell, Vince Basser, and several of those associated with the above in Denver, Louisiana, and on the road.

JACKIE ROBINSON

As expected, he faced racial taunts from opposing players and fans his first few years in organized ball.

He shone at second base for Montreal in 1946, where he hit .349, stole 40 bases to lead the International League, and was voted the MVP. Moving up to Brooklyn in 1947, he played first base, hit .297, and was picked as the National League's rookie of the year. In 1948, he switched to a more comfortable spot at second base. There, he became part of the outstanding infield of Gil Hodges, Pee Wee Reese, and Billy Cox that continued into the 1950s. Robinson hit .342 in 1949, to lead the National League, and collected another MVP award in doing so.

Robinson was the energetic sparkplug that brought the pennants to Brooklyn's Ebbets Field that Branch Rickey so desired in 1945. The Dodgers captured the National League flags in 1947, 1949, 1952, 1953, 1955, and 1956, not to mention close second-place finishes in 1950, 1951, and 1954, and a third place in 1948. Thanks to Robinson and his leadership, the Dodgers became a powerhouse.

Robinson retired after the 1956 World Series, a lifetime .311 hitter, and found himself in the Hall of Fame in 1962. He left his mark on baseball as one of the greatest players ever, and certainly one of the fiercest competitors. He died of heart failure in 1972 at the age of 53, more than two decades after he had paved the way for blacks to enter the major leagues.

BRANCH RICKEY

Branch Rickey cut his close ties with Gus Greenlee and the United States League mid-way through the 1945 season.

He was maneuvered out of the Brooklyn front office after the 1949 season by ambitious Walter O'Malley who took over the Dodgers and eventually pulled them out of New York in 1957 for greener pastures in the grapefruit-and-sunshine state of California.

In 1951, Rickey staked out new territory, taking his organizational talents to the lowly Pittsburgh Pirates. As vice president of operations, he soon discovered the likes of Dick Groat, Roberto Clemente, Elroy Face, Bob Friend, Bill Mazeroski, Dick Stuart, and Bill Virdon, all key members who went on to snatch the World Series from the heavily-favored New York Yankees in 1960, topped by Mazeroski's dramatic homer in the bottom of the ninth of the famous seventh game.

In 1963, Rickey returned to his alma mater, the St. Louis Cardinals as an advisor. Two years later, they fired him. He died that fall, eleven days shy of his 84th birthday. He was elected to the baseball's Hall of Fame in 1967, a cenotaph to boardroom greatness second to none.

SATCHEL PAIGE

Paige was given his shot at the majors as an over-forty-year-old rookie in 1948 with Bill Veeck's Cleveland Indians. He still had enough magic on the ol' bat dodger and blooper ball to throw two shutouts, win six games, and record a 2.48 earned run average in 72 innings in the Indian stretch drive that saw his team win a World Series in October. He later pitched in relief for the St. Louis Browns and the Miami Marlins of the International League in the 1950's, and the Kansas City Athletics in a 3-inning promotional stunt in 1965, arranged by owner Charlie Finley.

By his own accord, Paige had pitched in 2,500 games outside the majors, winning 2,000 of them, over one hundred of those no-hitters. He was voted to the Hall of Fame in 1969, not for his efforts in the majors, but for his decades in the Negro Leagues before integration came his way, too late to see what he really could have done against the best of competition.

Josh Gibson

Considered the greatest of Negro League sluggers, his name also found its way into Cooperstown's Hall of Fame based on his career in segregated ball. It was the same day that his Homestead Grays' teammate Buck Leonard was canonized in 1972. Had he a shot at the majors, Gibson might have been a challenge to Babe Ruth and Hank Aaron for the lifetime home run title.

Gibson was one of the saddest cases of all Negro League ballplayers. A heavy drinker and a drug addict in his final years, he died in early 1947 at 36 years of age, disappointed he hadn't gone to the Bigs. For years no one knew where his grave site was—only that it was somewhere in Pittsburgh's Allegheny Cemetery—until ex-teammate Ted Page took it upon himself some twenty years after his friend's death to search for it, finally finding it under overgrown weeds in an unmarked stone. The office of the commissioner of baseball offered to pay for a new marked gravestone, giving it the splendor it now richly deserves.

Other Pioneers

Larry Doby of the Newark Eagles was the first of the black players to go directly to the majors with no minor league time. He was also the first black man in the American League. Called up to the Cleveland Indians in 1947, he did very little, other than hit an anemic .156 in 32 at bats. But in 1948, he blossomed into a star, boasting a .301 batting average in the regular season and .318 in the World Series. He twice led the American League in home runs in the early 1950s and was one of the better center fielders in the game during his day.

The St. Louis Browns found the Kansas City Monarchs' lineup to their liking and signed Hank Thompson and Willard "Home Run" Brown, ten days after Doby's rise to the Indians. They both played for a few weeks, then were sent back to Kansas City. Past his prime, thirty-six-year-old Brown hit .179 in 21 games. At 21, Thompson fared better, hitting .256. The Giants signed him in 1949, and he went on to play seven seasons for them, hitting .302 one year, enjoying three 20-homer seasons as a regular third baseman.

Newark Eagles' Monte Irvin was already 30 when the New York Giants took him on the roster in 1949. He didn't disappoint the Polo Grounds' fans. He hit .299 or better the first four regular seasons in New York. In two World Series, in 1951 and 1954, he smashed the ball at a vicious .394 clip in 33 trips to the plate. He followed Gibson, Leonard, and Paige into the Hall of Fame in 1973, another player who made it on his Blackball credentials.

THE NEGRO LEAGUES

The Negro Leagues died a slow death once Robinson signed with the Dodgers. The United States League was the first to go, after finishing a disastrous 1946 season. The Negro American League and National League competed for its final World Series in 1948, then consolidated into one, the Negro American League which sputtered in fragmented form until 1960, only as a farm system for the majors.

From the new Negro American League, stars were born. Three were extremely noteworthy. The New York Giants paid $14,000 to the Birmingham Black Barons in 1950 for Willie Mays. In 1952, the Boston Braves bought Hank Aaron for $10,000 from the Indianapolis Clowns. The highest price paid was the Chicago Cubs' reported $25,000 for Kansas City Monarch shortstop Ernie Banks. All three players saw time in the minors before reaching their respective clubs.

In 1949, thirty-six Negro ballplayers were plying their trade in organized ball. Fourteen of those were with the Cleveland Indians, and twelve with the Dodgers. By the middle of the 1950's, fewer blacks were making a living at professional baseball than at any time since the beginning of the century. All because of Robinson and integration. The last black player to go directly from the Negro American League to the majors was pitcher Pat Scantlebury of the New York Cubans, who donned a Cincinnati Reds uniform briefly in 1956.

The Boston Red Sox was the last major league team to field a black player, a flaky, mediocre infielder named Pumpsie Green in 1959. It's ironic. Boston could have been the first during the war, when they had a chance to sign Robinson, Sam Jethroe, and Marvin Williams in 1945, following a tryout. The Red Sox weren't the first to bring up colored, so they opted instead to hold out, be stubborn, and be the last.

THE DODGERS

A wave of colored ball players quickly flowed into Brooklyn during the Robinson era to give the Dodgers a potent lineup. . . Roy Campanella, Jim Gilliam, Joe Black, Don Newcombe, and Sandy Amoros.

Reborn in their Los Angeles home, the Dodgers winning tradition continued unabated. Gilliam followed the move west and teamed up with black speedster Maury Wills, and black sluggers Willie Davis and Tommy Davis to grab more National League championships in 1959, 1963, 1965 and 1966.

For many years the Los Angeles Dodgers were one of the richest teams in baseball. Branch Rickey's 1945 plan proved correct. Colored ballplayers would bring the Dodgers pennants. . . and money to boot. First and foremost, baseball was and still is a business, something that Branch Rickey never lost sight of more than fifty years ago.

www.ingramcontent.com/pod-product-compliance
Lightning Source LLC
Chambersburg PA
CBHW021228020726
47498CB00008B/2744